THE
PARIS
Apartment

sophia karlson

Cover Art & Formatting by Qamber Designs & Media W.L.L
Editing and proof reading: Leanne Rabesa
Proof reading: Isolde Dittrich
October 2018 Edition
ISBN: 978 1 7238 593 73
Published in the United States of America

To my husband, as always
And
To the Book Club Babes —
Alison, Natsuko, and Martha

Chapter 1

WHAT HAPPENS IN PARIS STAYS in Paris. Mila's best friend's voice rang in her head as she tossed her backpack into the corner of the apartment's foyer. Stacey might have lured her to Paris with this golden rule, but what happened in Paris *did* stay in Paris, especially if there was no one to share anything with.

For now, she had to indulge solo in all things French. Stacey would arrive the following week, having finished her two re-writes. Trust her BFF from grade school to mess around so much that she had to re-sit papers for two of her final year classes, which she'd already repeated twice. Stacey's dad appeared to be happy to foot the bill, but at some point, Stacey would have to grow up.

Mila paused. In some ways, Stacey was much more grown-up than she was... or at least more worldly. Stacey had lost her mom in a tragic car accident, but it was more than that. Stacey had some fabulous male friends in Paris, or so she had insinuated, and they would have fun together. She pushed the thought aside, ignoring the tingle of anticipation in her body—a tingle that was heavily spiced with nerves. She had no misconception of what Stacey's idea of *fun* was. She had no objection to Stacey enjoying herself on all levels, but on a moral level, she and Stacey were from different planets.

Never mind her best friend's well-meant if naughty intentions—she was lucky to be in Paris.

The windows beckoned her. As she reached them she struggled with the latch until it swooshed open. Hot air oozed into the room, and she pulled a deep breath of the Paris summer heat into her lungs. The traffic, which had been a dim hum, buzzed louder.

But the view…

A narrow terrace led the eye to the rooftops across the street, where windows in the opposite apartments blinked. Clusters of chimneys poked into the air, and roof tiles, stained black and grey on the rusty brown clay, baked in the sun. The Eiffel Tower stretched into the deep blue that crowned it all, a blue which slipped into a lighter icy hue and then hazy yellow as it melted into the sun.

Mila reached out with her hand as if she could touch the picture it made. Her fingertips itched, feeling empty without a paintbrush in them. She burst out laughing, giddy with joy. She would make the most of her time in Paris, whatever that meant. Right now, the world was her oyster and she would be happy to discover anything and everything Paris had to offer. She had, after all, managed to escape from home and that had been hard to contrive.

A scuffle of feet behind her reminded her of Madame Leborgne's presence.

"Thank you for opening up. I—" She broke off. Madame Leborgne's English had been limited from the moment she rang the bell to be let into the apartment. It would not have improved with the lift ride or the opening of the apartment door… and neither did her non-existent French.

The elderly housekeeper nodded, didn't smile but jingled the keys and settled them in Mila's palm. She made a gesture with her hands, which Mila translated as "welcome and enjoy your stay" and then walked out of the apartment, closing the door behind her.

"*Merci,*" Mila whispered, as an afterthought.

With a grin, she turned back to the interior of the apartment and for the first time, the slight echo in the room hit her. She took in the vast space. One wall had windows and a set of French doors leading to the terrace, while the opposite wall was covered, almost completely, with large pieces of modern art. She walked the length of the wall, studying the works one by one. The apartment might have been a modern art gallery. The only furniture in the lounge was a lone wingback chair, a side table, and a modern rug, which was still pockmarked where other furniture had stood.

Weird. Stacey's brother James owned the apartment and seemed to be in the midst of a move or something. He was hardly ever here, apparently, and it suited Mila just fine. She hadn't seen James in more than twelve years. An ache whispered up from her subconscious, reminding her that twelve years was a long time to miss someone. He might have been ten years older than them, but James had been an anchor in Stacey's life, and Mila had been happy to barnacle onto that ride. James had none of the brotherly superiority that came with such an age gap, but had looked out for them, chauffeured them around, joked and teased in such a good-hearted way that his absence had reverberated long after he'd left to work overseas.

He'd understood her. Maybe because he'd understood Stacey. And when he hadn't understood, he had made it his business to figure it out.

James had been nothing like Mila's pack of brothers, and that had made all the difference. In his eyes, neither she nor Stacey were mistakes. To him, they'd been pure perfection. Her lips twitched as she recalled how he used to call them *The Princesses* in his deep voice as if he'd be their servant forever.

But time changed people... as much as she ached to see him again, she wasn't ready to find out if the James of her childhood was gone. She liked him floating around, drifting like a soap bubble in and out of her happier childhood memories, from when she and Stacey had still been allowed to be friends.

Mila shrugged off the whimsical thought and turned to find her things. She picked up her backpack and strolled back through the lounge, past the empty space where a dining table should be. There followed an open-plan kitchen and a guest bathroom. A corridor led to three doors, of which two were locked. The last door took her to the master bedroom. A king-size bed looked lost in the open space, basking in the light from a slanted skylight. She dropped her backpack, took a lunge and plonked down on the bed. It was pure luxury, the duvet huffing with her weight, the pillows caving in under her head in a slow, dreamy puff.

Thank you, James. In your bed, at last.

She giggled. James might have left home, but he'd been everything a girl in the throes of puberty from hell could possibly fall in love with. Hunky, tall, dark, brooding. A provincial rugby player until an injury curbed his career. He'd shaken it all off as a matter of fact and had gone off to make money another way. Hedge funds or something totally dull and overly complex.

Who cared? Paris called. She'd leave him a thank you note for allowing her to slum for two weeks in his luxury apartment. And would fervently hope that he would even remember who she was.

Chapter 2

JAMES OPENED THE APARTMENT DOOR with a sigh. He was bloody exhausted. But that was nothing new. The past year's constant travel had been crazy, but it came with the job of managing the hedge fund branches in Paris, Singapore, and New York for the bank he worked for. Then there was the bond issue he'd been working on with an international consortium, which would finally be signed off in the next few days. He needed the break and was in dire need of catching up on some sleep.

For the most part, he was thankful for his busy schedule; it helped to take his mind off things. He wheeled his suitcase and laptop bag in, closed the door and tossed his keys onto the table in the small foyer. They clanged menacingly and he closed his eyes at the echo. Marlène had made good on her promise. She'd emptied the apartment of her things. As he walked into the lounge it was nearly empty. He smirked with disgust. She'd left him a lone wingback armchair and side table, lost in the vast space of the lounge. He scanned his artwork in the last of the summer light and let out a short, haggard breath. They were all still there.

He'd been so busy with work that he'd stopped stewing over what had happened with his ex. His gaze fell to the side table where an uncorked bottle of red wine stood with a lonely wineglass.

Marlène.

She'd better not be here. It took a split second for him to remember that Marlène never drank red wine because it stained her teeth. He picked up the bottle and read its label. Neither did Marlène drink an odd four euros' worth of plonk. She preferred champagne. He stifled a yawn as an unexpected sense of relief drained to his feet.

Was he supposed to have visitors? Nothing had been noted in his calendar.

He put the bottle down and an open watercolor pad drew his gaze. Some pencils and a watercolor palette lay on the seat of the wingback. Picking up the pad, he studied the rough drawing and immediately recognized it as the view from the rooftop terrace. The drawing was gorgeous, almost wild in the haste in which the artist had drawn the lines of the apartment building across from his, the roofs, the chimneys, and the Eiffel Tower. Splashes of color had been added in places, bringing the pencil drawing to life.

His heart tugged as slow desire rose in him. With a piece of art, it was usually love at first sight and he recognized this connection instantly. This rough drawing needed a frame and a safe spot on his wall.

A soft creaking noise came from the corridor and he looked up. Somewhere in the apartment, someone had stirred. The inner silence was almost unnatural now. He put the pad down and walked down the corridor to check the doors. The second bedroom was locked and he cursed under his breath; the guest room was locked too. She said she'd changed the locks. No need to try the old keys—he should have known Marlène would go down crazy. She hadn't emptied the apartment; she'd locked all her belongings in the two extra rooms the last time she'd been here. As if he cared a toss about auctioning off her things or throwing them out of the windows.

The master bedroom's door was ajar and as he pushed the door wider a soft scent drifted to his nose. It was flowery, but not overwhelming; it was the type of scent that lingered after a shower, slightly moist, promising. And womanly. His dick stirred as he tried to remember who had a copy of his apartment key. Madame Leborgne and Marlène.

There was no one else.

And yet there must be. Light from the skylight revealed a woman who was asleep on top of the covers, her dark hair gathered in a ponytail, spread over the white pillows.

The room was hot and the other windows were closed. Whoever his intruder was hadn't known how to close the shutters to block out the midsummer's late light nor had she realized he had air conditioning in the room.

He took in her body, her legs that were splayed against the heat, their length inviting his gaze to travel to her sex, neatly packaged in white cotton panties, so different from what he was used to. None of his sexual acquaintances waited for him in cotton panties. At a minimum, it was La Perla or Chantal Thomass.

He took a step closer, intrigued. His gaze traveled upwards to her navel that was a perfect little button in the plane of her stomach, surrounded by curves and dales for his fingers to trace. He looked higher to her breasts, which seemed almost flat as she lay on her back. Nothing in them screamed silicone implants and the notion heated his budding arousal. Her nipples were relaxed in deep sleep and he groaned. She'd be a blessed handful once she sat up straight.

Pure lust overtook him and he drew in a slow breath. This was what eight months of celibacy did to a man—his cock was jostling within his trousers as if he'd just turned thirteen. He would have laughed but the situation was hardly funny. The idea that this woman was waiting for him, almost innocent in her allure, was painful, as it amplified how lonely he'd been.

He brushed his fingers through his hair as he took a few steps closer. Her arms rested around her head, almost as if she'd given up against the heat. He searched her face. She was young, not a wrinkle in sight, and her brow was smooth. Her long lashes threw shadows under her eyes and her slightly parted lips were full of promise. There was something familiar about her, but he couldn't place it.

He shrugged as he turned to switch the light on. This situation might turn out to be a lot of fun, and a much-needed interlude from his solitary confinement, but in providing him with entertainment for the night, Madame Leborgne had gone beyond the call of duty this time.

Chapter 3

"GAHHH!" MILA CRIED OUT AS she scrambled up straight, blinded by the sudden light. Her heart was in her throat, clawing to get out as it beat so ferociously she was sure to have a heart attack.

A man was in the room—was she about to live the most horrible episode of CSI she'd ever watched? She scooted back against the pillows, her body hitting the upholstered headboard. By instinct, she reached for her glasses on the bedside table but didn't manage to put them on. Her fingers were trembling in unison with her innards, uncontrollably.

"Breathe, baby," he said. "Didn't mean to give you the fright of your life."

"What the devil did you mean to do then?" she gasped, finally managing to shove the dark-rimmed glasses on.

The world blurred into focus. "Jeez, James!" she called out as she recognized his face and took in his tall frame at the foot of the bed. "What the f—" She stopped short of saying the offending word and collapsed back, pressing her palms against her sternum, willing her heart to calm down. The world had not imploded. It was just James.

She closed her eyes.

It was just James.

And from his facial expression, he had no clue who she was.

When she looked at him again he hadn't moved. God Almighty and all his angels help her, but he was more handsome than the last time she'd seen him. A naughty smile played on his lips, never mind the dark stubble that covered his jaw and the sparkle in his sky blue eyes as he studied her leisurely. He had a certain solidness about him, an unwavering strength that made her knees weak. Not that it mattered. Shaken as she was she wouldn't even be able to roll out of the bed, never mind climb out of it. She let her gaze travel down his body, jolting to a halt halfway.

He was hard. Unabashedly so. A slow burn settled on her cheeks and she wished the bright lights away.

As if he'd read her mind he dimmed the lights, then rested his hands on his hips as she lifted her eyes back to his. "You're a step ahead of me here…?" he said, waiting for her to provide her name.

Maybe not quite… a whole step… Yet inside her, desire flared up to match the heat in his eyes. If she were honest with herself, that flame had been turned on since the moment she'd stepped into his bedroom, plunging into his world and being surrounded by his things. In a split second, he'd turned it up full blast with just being present. She shook her head, taking another deep breath. "Mila. Mila Johnson."

"Who?" he asked, lifting his brows in question and leaning slightly forward. Mila Johnson meant nothing to him.

"Stacey's Mila?" she ventured.

His face blanched when the information hit home.

"She's invited me over for two weeks."

"Bloody hell," he murmured as he turned his body away from her gaze, which she desperately forced not to drop to groin level. He dragged his fingers through his hair with an ill–suppressed sigh. A second later he switched the light off completely.

She wanted to laugh, but adrenalin still rioted through her system, had made her forget that she was naked. She clutched a pillow to her chest but it was way too late to cover up her breasts... he'd had his fill of them already.

He seemed mortified at having shown his hand so blatantly, but here she was spread-eagled and panting. Her gangly legs were slow to close in a ladylike fashion and her face burst with heat. She fisted the linen, wanting to cover herself, but she was lying on top of the covers. The only way to hide all that skin was to get under the duvet and boil away. She'd look like such a prude.

"I forgot that Stacey said she was coming." He tugged his shirt from his trousers, letting it hang out and cover everything up.

"I didn't mean to... I'm sorry. This is the only bed." She shifted uncomfortably when he didn't move. "I—"

"Mila Johnson. All these years and you still have apologies running on tap?" He turned towards her, his lips twitching. "Stacey did send me an email some time ago, but I never read the whole thing. Got distracted. If I missed something, the fault's mine."

She blinked as not a single response came to mind, except the profuse need to apologize again. She had to keep this impersonal. "Stacey will be here next week, once she's done with her rewrites."

"So here we are then." He walked around to the other side of the bed, fished for a remote in the bedside table's drawer and switched on the air conditioner. "Welcome to Paris. I just got off a long-haul flight from Singapore."

Their eyes locked across the plump feather cushions, mutual recognition of their situation sinking in. The other two rooms were locked. Why did she sense he didn't have the keys for them? Between them, there was a king size bed and a wingback chair.

The need to get out of the confining space, a space that tightened by the second, overwhelmed her. There was no way she'd be able to get any shut-eye now. Not with him in the room, her heart hammering and her body begging for something she shouldn't have. She flung her legs to the floor, forcing the jelly in them to solidify. "How about a glass of wine?"

He grinned. "Sure, if you're up to it?"

"I'm always up to it." What a lie.

"Let me shower first."

This was her cue. "Sure." She got up, grabbed her discarded Hello Kitty PJs from the floor and scuttled out of the bedroom, pulling her nightshirt on.

Chapter 4

JAMES TURNED ON THE SHOWER and paused. *Little Mila Johnson.* She was the last woman he'd expected to find in his bed.

She'd changed a lot. The last time he'd seen her she was a dangle of limbs, out of proportion with a body that had been so skinny nothing had predicted the curves she ruled now.

Now her firm breasts had jutted up to him, their rosy tips hardening with each second he'd stared at her. There was something irresistible in a rising blush on a woman's cheeks when she was perused, openly and with sexual interest. It got him going every time.

And then there were those lips… he'd have to keep himself in check. That mouth was thoroughly fuckable. And thoroughly kissable.

He pulled his shirt off and tossed it into the laundry basket, then tugged off his shoes and socks. His fingers quivered slightly as he reached for his belt, which he unbuckled slowly, drawing out the moment in which he could take himself in hand. His cock was straining against his jocks, harder than it had been in months.

That a pair of white cotton panties could pull him out of his slump was a wonder. Had he known he would have investigated the matter sooner... but surely it was more than that? Maybe it was the look in her eyes, the way she'd pulled her legs up when he'd scrutinized her, closing up, hugging her pillow so tightly, hiding her body from him. That was new. Women usually flaunted everything they had.

He didn't know what it was.

His trousers and jocks dropped to the floor and he groaned in relief as he gathered his sack and stroked himself in long, languid pulls.

Fuck, she'd feel good right now. His fatigue from earlier was long gone. The notion of burrowing himself in Mila's tight, moist velvet would be the perfect release of months of underlying tension, tension he'd consciously chosen to ignore.

He stepped into the shower, testing the water with his back, enjoying the scalding burn as the heat engulfed him. He soaped himself down, spreading the lather over his chest and lower. Closing his eyes as the suds smoothed his hold on his cock, he let his hands slide over it, one trailing after the other, visualizing how she was waiting for him... had been waiting for him. At the current rate, he would explode within a minute of slipping into her tight pussy.

The mental visual made him pause.

Little Mila Johnson. She was Stacey's age, so around twenty-four, and his sister's best friend since playgroup. Until the time when Mila's parents had forced the two girls apart. The pastor's only daughter was not to be seen fraternizing with the town hussy's offspring. He'd never had time for all that holier-than-thou bullshit that seemed to permeate the middle-class neighborhoods of their youth. But for those years of intense friendship, with them

14

living a few houses apart, Mila was like Stacey's twin. Fucking her would be like sleeping with his sister.

The idea was enough to cool his mounting desire and he let go of his cock to lean both hands against the shower wall. He let go of a deeply buried groan.

There was always the club. He could go. Alone. After that glass of wine. As it was he had a meeting there later in the week, but one night there could be all he needed.

The thought lasted all of two seconds before he wilted. The mood wouldn't come back to him. The notion of the club had become a complete turn-off. With Mila in the apartment, he should be thankful. Thinking of the club would keep his cock in check.

He turned off the faucet and reached for a towel. As he rubbed dry he took stock of the situation. Tomorrow he'd be leaving for work again, if only for two nights. He could make arrangements for a sleeper couch or something in those two days. Whatever.

Did Mila Johnson even know she was hot as hell?

Rein it in, boy.

One night. He could do it. He was the master of control, after all. Wasn't he?

He groaned. He didn't need to look down to know his dick was giving him the one-eyed stare. Fuck. He hated his life.

Chapter 5

Mila's ears pricked with every sound coming from the bathroom. The shower turned on and she exhaled, relaxing her grip on the wine bottle. She poured two glasses, so eager that she spilled some. The drops pooled like blood red watercolor on the white granite and she wiped them off with the side of her palm. Her fingers were trembling as she licked the liquid off her hand.

He gave her such a shock barging in on her.

Yeah right. That was it.

She closed her eyes and leaned against the kitchen counter. Nothing Dutch courage couldn't fix. She took a breath and downed her glass.

The liquid settled in her stomach in a slow, easy swirl of warmth, and she produced a little cough.

Ugh. The last thing she needed was to get drunk before he came out of the shower. She'd be passed out before they'd discussed the weather. Because the weather it was going to be. Her tongue was twisted into a thousand knots. What was she going to say to

James Sinclair?

She refilled her glass and crossed to the French doors that led out to the terrace. With one hand she struggled with the latch but got it open to let in the night air and the cooling breeze. She'd never thought it could be so warm in Paris. The city lights twinkled in silver and gold and the lit-up Eiffel Tower shone as if encrusted in gold leaf.

Settling in one of the wrought iron chairs on the terrace, she let the wine do its thing, sipping at it demurely.

When James padded in ten minutes later, wine glass in hand, she'd mellowed completely. He was barefoot and wore shorts and a T-shirt, looking at ease. Heat radiated from his skin and a soft mist of freshly showered male drifted over to her.

Heavens, he looked good in anything he wore. But she bet butt naked was his best. She took a heavy gulp of wine, praying she wasn't going to slur.

He smiled at her as he sat down, facing the same intoxicating view. "When did you arrive?"

"Only this morning."

"You found the apartment easily?"

She shook with a slow laugh. "It was quite an adventure to find my way here. But yes, eventually I did."

He grinned. "What are your plans until Stacey arrives?"

"Visit every art museum twice? Three times if possible."

"That's a lot of art." He studied her face in the dim light and leaned closer. "You did the drawing in the lounge?"

For a moment she had no idea what he was talking about. Her wild sketch of joy, her first one of Paris, came back to her in a rush. "Yes… I was just fooling around."

"I like it."

"You do?"

"Yes. You're studying art?"

"Final year of my masters. I'll have my first solo exhibition in three months. It's only at the local gallery, nothing huge—" She broke off. The exhibition didn't bear thinking of. It petrified her. Lately—or had it been forever?—things just didn't jell. Another reason why coming to Paris had been a brilliant idea. She needed some inspiration... amongst other things.

"Really?" He chuckled. "You were always doodling around. I should have known you'd end up an artist."

She shrugged. "My folks wanted me to do something more solid. Something that brings in a secure, decent salary. I finished my first year of law and then absconded to the art department."

He laughed. "Absconded?"

"Pretty much." She'd never expected her parents to have so much grief to give. She still got it every now and again, redefining the idea of a gift that kept on giving.

"There's no reason why you can't make a good living with your art." He raised his glass in salute. "Good on you for sticking to your guns. Law would've been the end of you."

"Yes, probably." Stacey was studying finance and corporate law, and had been flunking it for how many years now? Did James even know how much Stacey hated her studies?

"Do you think you'll have it finished before you travel home?"

"What?"

"The drawing? I'll buy it from you once you're done. Put a sold sticker next to it at your exhibition to get things started," he said with a little smile.

"You can have it." She swallowed, at last managing to look

him straight in the eye. "As a thank you for having me."

His gaze bore into hers, his one eyebrow slowly raising in a subtle question. "So… I'll be having you?"

Splotches of heat spread over her neck and face. Oh for the good Lord's sake. Did she have to put her foot in it so thoroughly?

His eyes dropped to her lips and he licked his own. "You still open yourself up for relentless teasing, Mila."

"For having me *stay* here, I meant." She blinked, her lips slipping into a smile. Half of her wanted to laugh, the other half wanted to run.

It's just James. She had to get over what had happened earlier, even if the same tenseness hovered between them now. He might as well have been her brother. One more of those hardly mattered.

She glanced at him but didn't meet his eyes. His gaze had dropped lower, to her breasts and her treacherous nipples, which had hardened under her ridiculous Hello Kitty nightshirt. It had been washed so often the fabric had thinned out and wasn't fit for public inspection. From the closed look on his face and his eyelids that had lowered as he scrutinized her, the material was non-existent and he could see every curve and shadow of her breasts, the Pink Lady shade of her areolas, the protruding tips begging to be kissed.

He shifted in his chair, the metal scraping mercilessly over the tiled floor, and took a deep swig of his wine.

"Right. About that." He stood and took two steps to the railing, his back to her. "I'm only here for tonight. Tomorrow I'm leaving for Brussels."

She could exhale in relief at no longer being under his thorough inspection. But somehow her breath caught in her throat. "Brussels? What for?"

"We're closing a deal. I'm blocked for two days, two nights.

It's enough time to arrange for a sleeper couch or something to be delivered here."

Two days. She could find somewhere else to go slum in that time, but it would chow through her handful of euros. But she was intruding on his space. There was no need for him to spend money on a couch.

Behind her, the empty lounge all but whispered that it badly needed some furnishings.

"Don't even think about it, Mila."

"Think what?"

"Going to some dodgy youth hostel. I'd hate to go drag you out of the one three blocks away and bring you back home."

Home. Why did he make it sound so cozy? It was wonderful to have the apartment to herself, space and luxury she'd never experienced before. Things had been crowded from the day she'd been born.

"We'd need it in any case once Stacey arrives."

True… but.

"Tonight?" Her voice croaked, giving every feeling away. She closed her eyes. If he could but read her mind. The good Lord forgive her but she couldn't help her body's reaction to James. This feeling had never been so intense. She wanted to share his bed with him, in every sense.

What had Stacey said? Mila didn't know what she was missing out on and she needed to lose her effin' virginity and start living life.

But she was a good girl and James was like a brother.

Keep on telling yourself that.

"The bed's big enough… if you don't mind. I don't have the energy to go to a hotel now."

He didn't have the energy to leave. She couldn't expect him

to leave. She'd been sharing rooms and spaces with her brothers most of her life. In his brotherly capacity, one night with James would hardly matter.

"Why did you bother to come home for one night if you're off to Brussels first thing? Why didn't you fly straight there?"

He chuckled. "I rather do like sleeping in my own bed when given half a chance."

She bit her lip. Only half a chance. Given half a chance she'd do some seriously stupid and very regretful things tonight. "I'm cool." Liar. She was hot, bothered and all clammy between her thighs. She wanted to open wide and let the night breeze cool her off in that particular department.

She and Stacey had made all kinds of plans for these two weeks in France. Hovering in the top ten was to "get thoroughly laid." That was what Stacey had prescribed and jotted down. She would've been a dumb nut not to realize that sleeping with every Frenchmen within a two-kilometer radius was ideally the first thing on Stacey's agenda. Mila glanced at the cityscape. That was a lot of Frenchmen. Her best friend had gone so far off the rails that she'd lost sight of the tracks.

Her gaze magnetized to where James leaned against the railing, his back to her. His body seemed rigid, his back muscles strained underneath his T-shirt. He drank deeply from his glass, inhaling sharply after the liquid had gone down.

He'd be the perfect candidate for her first time. Built and equipped for the job of satisfying every woman in said radius. And somehow, she couldn't imagine ever doing it with a complete stranger.

Best of all, Stacey wouldn't know. Stacey was still hanging on the thin thread of hope that Jamie and Marls—was it Marls? Short for what again? Marly? Marlène?—were going to patch things up and make her a bridesmaid or something that involved an expensive dress.

Sleeping with James would be trespassing on sacred territory.

Mila seeped out a slow, dense sigh. Never mind that, she wasn't going to engage in the remedial activities Stacey had in mind. She couldn't. Not only would she be flogging herself mentally for the rest of her life if she dipped her toe in Stacey's sordid habits, she'd feel plain filthy.

Then why was she considering the world of possibilities with James seconds ago?

"I'm going to bed," James murmured. "I'm catching a train in five hours."

He turned and walked back into the apartment, his wine glass empty, ignoring her completely.

She stared down at hers. Despite her eager consumption of alcohol, her body was as stiff and taut as a freshly-primed canvas.

She had a good half glass to go. "G'night."

Her words were lost between pedestrians calling and the erratic hum of traffic a block down. Her heart was beating in her ears, amplifying every sound.

Round one survived. Tick.

Except… James didn't look like the type of guy who owned any kind of pajamas. What was she going to do if he was waiting for her in bed—stark naked?

Chapter 6

J AMES REACHED HIS BEDROOM AND paused to rub his shoulder muscles. He dropped his head back with a groan. Mila Johnson. She'd come a bloody far way to ruin his peace.

What a joke. Peace wasn't how he'd describe his life, but honestly. She couldn't be in his bed when he'd arrived, wear nothing except knickers, then cover up in some girly Hello Kitty garb and think he was going to be immune to her. He was only a man.

He sighed and pulled himself tall. There was only one way he was going to deal with this situation. Pop one of those jetlag sleeping pills he had on hand and get mummified under the covers before she even came back to bed.

He glanced around the room, traces of her being there filling the empty space. Her backpack and handbag leaned against his closet, reminding him that he still needed to pack for Brussels.

He picked up the items to move them to the corner. The backpack's zipper was open, revealing a scrum of clothes. Sticking out from the folds was a box of condoms.

His eyebrows shot up. Little Mila Johnson wasn't as innocent as she seemed. He lowered the backpack, going on his haunches. He tugged the box from the clothes and paused. Wet & Wild. He swallowed involuntarily. An unopened twelve pack.

Museum visits were not the only thing on Mila's agenda. He could get Wet & Wild with her and make her trip to Paris truly memorable.

He rose with a blink, shoving the box back between her clothes.

Why did he keep losing his grip over everything going on here?

He opened his closet and jerked out another suitcase, mentally forcing Mila back into the realm of sisterly affection. He quickly packed everything he needed for Brussels.

After he'd placed his suitcase with his laptop bag at the front door, he strolled back through the empty lounge, searching through the windows. Mila still sat on the terrace, her hair pulled loose from her ponytail and hanging over the back of the chair. She sat so quietly, she appeared mesmerized.

With a shrug, he walked to the bedroom, popped the sleeping pill he'd left on the bedside table, and got under the covers.

He couldn't get comfortable and ended up with his hands cradling his head, staring at the skylight.

He hadn't seen Mila for over twelve years. It was an easy calculation. Mila's parents had severed the cord between Stacey and Mila the moment the sordid details of his mom's affairs had erupted to the surface. The whole business had been quite a spectacle and the gossipmongers had revelled in the details that had seeped into society over the weeks. It had been like watching a fucking soap opera in which he played the minor role of the whore's son. Nothing had been news to him, simply a rerun of the same show he'd been watching for years.

Mila came into the room, one arm crossed over her breasts, clutching her elbow tight. Their eyes met across the dark space.

"You're good?" she murmured, inching closer to the other side of the bed.

"Yes." Inside him, he could feel the sleeping pill working, relaxing every tense muscle.

"It's cold in here now."

"Get under the covers." He gave her a surreptitious inspection. That wash-worn nightie might as well be non-existent. "If you're still cold, we can adjust the air conditioning."

She got into bed, her breathing strained as she turned her back to him.

He should dismiss her too, but he couldn't. Not quite yet. "We haven't seen each other for ages—I reckon it's more than twelve years," he said into the heavy silence.

"You did leave," she murmured into her pillows.

He had no response to that. He had *had* to leave; the whole universe had wrenched him away from home. It had been the best decision at the time and he'd never regretted leaving. Over the years his visits home had reduced to none. He'd preferred to see Stacey and his dad off home territory.

"You weren't at my mom's funeral." He should have seen her there, six years ago, the last time he'd been home.

She stirred and turned to face him. "I..."

"You knew about the accident?"

"Yes."

Everybody had known. Towards the end, his mother had done nothing quietly. Least of all her parting from this world.

"My dad did the funeral, James. Of course I knew."

He smirked and uttered a bitter, flippant sound. "He refused to do the service, initially."

"What?" She propped on her elbow. "Did he? Refuse?"

The shock in her voice vibrated through him. She wouldn't have known. Mila's dad wouldn't have publicly refused to bury his mom. It had been a backhanded dispute between their fathers, a fight he was probably not supposed to be aware of either.

He sighed and wiped at his eyes. "Your dad insisted on a memorial service, as far away from his church as possible. I'm not sure how my dad convinced him." His mind was grinding to a slow halt. "Despite everything, my dad still had to send her off in some proper way." As he thought about it now it was more like his dad had gotten in the last laugh.

Her hand reached for him and soothed over his shoulder. The warmth of her touch was calming and he shifted on his side, slipping her hand into his. Her fingers were the perfect fit and she didn't pull away.

"I'm so sorry, Jamie," she whispered. "For your loss, for everything."

"It's okay, Princess," he breathed, the last of the apprehension between them dissolving.

"They didn't allow me to go to the funeral." She spoke so softly he'd hardly heard her.

"Really?" How could he not have guessed?

"I wanted to be there… for Stacey, for you. But they stopped me." Tears were shallow in the back of her throat, her emotions shredding him. That mother of hers wouldn't allow her close to the Sinclairs, even at a time they'd needed comfort.

Tears from Mila were the last thing he wanted. Seeing her or Stacey like this always crushed him.

"Hush," he said as he squeezed her hand softly, relishing the anchoring warmth. "We can't go back there."

"No."

She edged closer, but there were still miles of space between them.

And he needed to keep it that way.

His alarm woke him up hours later and he muted it fast. Mila stirred against him. Her sweet, rounded ass pressed against his thigh and if he had the time and audacity to take this further… he'd only need to roll onto his side and cradle her in his arms. Things would fall naturally into place from there.

He sat up and swung his legs out of bed, away from her allure, needing to hide his reaction to her.

"You're going?" she murmured.

"Yes. You stay right where you are, Princess."

She chuckled, settling on her back. Her gaze found his. "I really missed you, James."

It sounded as if they wouldn't meet again for ages, as if this was good-bye. "You'll see more of me soon enough."

She tugged her pillow closer, scrunching it under her head. "When you're back, you're not leaving for somewhere exotic again?"

"Brussels is hardly exotic," he teased. "I've taken some time off to deal with admin." With Mila being here last night, he'd forgotten all about the shit he needed to sort out.

"Enjoy Brussels."

He reached for her cheek and ran a finger along the soft curve to her chin. "Enjoy Paris."

He shouldn't have touched her, but he couldn't stop himself.

Chapter 7

MILA BURROWED DEEPER INTO THE covers and feigned sleep, the trail of James's touch burning on her skin. Her whole body begged for more of his slow touch, spiced with more intent.

James moved around the room noiselessly, only the shower's splatter disturbing the early-morning quiet. When he came out of the bathroom, she peeked at him. He'd dressed and was pulling on his suit jacket.

"Sorry I woke you."

"Comes with the territory," she sighed. She was in his bed, after all, missing the feel of him next to her.

"Everything opens much later in Paris," he said. "You can catch two more hours of sleep." He paused and took a breath. "And don't ship off to go somewhere else while I'm gone, okay?"

"Don't worry, James Sinclair, I'll be right here when you come back."

He gave her a slow grin. "I rather like you right here, where you are now."

Heat spread through her body and her cheeks caught fire. There was no doubt where the conversation was going. Was he flirting with her?

"Don't get too used to it," she murmured. "I've got places to see, people to do."

His eyes widened and that seductive smile of his tugged at the corners of his mouth.

Something had sounded off. Her words chased through her mind. Heavens, did she really just say that? Those words had come out all wrong but she couldn't pinpoint where.

He adjusted his tie and headed for the door with a laugh. "Easy does it, Princess. I'd hate to see you get hurt in Paris. Under my watch."

"Oh, be gone with you!" She grabbed a pillow and flung it in his direction.

He caught it nimbly and laughed as he tossed it right back at her. "We'll catch up later."

She swallowed involuntarily. "Whatever. Bye."

He was gone, his footsteps ringing down the corridor and echoing from the empty lounge.

She gathered his pillow closer and plopped it on her face. Her embarrassment sat so shallowly, she didn't want to breathe.

She tried to fall asleep again but it was useless. After twenty minutes of rolling around, wondering what she was going to do with the empty itch that lounged in her body, she got up, stripped, and went to the bathroom.

The scent of James's cologne teased her, and she inhaled deeply as she stepped into the shower. It was a good thing he'd left so early and had a reason to leave. After her stupid slip of the tongue things could have gotten interesting.

Places to go, people to see. *Do* didn't even feature in there. Heaven only knew what James thought of her now.

She let the water run over her body, turning her face to the showerhead. She was exhausted, not used to sleeping with an air conditioner on or with someone next to her.

Not just someone. *James.*

His words had her blinking in the darkness long after he'd fallen asleep. Her dad, Pastor Johnson, had actually refused to do the funeral service for James and Stacey's mom, Cecile Sinclair.

She couldn't believe it, and yet… her dad was prim to the brim. Her dad might be religious, but he was judgmental to the bone. Her mother was even worse.

That her dad had been so self-righteous had made her battle with anger, but she'd had to contain every emotion as she'd listened to James's rhythmic breathing. How could her dad have done something so callous?

Her parents had never taken to the Sinclairs because they weren't churchgoers. Despite her friendship with Stacey, despite James coaching all her brothers at some point at the school where he'd volunteered while he still played rugby. That had been ages ago.

She took up the soap and lathered herself down, but nothing could rinse away the memories that had been lurking in the back of her mind. None of them were pleasant. Had bumping into James set them all loose?

Apparently, Cecile had had many affairs and had gotten away with all of them. James and Stacey's dad never filed for divorce. That was all Mila knew, but if she'd wanted to eat up the gossip she'd have had her fill a million times over. Mila had cut it all off, for Stacey's sake. Not that it would have mattered since her parents had moved her to another school—away from the unsavory influence of Stacey Sinclair—and they didn't see each other for years until they reconnected at university.

It was clear to Mila now, the moment in which the rift between her and her parents had started. When they'd refused to let her be friends with Stacey anymore. Some things were just meant to be. Her friendship with Stacey had become a lifeline these past few years. Stacey had prompted Mila to change her studies and had supported her through every difficulty at home. Stacey might have turned out as wild as Cecile Sinclair, but Mila wasn't going to judge her for it. Mila looked out for Stacey, and Stacey looked out for her.

The stronger her friendship with Stacey had grown, the bigger the rift back home gaped. And she couldn't take it anymore.

She got out of the shower and rubbed herself dry. Why did everything go back to her parents? Her mom and dad had a mean streak in them, despite being devout Christians. That mean streak had been aimed at her so many times, subtly, shrewdly, that she was only able to see it for what it was once she'd rebelled and changed her studies to suit her, and not her parents. Then the mean streak came out in full force.

Being away from home was balmy, if not pure bliss.

Maybe she was naïve. Everybody had their faults.

Mila wrapped the towel around her body and walked to the bedroom. She picked up her backpack and pulled out clothes from the cavity with disinterest. The packet of condoms tumbled around until she'd emptied the backpack. Then it stared at her with a naughty grin. Stacey's parting gift. The *Starter Pack* Stacey had called it.

Mila chuckled as she tossed the box on the bedside table. The *Starter Pack* wasn't going anywhere soon. The museums in Paris awaited, and being up so early, she might as well walk to the D'Orsay, first on her list, and get to see Paris wake up.

Chapter 8

JAMES STARED AT THE NUMBER on his phone, newly saved. Mila Johnson. He'd had to nag Stacey the whole day for Mila's number, but Stacey hadn't answered her phone or read his messages. At last she'd let him know that she'd been studying.

Ha. He bet she was studying her butt off.

Day from hell didn't quite describe the mental tossing and turning he'd been doing over Mila. When the deal was signed and sealed sooner than he'd anticipated, there was nothing left to do but to have dinner with the relevant parties.

It was wrong, but he'd cut dinner short as soon as politely possible.

James pocketed his phone, took up his unnecessary suitcase and boarded the train for Paris. Given half a chance he always slept in his own bed. He couldn't help it if said bed was occupied by a gorgeous brunette who'd also occupied his mind and bulged his dick the entire day.

He shouldn't, but honestly? If she was going to explore Paris, *do* Paris, then she might just as well start at home. And stay at home. The idea of Mila working her way around his *arrondissement* gave him the creeps.

An hour and a half of itchy fingers later, he exited the train station and hailed a taxi. In the current traffic, it would only take him ten minutes to get home.

James leaned back in his seat and forced himself to wait. It was the first time in months that he had had any interest in a woman and he couldn't let her slip through his fingers. After a night—or a few—spent with Mila, life might return to normal. Whatever that was.

The taxi stopped in front of his block and he paid the driver, grabbed his luggage and got out of the taxi. Outside the double street doors that led into the apartment block, he paused to take his jacket off.

He punched in the code and entered the lobby. It was empty and he dialed Mila's number, his heart skipping a beat in the anticipation of talking to her. Dirty. He needed to test that honeyed tongue of hers to see what witticism she'd come up with, with those sweet, fuckable lips.

After two rings she answered. "Hello?" Her voice was husky, doused in sleep.

"It's James." He rubbed the frown lines on his forehead with his thumb. What the fuck was he doing? It wasn't that late. Was she sleeping already?

"James?" She gave a soft chuckle. "How's Brussels? Sprouty?"

He chucked. "Brussels is signed and sealed."

"Well done."

"What are you doing?"

"I'm right where you left me this morning."

"Hmm…?" He ran a finger around his collar. *Here we go…* she was much quicker than he'd anticipated. "In bed?"

"You did say I should stay right where I am."

She was a tease. He could be a tease too. "The entire day? What did you do with yourself in bed the whole day, Mila Johnson?"

She breathed into the phone, a little laugh escaping. "Don't be silly. I went to the D'Orsay and now my feet are killing me."

"Sounds like you need a foot massage." He tugged his tie loose and shoved it in his pocket.

"Sounds about right."

"Anybody there to help out?"

"With a foot massage?" she murmured. "No."

"You're alone?" Instead of waiting for the lift he took the stairs two at a time.

"Of course I'm alone. I don't know anybody in Paris."

Good. He planned to keep it that way.

"You really shouldn't be."

"What?"

"You really shouldn't be alone in Paris, Mila."

"Wasn't exactly my plan either," she said, then sighed into the phone. "What are you doing tonight?"

"I've eaten the obligatory dinner with the bond folks. Now I'm off to bed." He fished his apartment key from his jacket pocket and pushed it into the lock and twisted.

"Oh. Wait—"

Through the line, he could hear that she was moving.

"There's someone at the door." Her tone was edged with concern.

She was more awake than the evening before. She hadn't heard a thing the previous night. He tried not to smile too widely. "Really?"

34

"Oh God. James!" she whispered. "Who's got keys to your apartment?"

"Only me." He stepped into the foyer, took the few steps into the lounge and met her wide-eyed gaze as she froze mid-stride.

She wore a white tank top and white cotton panties. Not a sign of that innocent Hello Kitty nightshirt. Her hair fanned loose over her shoulders. She had her glasses on, looking bewildered. The devil himself couldn't help him now.

"Stop doing that!" she reproached. "Two nights in a row! I feel like vomiting my heart out."

He laughed as he dropped his things to the side. "Please don't!" He took a tentative step closer. "Now you're no longer alone."

She didn't look away, didn't even blink behind those black frames. The glasses suited her, but he was looking forward to stripping her bare and he'd start with them.

"I'm here to give you a foot massage." Bar asking for sex outright he couldn't muster a more straightforward invitation.

"A foot massage?" she breathed, her hands swiping down her tank top. "I might just take you up on that."

Sweaty palms much, Miss Johnson? "Might just?"

Her face was flushed, maybe from the shock of him barging in on her again, or maybe because she understood his meaning exactly. Fuck it, she was too sweet.

"That depends," she chuckled. "My feet are all blistered and if I have to stand for another second—"

He closed the gap between them, took her by her waist and heaved her over his shoulder. "I'll have to sweep you off your feet then."

"Ahhhh!" she laughed. "James!"

He strode with her to the bedroom, Mila shaking with laughter and slapping at him in careless protest.

"Put me down!"

"Sure, Princess." He let her slip down slowly against his chest, their bodies flush, every curve of hers teasing his shoulder muscles, his chest, his thighs. His erection was soon going to battle for space in his slim-fit trousers. Grasping her hips, he tightened her to him, to his very essence that craved release.

She didn't let go, her arms following the rest of her, except that they hooked around his neck until she found her feet. Then she leisurely eased her hands over his shoulders, leaving a spread of heat over his skin. They paused on his chest and when she gazed up at him her lips parted, wet and begging.

He wanted to kiss her, deeply. So badly.

The thought stalled every further action.

This was pure fucking madness.

Instead of giving in to the craving that burst to his lips he leaned in and kissed a slow path down her neck.

Her pulse raced under his lips, her chest heaving against his.

"We shouldn't, James," she whispered as she tilted her head, making space for him to suck and nibble.

"No, we shouldn't," he echoed back, tortured. She smelled of spring flowers, tasted like lazy Sunday afternoons filled with sex.

"But we're going to, aren't we?"

What had he been thinking? Now that he was here, with her in his arms, he didn't know how to stop. He fucking needed to. This was Mila.

He was a man who didn't acknowledge the concept of sin.

He should have stayed in sprouty Brussels.

He closed his eyes and dropped his head back with a heavy

exhale. "Give me five minutes. I'll give you five minutes. Make sure this is what you really want."

His eyes met hers in a moment of weighted silence. She searched his gaze, lost. "Why?"

"Mila." Was he trying to talk sense into her head, or his? "Being in my bed… comes with certain risks. Or risqué certainties. Whichever takes your fancy."

She nodded slightly; her eyes sparkled and her lips twitched. "Risqué *certainties*?"

She was so not helping. But he needed to give her every chance to opt out.

"What's your risk profile, Mila?" he whispered as he leaned in to taste her again.

She shivered at his touch on her sensitive skin. "I don't know. I've never considered it."

Fuck knew how he was going to contain himself and not fuck her six ways from Sunday. He let go of her and walked into the bathroom. "If you're the conservative, skittish type, stick to the far end of the bed. I'll get it and leave you alone. Otherwise… rough times ahead."

Chapter 9

MILA HELD HER BREATH AS she listened to the movements in the en suite bathroom. James was brushing his teeth and she instinctively ran her tongue over her own.

For the duration of James's shower, she'd conjured images of them, together, and those visuals did nothing to slow the rising heat between her thighs. Her heart was beating in her throat and butterflies were high on something and partying in her stomach.

There was no misunderstanding James's intentions and her pulse sped away in anticipation. There was only one problem—how she was going to hide her inexperience? What if she disappointed him? The thought was too intrusive, so she shut every door in her mind, forcing her focus onto the physical.

Focus on her hymen. On that sneaky little bit of evidence that would give her innocence away without her even trying. She doubted it was still fully intact. Tampons, horse riding, doing ballet and splits… those were all hymen-tearing activities, weren't they? She hoped it wasn't still fully intact. Maybe he wouldn't notice.

Dear Lord. Let the hymen be gone. Please. Amen.

She shuddered. Good girls didn't pray for that.

But the good girl in her had walked out the moment James had walked in. He'd been in the forefront of her mind the whole day, with every step she'd taken and every blister she'd rubbed on her tired feet.

She let out a deep breath, calming herself. He was the proverbial sex-on-a-stick. She'd been fantasizing about him for as long as she could remember, and now everything seemed ripe—she even had condoms with her.

She glanced at the box that still stood where she'd tossed it that morning. She took the package and ripped the cellophane wrapping off, scrunched it together and threw it in the direction of the bin.

There. That should do. Risks covered.

Right.

This was a bad idea.

She got back under the covers with a suppressed giggle, sticking to the middle of the bed. The bathroom door opened and James walked out, still wet and dripping. His towel was wrapped around his hips so tightly that it held everything nicely together. Maybe he was no longer in the mood. Maybe he'd changed his mind. Maybe his cock was just really long... and he'd trapped it with the towel against his body.

He stared at her for a moment, searching her face.

"We need help here, Mila," he hissed. "Fuck knows I can't walk away. Aren't you the conservative type?"

"No." Why was she lying? He should know she was conservative to the marrow in her bones. She wanted to hide her face, which buzzed with prickles of heat. "We could just fool around?"

He tugged the towel from his hips, baring himself to her, then started rubbing his hair dry. The towel which dropped from his hands covered him… hardly.

Lord Almighty. Did it have to be so big? Where was it all going to go?

A lump jumped to her throat and wouldn't budge. It was nerves, and her fingers curled into the duvet as his eyes settled on her.

His gaze swerved to the box of condoms and back to her. "Not fooling around at all, are we?" he said, his lips tugging into a smile.

She didn't have to answer.

He stepped away and threw the towel toward the bathroom, exposing his toned glutes and a smoothly-muscled back. He switched off the lights and closed the shutter blinds until only a yellow haze of the city's glow scantly lit the room.

He padded over, his figure dark against the window. As he got under the covers, the heat of his body filtered through the linen. The dark room enveloped them, the bed's covers like a cocoon, trapping their bodies' heat.

She had to keep her cool. Doing it in the dark would be a breeze. Her face wouldn't give her away in the dark—the heat of embarrassment had settled like a faint layer of red watercolor on her skin.

He tugged at the cover, sliding it over her breasts and lower, exposing her to the cooler air, which was thick with the scent of his moist hair and freshly-showered skin. Her nipples puckered against her top, sending a shiver of goose bumps over her arms and stomach. He hadn't even touched her yet, and he was doing this to her.

He edged over, his muscular shape silhouetted in the dark. She inhaled because he was so close, so close that his breath caressed her cheek. Her pulse jumped when he touched her forehead gently, tracing a line down to the bridge of her nose with his forefinger. She turned her face to his palm, into the harder skin of his male hand.

"You don't sleep with these, do you?" he quizzed as he pinched her glasses at the bridge and carefully slid them off. A sense of being exposed flitted through her, more so than when he'd removed the sheet.

"No," she whispered, already missing his fingertips on her body and the small pools of warmth they'd formed on her skin.

The sheet rustled as he reached over Mila to put her glasses on the bedside table. There was a slight pressure of his body on hers, a promise of the weight to come, a small hug of encouragement. He settled back next to her, shrugging the sheet down to reveal her body. Her white tank top and cotton panties seemed totally insufficient as his eyes rested on her. She felt his gaze traveling over her, the white fabric illuminated in the soft shards of light that beamed in from the skylight.

"Do you usually sleep in this?" His finger was back, this time tracing the thin strap of her tank top, tugging it gently until it slipped off her shoulder. She closed her eyes as his finger hooked the strap, pulling the top lower, peeling the fabric from her breast.

"No, I—" Her voice stalled as her nipple broke free, the cool air mingling with his breath as he blew over her skin and nipple. Her back arched and her breast brushed against his smooth palm.

He paused, his hand connected to her, his fingertips resting on the soft under-curve of her breast. "Hmm?"

"It's too hot for my Hello Kitty PJs." Why did it sound so… schoolgirl?

A quiet laugh slipped from his lips. "I like Hello Kitty." When his fingers ambled over, lazily catching her nipple, she inhaled at his touch, at the warmth that shot from her breast to her deepest part. His fingers rode her nipple, up and down, toying with her, so gently, almost in reverence as it puckered in a painful desire for something more.

When was he going to kiss her? She would be calmer if only he'd kiss her.

As if he sensed some need in her his hand traveled to her other shoulder, pulling at the strap. She rolled onto her side, trying to make out his face in the dark, wanting to touch him, too. Wanting to find his mouth.

His eyes glinted as he perused her openly. "It's too hot for clothes. Don't you agree?"

She wanted to nod, but he was already on his knees, his penis jutting out, silhouetted in the dark, to which she had grown accustomed. He was so comfortable in his skin, and on hers a permanent blush had gathered, intensifying the pools of heat generated by his touch. He was so close she could cup him in her hand. Her fingers twitched, wanting to reach out and touch him, but she hesitated. The size of him made her quiver. Inside she clenched, unclenched, and burned.

He nudged Mila onto her back and gathered her tank top with his fingers, pulling it lower. "Up with your hips," he instructed, and, before she could even grasp what he was doing, he had both her panties and top hooked with his thumbs and was pulling them downward. She lifted her hips in time with his actions. "Do you sleep in these?" he asked as he separated the two pieces, wriggling her panties in the air, staring her right in the eye.

"I do keep them on—"

"Not when in my bed." He tossed everything to the floor, not shifting his gaze. She suppressed the urge to cover herself, to reach for the sheet and drag it over her exposed body. She forced herself to relax her legs, allowing them to fall apart.

He leaned onto his hands, pinning her between his arms. He moved his body over hers, but sliding lower. His cock grazed her knee, leaving a wet trail of his arousal over her skin. Dipping his head, he kissed her hipbone, blazing a path above her trimmed pubic hair. The tender touch sent a gush of heat through her stomach. She dug her fingers into his hair, wanting to pull his head away, but instead found that she steadied him there, edging him down to where she wanted his lips the most.

"You're such a greedy little thing, Mila," he smirked as he kissed the soft skin leading to the apex of her thighs, trailing his tongue along the edge between the lips of her sex and inner thigh. "And I'm sure pretty tasty too."

Her insides oozed at his words, and a drop of arousal trickled between her thighs. He was working his magic way too fast for her, and in a moment of panic, her legs muscles contracted to clamp closed on her sex.

"Baby," he berated, then shifted, a hand on her knee, pressing it aside and up, splaying her for him, for his hot mouth and rough stubble that scrubbed against her skin. "Ticklish, are you?"

"No…" No one had ever been there before. She probably was ticklish but in that moment, every sensation was too much, desire overriding everything else, creating havoc in her body.

"Relax, I'll make it good," he whispered into her skin. He didn't let go of her, but slipped off the bed and pulled her legs until her bum rested close to the edge. He dropped to his knees on the carpeted floor, making himself comfortable.

A wild fear settled over her—a fear that he would actually kiss her *there* before having kissed her lips. Every muscle in her contracted away from him, when at the same time she wanted to push her sex to his mouth before he changed his mind. It was wrong, yet the promise of it sent waves of desire through her core.

She quivered when his hands stroked down her legs, spreading them wider. A part of her wanted to bring her knees together and roll away.

"Hello, Kitty," he sighed as he traced her sex's outer lips with his fingers, leaving a tingling path. "What do you like?" he quizzed, blowing a heated breath on her exposed, gaping slit. "Tell me?" The impulse to cover up was too strong. She propped up on her elbows, her knees almost catching his face between them as she closed her legs. But as if he anticipated this move he clamped her down. "Relax, Mila."

"Are you for real?" Was he having verbal intercourse with her *kitty*?

He met her gaze, eyes shining. "Very." He looked down at her sex again. Unable to move under his steady grip, her clit beating as if it had its own little heart, she dropped back and covered her eyes with her hands. She couldn't deal with this. It was torture.

"Just trying to figure out what makes you tick, baby," he said then, probably sensing her surrender because his steel grip on her knees loosened and his hands moved so that he rubbed his thumbs over her again, this time the merest fraction closer to her clit, each stroke bringing him closer, each stroke becoming smoother as he lubricated his thumbs with her juices.

"So deliciously wet, you needy little thing," he purred as the soft pads of his thumbs circled her clit, rotating one after the other in an agonizing, titillating game. He wasn't touching her clit; the build-up of desire to feel him there, where he wouldn't go, was almost too much.

She anchored her fingers in his hair as her hips started to

roll, mimicking his movements. "Kissing usually gets me ticking," she choked, wanting to slow him down, to distract him, and herself, from what seemed to be an unavoidable collision. *On the mouth.* Her lonely mouth, which, apart from a few lost words, had received zero attention from him. It felt wrong.

"I'm happy to oblige," he murmured and his mouth welded to her clit in a tender suck that sent an electric shock through her.

Her whole body jerked. "God!" she yelped, springing away from him, breathing hard against the current that still zapped through her. She clamped her lips down on the blasphemy that slipped from her lips, but no other word had come to mind. Her heart was beating, everywhere, as if it had taken over every other organ.

"Too much?" He stared at her from the foot end of the bed.

"Y-yes… no." How was she going to tell him that everything was too much?

He was studying her face, waiting for her to explain, his hands still on her legs, letting her know she wasn't going anywhere, and neither was he.

"I'm just used to doing things from the top down, not from the bottom up," she said—another white lie to help her out in this tight situation. She'd beg God for forgiveness for this, and everything else, later.

A soft chuckle broke from him as he took hold of her feet, stroking them tenderly. "I did promise you a foot massage."

He inspected her feet, which were more tired than blistered, except for the blisters on her heels. He started a deep massage on her soles, easing the tension from this part of her body with his expert touch. How did he know how to do this to her?

"Change is as good as a holiday." He got up and walked to the bedside table. He slid the drawer open and pulled something out of it. She eyed him warily.

"We don't need lube in the middle section but I enjoy this bottom-up-business," he teased. "We might just as well do this properly."

She could swear he'd winked at her as he drizzled something that smelled like lavender into his palm. He closed the bottle and dropped it onto the bed next to her. As he walked back to the end of the bed he lathered his palms.

His hands were warm as he touched her, oiling her feet with massage oil, spreading it to her shins and calves. "Breathe, Mila. Try to relax," he said after a minute. "Did I scare you too much earlier, barging in like that?"

The concern in his voice was real, and for a second she almost caved in and told him she was a virgin. He was sensing something was out of tune but would he sleep with her if he knew the truth? She was not going to risk finding out. The embarrassment of his rejection, the notion that he wouldn't want her would be too much for her right now. He'd kissed her *there*; it was as if she was already marked as his. She'd rather see everything through and, with any luck, he would be none the wiser.

"Yes, I'm rattled," she whispered. "I had no idea you'd be here tonight."

"Shhh," he said as he worked her soles, "you're safe with me. We won't do anything you don't want to do, so just say stop if it goes too far, or too quickly, okay?"

The rhythm of his hands, the pressure of his thumbs as he massaged her feet and edged his way up to her calves, told her he was looking after her, taking charge, giving her time. He was being generous, waiting for her to relax, to become the clay in his hands that he could shape as he saw fit. He seemed to know each knot as he went higher. Her nervousness had evaporated by the time he reached her thighs and urged her to roll onto her stomach.

It was a relief to hide her face in the soft duvet as he dripped the oil onto her back. Then his hands were on her, still sure and steady as he massaged her, luring and guiding her to what they were going to do together. He went higher now, his touch changing, becoming softer, more erotic. She shivered as he stroked the back of her knees, and higher to the curve of her butt. He palmed her, running his fingers over her buttocks and up her sides, to where her breasts swelled out from her body weight. Her breathing hitched; he was doing it again, making her want to squirm. Her pussy was clenching and unclenching, feeling empty.

"You're beautiful, Mila," he said as he gathered her hair away from her face, his body's heat a whisper against her back. He wasn't pressing down on her yet, but his shadow was falling over her.

"You're not so bad yourself," she sighed, suspended between the erotic laziness that had settled over her and the incongruous undercurrent of anticipation that undulated within her.

"Feel what you've been doing to me, ever since I saw you in my bed yesterday, waiting." He whispered the words in her ear, his lips caressing her lobe, setting fireworks of goose bumps loose over her skin. He shifted then, and with his hand, ran his cock down the crack of her butt. The ripple of lust that ran through her at this touch was almost as intense as when he'd licked her clit. His cock was wet, warm, and rock hard. He pressed down, rolling his hips. Her body went with his, almost instinctively. "Do you have any idea how much I want to fuck you right now?"

She moaned, wanting him to do as he'd promised already.

"Tell me you want this; tell me you want me." He kissed her back, sliding his lips in a soft line to her temple.

"Yes," she whispered, knowing that he was asking her honest consent. There was no way she could turn back now. She didn't want to turn back.

His weight lifted and he took the condom box that was still on his side of the bed. He busied himself opening the package, ripping the foil, whilst straddling her legs.

"Which fantasy of yours is this, Mila? Don't tell me it is One-night-in-Paris."

His frank question caught her off guard. He was so verbal, so open, so at ease, that deep down it made her afraid of failing him. Thinking about what she was about to do, she wanted to creep back under the covers, into the dark, where no one could see her sin. Her want. Her need. "Strangers in the night."

She should have kept it at that. It was too late now. Hit and run was no longer an option.

"Strangers in the night," he murmured. "Not after tonight, baby."

It was true; he'd know more of her than anybody else. She was fruitlessly trying to hide behind a fantasy, because deep down she wanted to hide her lie to him, the one man that in a way had known her the longest. "What's yours?" she asked, not wanting to think any further.

"Having the pastor's virgin daughter." He chuckled. "After a very long and boring sermon. During which I could think of nothing else but how I was going to fuck her sweet pussy until she came."

At his words every muscle in her lower abdomen pulled tight, upping her desire. A cold sweat settled over her back, and his hands became islands of warmth on her skin.

He knows.

She wanted to laugh, wanted to cry. She defaulted, chuckling. "Do you want me to play the part?"

"Hell yeah, if you want to," he said softly, his hands back on her butt, massaging her lower back. "Nothing like a bit of forbidden fruit."

She could paint this picture; it could work for her. She could slip out of her own skin, and yet she could totally be herself. She shifted under him, and he dropped back down on her, his legs sprawling over hers. He trapped her between his arms and his abs flexed against her back. His hands were fisted right next to her face, and she leaned in to drop a kiss on his thumb, licking it. He reacted, lifting his thumb to her lips, and she drew it into her mouth, sucking it as deep as she could, then back. He inhaled sharply, and she did it again.

"Fuck, Mila."

She arched up to meet his lips, but his cheek grazed against hers.

"Missionary or doggie, baby?" he whispered against her neck, whilst pressing sweet kisses along the ridge of her jaw, idling around her ear, sucking her lobe.

"Missionary," she murmured, breathless, "it's appropriate, don't you think?" She hadn't imagined losing her virginity any other way, to be honest. So traditional.

He didn't answer but eased her around. When he met her gaze in the dark, his eyes glinting, there was something in them she couldn't grasp. She reached for his face, stroking his cheeks, wanting to pull him closer for a kiss. But he cupped her chin in his hand, his thumb sweeping over her lips, dipping into her mouth. She licked and sucked him back, letting her movements echo his breaths that became more strained.

"I'll fuck this mouth later if you'll let me," he said as he slipped his thumb from her lips, his hand following the column of her neck, applying gentle pressure, making her catch her breath.

"What if it's too big?" she moaned, arching up to present her

49

breasts to him, knowing he'd know she was talking about his cock.

"Sweet baby," he breathed, "I'll be gentle. Only the tip, until you can take more. I promise."

"What if I'm too tight?" she asked, aching for him to touch her there, getting her head into this game they were playing. She reached for his cock, feeling it beyond the rubber of the condom that was straining over it. She ran her fingers down the thick length, knowing he would never fit inside her. It was mesmerizing, how it kept upright for so long. He sighed deeply, letting her toy with him, exploring, clasping his balls in her palm. Her fingers were dumb, fumbling, not hiding the fact that she had no clue what she was doing, but his breathing became heavier, slower and he groaned his pleasure.

"I can't get any harder than this, Mila," he said after some time, catching her hand and bringing it to his mouth to kiss her palm. "At least not without coming."

He dropped down, kneeing her legs wider. She was so drugged with desire she could do nothing but open to him. "Just the tip, I promise, slowly taking more, stretching you bit by bit."

"What if it hurts?" she asked, not funning anymore.

His hand was reaching between her thighs, to her clit, which was begging for a release of the ache that throbbed inside and around it. He slipped a finger inside her, softly, gently. "Does this hurt?" he whispered.

"No—" Her answer caught as he pulled out, ran a featherlike circle with the tip of his finger around the entrance, and slipped inside her again, going a bit deeper. God help her, but she wanted him so deep.

"More... please."

"Asking so prettily. Every part of you is begging for it, isn't it?" He pushed two fingers deeper and she bucked into his hand. "You're so wet," he groaned as he pressed down with his palm, letting his fingers ride in and out, sliding over her clit, into her entrance. "So ready..."

He shifted, his cock in hand, pressing the wide tip to her entrance, hovering, letting her feel him. He trapped her between the pillars of his arms and looked into her eyes. She gripped his wrists with her hands and bit her lip as she hooked her legs around his hips, lifting herself against his rigid cock. He kept still, looking at her with wonder. "Take it slowly, baby. Take it all."

He pressed down, holding still as she rode him, taking him slowly deeper, until he closed his eyes, his hips starting to roll with a low murmured *fuuuuck*.

She bit harder on her bottom lip, suppressing the gasp when he hit her tight barrier, but all resistance gave way to the thrusting of his hips, which were now working with her in a decisive rhythm. The moment of discomfort was gone, and having him inside her was weird, intrusive... and delicious. She fought the incongruous sensations, forcing herself to relax her legs and the clasp around his hips.

James seemed oblivious that she'd just been penetrated for the first time, and in her everything slipped, fell towards some abyss she didn't expect. He was fucking the pastor's virgin daughter, and she was letting it happen, a sweet revenge fuck, for wouldn't her mother and father just loathe learning that James Sinclair was her first?

It wasn't the heavy rising throb of an orgasm that built up to release, but the slow, dark suffocation of every physical sensation as her mind took over.

She blinked. She was *not* going to freaking cry.

"You're so fucking tight," he murmured then, their bodies mingling sweat. He gripped her head with his hands, kissing her neck, her closed eyes. "Don't hold back, baby, come with me," he murmured, a tortured moan slipping from him as she grabbed his ass, drawing him to her, making him dig deeper, deeper into her shame in an attempt to chase that nagging little voice that had surfaced away.

This was something one did in love. Her mother's words swamped her thoughts. *After marriage. Anything else was pure, unforgivable sin.* Regret washed through her as he ground into her, a tight gasp breaking free from his chest as he let go of her, thrusting with the force of every muscle in his legs and glutes, so deep it hurt.

"Fuck, James," she whimpered, almost pleaded, her pelvis clashing against his, her fingers digging into his butt as he spurted his seed. He held his position for a long minute, pulsing into her. When he leaned down, he took in her face, traced his nose along hers in such a gentle gesture that her heart slowed down. When he kissed her tenderly on the forehead she breathed tightly, trying to contain the emotions that swarmed her mind and heart.

"You came?" he asked softly, searching her eyes.

Thank God it was dark. "Yes," she lied. She'd never been so close. Had never lost it so quickly.

He pulled out of her, busying himself with the condom, which he knotted, wrapped in a tissue and placed on the bedside table.

He sagged back onto the bed, pulling her into his arms. He held her for a long time, tracing lazy lines down her arm, pressing his lips against her temple. She breathed easier but was all clogged up.

"You like sleeping like this or must I leave you alone, my little stranger?"

Always so freaking considerate. She had no clue. "I sleep on my side."

"Then tuck in." He shifted his arms, allowing her to turn

obediently on her side so that he could spoon her. He cuddled her close, the warmth of his skin against hers soothing, even if it was only on the surface.

He hadn't kissed her once.

She stared at the thin beam of light from the window as his breathing steadied. He fell asleep quickly, and only then did she let the tears slide down her cheeks.

Peace was elusive, and the idea of finding it in prayer seemed foreign.

There was no reversing the clock. She'd never be the same again and she couldn't share what had happened with Stacey, or with anybody for that matter.

That pesky little voice in her head whispered that revenge was never sweet, and doing wrong things for any reason never paid.

Bad, bad girl.

Chapter 10

JAMES DREW HIS ARM FROM underneath Mila's neck and paused as she stirred. He gathered the long strands of her dark hair away from her back, extracting himself completely. She rolled on her stomach and resumed the even rhythm of her breathing, her face turned away from him and the pink light of dawn falling on her naked back.

He scrubbed his face and stared at his least-favorite mistake. A mistake he hadn't made in a good six years. The last time he'd had a one-night stand was pre-Marlène, and back then, he'd always connived to leave in the dead of night, making sure he didn't wake up beside a stranger in the morning.

This one took the bloody cherry. Sweet Mila Johnson was in his bed and he was going to regret it.

There was no such thing as a perfect one-night stand. It was always laced with a bit of desperation, a bit of folly, sometimes a bit too much liquor on one party's part, if not both. But this was the first case of pure soul-driven lust that got him into this situation.

A slow breath reverberated out of his chest. If a one-night

stand wasn't well managed, it came with a good dollop of regret, regret he avoided by not taking the risk of waking up next to the lady or ladies in question.

Mila wasn't one-night stand material. He'd known this from the start, irrespective of the evidence to the contrary that littered the apartment.

Something was off and he couldn't put his finger on it.

Bottom line: Mila wasn't going anywhere soon. She was here to stay for the entire time he would be in Paris—and she was a complication he didn't need. Even if his cock was ready to take on complications.

He couldn't remember the last time he'd fallen asleep so easily. And he hadn't slept so well in years. He took in the smooth slope of her back and the dimples above her butt, barely visible before the rest of her disappeared under the covers. He reached for the air conditioner's remote and beeped the temperature as low as it would go, kicking the covers off his legs.

If he hadn't been so horny, or so desperate, or such a bloody idiot, he would've gone somewhere else to sleep. But the temptation of her had been too big. He was risk-averse when it came to leading women on. He never spent a night with someone without ensuring all lines were deep grooves in the sand.

But here he was with Mila. She had been a rather playful lay, but that was probably not to be repeated if he was to keep all emotions out of the equation. Why hadn't he thought it all through the night before? Stopped himself? She was Stacey's best friend—his sister would not only jam her knee into his balls for sleeping with Mila in the first place, but she'd be pissed to the eyeballs if he messed with Mila's feelings, or worse.

He ran the events of the previous evening through his mind's eye. Mila had been keen, oscillating between playing the shy nymph and urging him on. Something towards the end of their little game had made him pause, but at that point, there had been no holding back. Had she even come? She'd been on the brink so many times. He chuckled as he got out of bed to use the bathroom. She must have, surely, given the way her pussy had been clutching his cock.

Mila had been fun, fooling around with him, as much as he had fooled around with her. She'd suggested fooling around in the first place. He rubbed the back of his neck, trying to ease some of the tension. Fooling around had come a long way since he last checked.

Deep inside he sensed they weren't done with each other yet. Maybe they could strike up some deal. A no-strings-attached sex fest while she was in Paris, and he'd get to satisfy the boner he'd be sporting for the time she was invading his apartment.

For an invasion it was. The scent of sex and lavender clung to his body where he'd rubbed over her oiled-up skin, and her few toiletries were scattered over the commode. Her clothes were draped over the edge of the bath, a confused pile of mismatched flowery fabric and sandals. He was no longer in the habit of having someone in his space. Lately, he'd spent most of his time alone in characterless hotel rooms, and Marlène had never shared his bathroom. She had too much stuff—samples, make-up and promotional beauty products of every kind used to clutter up her bathroom in the second bedroom.

He finished brushing his teeth when a rattling noise made him pause. He turned toward the bathroom door that hadn't closed properly to listen. The shutters were rolling up in the bedroom.

He opened the bathroom door to find Mila sitting with her back to him, her hair cascading down her back, almost to her waist.

She was wearing those seductive white panties she'd worn the night before. She turned to glance at him, fumbling with the tank top she still held in her hands.

"Hi." He needed to break the ice and cursed at being so out of practice.

"Hi." She turned away to the window, to the view of the Tuileries and the line of trees bordering the street.

Why hadn't he gotten up earlier? He could have gotten over this moment by plying her with a buttery croissant and coffee, then sending her on her way with a loving pat on her sweet ass.

Fuck it. She wasn't going anywhere.

He strode towards her, his dick, as always, two steps ahead. "Slept well?"

Her hair covered her breasts, her feet and knees pressed together. She didn't look at him, her eyes averted behind her glasses, as she busied herself turning the tank top right side out. Her lips were moist but she ran her tongue over them again, and his cock saluted the gesture, doing a little push-up. He'd forgotten how, with her sitting on the bed, his cock could be a bit in the face, never mind that he'd told her he'd fuck her mouth if she'd let him.

Another reason why morning-afters were never good. He could keep going all day long, whereas women always seemed to be fucked tired and sore after round one.

He sat down next to her, gathering her hair away from her chest, opening her body to him. He had to see her beautiful breasts again before she put on her top. "Did you enjoy yourself last night? I know I did."

"Yes," she spurted out, her fingers trembling, her shoulders hunching to hide her breasts.

"Mila…" His gaze wandered down the curves she was trying

to hide, to her nipples that were hardening silently, voicing how she felt when he looked at her. His gaze dropped lower, to the apex of her thighs.

He did a double take. "Your period?"

On her creamy upper thigh, a faint red smudge disappeared under her panties.

She didn't answer, a deep blush settling over her cheeks.

"Don't be shy, baby," he murmured. "If you don't have tampons with you, there's a shop—"

She stiffened, her breasts lifting in a tantalizing tilt as she raised her arms to pull on the top. "I've come prepared for that eventuality, thank you."

He turned away, looking at the debris that was Madame Leborgne's perfectly made bed. "You don't need to hide anything so natural from me. You know that?"

The faint sweep of blood that stained the white linen wasn't contained to where she'd been lying. He narrowed his gaze to where he'd probably pulled the condom off, and to the condom that lay discarded on the bedside table, a tinge of red crusted on the tissue. His pulse heaved and his head spun a turn as he looked back at her. She didn't need to hide anything from him… she couldn't hide anything from him.

She still hadn't looked him in the eyes, but her breathing pitched in the silence, her hands fumbling with her tank top's edge, fingers quivering. He cupped her cheek to force her to look at him. "Mila—"

"I need the bathroom."

He ran his thumb over her moist lips, but that sweet tongue did not peek out to tease him. "Not until we've talked about this."

She still looked down, trying to shrug his hand away, but he

58

touched her more tenderly, his fingers reaching to the hair at the nape of her neck, then retracting, tracing soft paths into her thick strands.

"Mila." He didn't want to sound commanding, but he knew she wouldn't trifle with him when he used that tone.

Her gaze met his, unwavering, her brown eyes wet with the truth as she blinked.

Fuck. He hadn't seen this coming. She'd been a virgin. A freaking virgin! A budding anger rose in him because playing games like this was the last thing on his agenda. "You cheating little minx."

She stiffened under his hold, trying to pull away, but he didn't let her.

All women needed and deserved tenderness, to be loved after the act and given the aftercare they needed. But virgins? That first time...fuck.

Mila needed to be held, to be kissed, needed to be made love to by the man she was going to marry, especially since she'd held out for this moment until the age of twenty-four. A virgin like Mila shouldn't be randomly fucked into oblivion by a man like him. Not her first time. His type should be last in the world to have the pleasure of...deflowering a beauty like Mila.

Fuck it. He would have taken it slower. He would have made it more—what—special? No wonder every movement, every breath, and every tremble had been in contradiction with the rest of her. If only he'd known. Had he really been that blind? They'd been playing a game, but it hadn't been a game at all.

"Was last night your first time?" He stopped short of cursing. He couldn't believe it. When she said nothing, his hand circled around her neck, pulling her closer, and he peered into her eyes. "Tell me, Mila?"

"Yes." The blush that tinged her cheeks spread to her neck and lower to disappear below her tank top.

"Why didn't you tell me?" He let go of her, giving her space to breathe because she'd been holding her breath.

She stretched the tank top down, trying to pull it over the evidence. He stilled her by clasping both her hands in one of his. She shot him a glance, then gave a strained laugh.

"Laugh all you want, but I want to know why you didn't tell me."

She shot up, forcing him to move and took two steps away from him. "I didn't know how to tell you, okay?"

"And?" By the strain on her face, she felt rotten about the lie she'd told. But there was something more here.

"I need the bathroom." And off she went.

Mila was avoiding the question, walking off like that. He sure as hell wasn't used to a woman closing up on him like this. The type he slept with normally spelled out what they had done, and would like to do—with him—and there was no guilt or repercussions. Not like now. There were stains on the linen... he *must* have hurt her. He crossed the floor in a few wide strides, catching Mila by the wrists and pressing her against the bedroom wall, trapping her, his cock nestling between them, still erect, wanting her.

"Did I hurt you?" he asked, his voice husky with the knowledge that he'd been too rough, too forceful and hasty in his drive to climax. She'd had no clue what was coming her way.

"No... it was fine."

FINE. Freaked out. Insecure. He couldn't remember the rest of the acronym Stacey always threw at him whenever *fine* came up in conversation. Had she been scared that she would disappoint him? Inside he felt himself shrink. *He* had disappointed *her*.

"Did you even come?" he asked, staring at her flushed face, into her eyes, which were brimming with tears.

Her breathing came hard and fast through those two beautiful, fuckable lips. They were rosy, moist, full, and had been playfully sassy with him last night. Playing the part. Which hadn't been a part at all.

"I don't know," she whispered, trying to break free. Their gazes clashed, her face flushed as he held her there.

Seconds passed, then he smirked at her answer, incredulous. This was a novel experience. He leaned closer to her, his mouth at her ear. "I can't guarantee you much in life, Mila, but I can guarantee you that, when I make a woman come, she knows about it."

He let go and strode away from her, trying to contain the anger that had erupted out of nowhere. Behind him, the bathroom door closed with a click.

Chapter 11

MILA LEANED AGAINST THE BATHROOM door, wanting to prevent James from following her. The door handle didn't move and she closed her eyes on an exhale, killing the sob that battled in her chest. There was no lock on the door, but as angry as he'd been she half expected him to stomp in and give her a spanking for not telling him he'd been her first. He would pull her over those muscular rugby thighs of his, push up her tank top and pull down her panties and smack her hard on her naked butt.

The notion of James spanking her made heat simmer between her thighs. She shuddered. One night with him and she was totally debauched.

Why had he been so angry? It wasn't as if he'd lost anything. She'd let go of the one thing she was supposed to keep sacred and unconditionally promise to the man she loved—the man with whom she was supposed to spend her life in married bliss.

So not James Sinclair.

He'd said he'd enjoyed it.

Dear Lord.

At least she hadn't been a complete failure.

It had felt all too good. Inside her, the brooding frustration intensified. She was wound tight by the feather-light strokes of James's hands, his kisses on her breasts, his body inside hers. She could still feel him pulsing inside her—sleep had done nothing to wipe out the traces he'd left everywhere.

She'd underestimated her body's reaction to his and hadn't expected this deep-seated sense of being unfulfilled.

She hated what her upbringing and small world had prescribed for her. She hated that her body and conscience were in opposition and that she couldn't please the one without sending the other into a diatribe of shame.

Her fingers longed to go where James's fingers had been, to find the release her body craved... *When I make a woman come, she knows about it.*

She didn't doubt him for a second. She couldn't touch herself, not with him on the other side of the door, waiting, knowing what she'd be up to. She hardly ever did. Good girls didn't do things like that.

She got on with her morning routine, fingers trembling as she brushed her teeth and combed her hair. If she could afford to, she'd go stay somewhere else. But this trip had already been crafted on a too-tight budget. Her little shopping spree of a luxurious bottle of red wine had chewed into two days' worth of her food budget. She'd had no idea things were so expensive in Paris, and being in the center of the city didn't help. And she'd rather starve than miss any of the museums and galleries she'd flown thousands of kilometers to see.

Had she known sleeping with James would mess things up

on more than one level, she might have taken her chances on the wingback chair in the lounge. But it had happened too quickly and she'd paid no heed to the secondary repercussions.

Because she'd wanted him. It was as simple as that.

And now his scent clung to her like fog on a cold window and she had to get it off. For her soul's sake, there would be no repeat performance of last night's intimacies. Her body would have to toe the line. She stripped and got into the shower, turning the heat up to scald her skin clean.

James stalked to the kitchen and tossed the crushed-up condom in the bin. He paced the length of the lounge, the carpet soft underfoot, the early morning light frank in its honesty: he'd fucked up. Big time. With Mila Johnson.

When had he become so out of tune? Okay, eight months without sex was an eternity, but given that he considered himself an expert in the field, he had just suffered a massive fail. If this were work, he would've lost millions of dollars.

He heaved a sigh, frustrated. When had he started comparing sex with money and million-dollar deals? Was it because there had been nothing else in his life for the past eight months? Had it always been like that? Breathing into his cupped hands, he tried to recall. Fuck it all.

He raked his fingers through his hair and stomped to the linen closet in the kitchen. He bundled together clean sheets from his housekeeper's neat stack.

Back in the bedroom, he changed the sheets, the silence from the adjacent bathroom deafening. If Mila was crying, she was doing it so quietly he couldn't hear her. He still had no idea why she hadn't been open with him.

Had she been scared that he would have rejected her? Would it have stopped him?

Nope.

Yes.

He had no idea what he would've done. Virgins had never been on his to-do list. Even his own virginity had been claimed by a schoolgirl who'd worked her way through his team when he was on a rugby tour in his final year of high school. He played flanker, position four or five, and this lady had been counting down from fifteen to number one. The memory made him curse. It had been a messy experience. Fast, furious and unfulfilling.

Had it been like that for her?

With Mila, he would've paused, that was certain. He wouldn't have pounced on her as he had but would have taken time with her and made sure it was memorable. Had she even enjoyed it? He couldn't be sure.

He exhaled slowly. Her virginity was lost now, and the least he could do was make it up to her somehow.

By finishing off what they had started last night. By making her feel good. By making her come. Preferably again and again.

His dick went straight back to high alert, and he groaned. What if she said no?

She was so going to say no. Pastor Johnson's daughter. Who had been fucked after a very dull sermon, living up to each part of his fantasy. He chuckled and his anger abated. Mila might have had a prudish, overprotected upbringing, but she'd been begging to be taught just how this game worked.

The toilet flushed, and the shower faucet turned on. He waited a minute, digesting the opening of the shower door, the water's change of rhythm as she got in.

He pushed down the door handle, peering into the steam that already hugged the ceiling and swirled lower. She stood under the stream with her face raised to the water, her hair a black waterfall caressing her butt. She looked down and scrubbed her body almost viciously as if she could get clean… clean of what they'd done.

She was unaware that he was watching her, her hands gliding the soap over her perfect breasts, down her belly, and between her legs. He stepped into the bathroom, walked to the shower door, and opened it with a click. At the sound, she looked up, and the soap slipped from her hands, thudding onto the tiled floor. She raised her arms to cover her breasts, her back pressed against the wall as he got into the shower.

"Let me." He reached down for the soap, giving her body a slow inspection as he straightened. Beautiful creamy legs, like silk, curvy hips but a flat tummy. A little mole close to her belly button marked its territory. And her breasts, which she tried her best to hide, were heavy, nipples jutting upwards, begging to be kissed. She was gorgeous.

"James—"

The burning water beat his back, his bulk blocking it from falling on her rose-tinged skin. "You think you're in hell already, don't you, for what we've done?" He turned the faucet to a cooler temperature and slipped the soap into the holder.

When he turned to her, he propped his hands on either side of her, hindering any means of escape. Her lips were slightly parted, her eyes wide as she stared at him, her wet lashes clinging to each other in sharp little points. Her face shone with water, probably mixed with tears because her eyes were red.

"I'm not thinking anything." Her voice was almost lost in the water's rush because she'd spoken so softly. She dropped her gaze but lifted it again to his upper chest. Away from his erection, but not meeting his gaze. He only had those lips, which were being shredded by a set of perfect teeth, to go on. Her mind was churning, all right.

"Do your parents know you are here?"

"No."

He raised his brows. "They don't know that you are here by Stacey's invitation?"

She shot him a glance. "No."

Of course not. The Johnsons would have a conniption if they knew.

"They think I'm at a youth camp. Somewhere in the sticks. Where there is no network or cellphone reception." She bit her lip to stop its quivering… or was it the start of a laugh? "My brother Ruben knows I'm here. He dropped me off at the airport."

He wanted to laugh. This little bird had flown the cage, but he was still ticked off at the situation. He couldn't give a damn about her condescending, two-faced parents or her brother. He cared about her.

A—she'd been a virgin.

B—she hadn't come.

Had he lost his touch? He sighed. "I wished you'd told me."

He felt a total idiot. The two most probably went hand-in-hand. Especially if he considered how she'd been brought up. He might not have been subjected to the same dogma as Mila, but he'd experienced enough of the thought process at school to understand what might be going on in her head.

"Are you angry?" She met his gaze, her face turning crimson.

Her question was frank, and so should his answer be. He was pissed off, but it wouldn't help her already-brainwashed conscience to tell her that he was unworthy of her gift. That indeed, he would have preferred if she'd stowed it away for someone worthy who'd kept to a similar set of morals. That he'd feel like a real man—not a defiling dickhead—if he'd earned her virginity, by being in love with her, and she with him... by fulfilling a desire fueled by love.

"I'm not angry. But there are a few things going on in my head."

She blinked. "A few things? More than one? How bizarre for a man."

Little Miss Sassy.

"That mouth, Mila... I've promised to do some things to it—with it." She slowly turned her face, inclined her head to meet him halfway, and he knew she needed it. Wanted it. Deserved it. He leaned closer, catching himself just in time to stall the kiss. He couldn't go there. It was so dead set in his rules—even if those rules no longer had any bearing—that he deflected to her ear. "The one thought that keeps on coming back to me is that I've been taken for a ride twice, and you only once. Without any success."

"James—"

"Let me," he interrupted, his nose riding the ridge of her ear to her lobe, which he nibbled, sucked, making her shift on her feet. She raised her hands but stopped short of touching him, dropping them back to her sides.

"James, I—"

"Let me—" He broke off to lean into her, sliding his hands up the tiled wall, bringing his body closer to hers. As his cock touched and rode up the flat of her stomach, wet and pulsing with want, she rasped in a breath, her nipples hard as they rubbed against his chest.

It had been a calculated move to make her feel him, make her realize that he still wanted her, to make sure she still wanted him. "Let me show you what we can do when we take our time."

The notion hung between them, full of promise and the release he knew she craved. Her body was speaking to him without saying a word, in the rise of her breasts against his chest, in the halting way she breathed, in the way she intuitively rocked forward to rub against his cock.

"James, I shouldn't," she almost pleaded.

A shouldn't—not a wouldn't or a couldn't.

"Just once, baby. To finish what we started. So that you can feel how good sin tastes."

Something caved inside Mila at his words, because she leaned forward and rested her head on his chest, hiding her face. Her shoulders shook as she sobbed and he pushed away from the wall to gather her in his arms.

James held her for a long moment, protecting her from the cleansing onslaught of the water that streamed down his back. He could only imagine what was going on in her mind, as her need for sexual release battled against her conscience. He caressed her back and waited for her to find herself. Eventually, her breathing evened and she hiccupped. He stroked her shoulders, then headed down her arms to her hands, which he clasped in his.

"Just once?" She looked up at him, her eyes shining with innocent desire. He'd never been worthy of that look in any woman's eyes.

He had to break away from her intense gaze and closed his eyes. He rested his forehead against hers. "Trust me?" he asked, for that was what her gaze imparted.

She nodded and he pulled her hands to his waist, flattening her palms against him. Her hands settled, uncertain, quivering, seeking as they shifted under his.

"Touch me," he whispered. He loosened his grip and she didn't pull away. The relief of this small acquiescence pulsed through his veins. She hadn't run off—yet.

Tame me. The words rushed through his mind, hovering on his tongue. He bit them back.

Chapter 12

JUST ONCE. THAT WAS THE deal.

Mila ran her fingers around the ridges of his stomach, James's forehead still resting on hers as he guided her hands over his body. It was magnificent, sculpted from years of exercise which he obviously still did. She lifted her mouth to his as her hands slipped to his back and his glutes, but he pulled away. He dropped his head back in a soft moan as he let go, steadying himself by stretching his arms to either side of the shower wall. Her lips melded with his throat and trying not to look like an idiot she worked her way over his Adam's apple and into the hollow of his neck instead.

With his guidance gone, she had no idea what to do. The water trickled from his broad shoulders in small rivulets, losing track in the hair on his pecs, diverting when it hit some oily patches.

"You smell like lavender," she whispered, lifting a finger to trace a patch on his skin where water and oil didn't mix.

"Hmm, you smell edible. Same as last night." He still stood with his head tossed back, but a smile played on his lips.

He was waiting for something. He was waiting for her, letting her set the pace.

For some reason the stress of expectation slipped from her, making her feel light and silly. Rising on her toes she pressed her lips to his ear, her breasts rubbing his chest. "May I soap you down?" The idea of her hands roaming over his gorgeous body, free to touch where she wanted, to see how he reacted, excited her.

He met her gaze. "Do whatever pleases you, Mila." He turned the water down to a slow trickle. "Explore all you want."

"I'm not good at any of it."

He stared at her, silent for a moment. "Then I'll teach you." He reached for the soap and slipped it into her hand.

"Shower 101?" She widened her eyes, mocking primly.

"Just a little lesson, baby."

His tone held a pinch of threatening tease, and she swallowed. A part of him was still pissed off. Why did she feel that she was going to pay for lying by omission? "I promise to be a fast learner." Remember. *Just once.*

"I won't mind you taking your time," he grinned, lifting an eyebrow.

His words made her quiver inside. Making deals with James was a bad idea because he already had the upper hand. Wasn't making million-dollar deals what he did for a living? If she took her time and failed, he might deem it fit that she had another... lesson. Her conscience was knocking heavily, but she went deaf as her body surged with lust.

Just once. She'd make it count.

She rolled the soap in her hands, then pressed her slippery palms to his chest, slowly sliding them to his shoulders. One hand still held the soap and she drew a path with it over his body, circling his ridges and valleys.

He settled his arms again on either side of the shower's walls, giving her access to every part of him. She didn't dare look down, for the tip of his cock brushed against the under-curve of her belly on every breath he took. He was warm and wet, the damp air heavy with the scent of his arousal. Her need intensified and her hands slowed of their own accord. She stroked him gingerly, running her fingers over the soapy fuzz on his chest, and back to his neck and sandpaper stubble.

He moaned as she retraced her steps, going lower to the V carved in his abdominal muscles, which beckoned where she was not quite ready to go. It was one thing fondling him in the dark at night, and another to touch him in the morning light that filtered through the bathroom window, where her inexperience was clear and embarrassing. Her breathing was strained as it was, her pulse jetting her blood through her veins as she blinked. His cock was begging to be touched.

Instead of going lower, she chickened out and slipped her hands around to his glutes, the soap slipping from her fingers as he shifted his weight.

He murmured something unintelligible and lowered his head. "I need more, Mila," he whispered as he guided her soap-sudsed hand to his penis, suspended like a bridge between them. "Touch me."

Her fingertips brushed against the silky skin of his shaft. "I—" His reaction to her touch was immediate, and her voice broke as he clasped his fingers over hers, wrapping them around his cock. His grip was much tighter than she'd expected, and she gasped as he thrust against their hands in solid, slow strokes.

His breathing became strained, and she quivered inside knowing she had this effect on him. She wanted to give him more, but after a minute he loosened his grip with a groan and she let go. "I'd love you to jerk me off right now, but this is about you."

She inhaled sharply at his soft-spoken desire. "I'd like to learn how to—" Inwardly she shrunk at her own boldness, wishing she could liquefy and disappear down the shower drain.

"God, you're sweet when you blush, Mila," he whispered, caressing her cheek with the back of his hand. She melted at his loving touch and turned to press a kiss to his fingers.

She hesitated for a split second, but she wanted this, as much as his body told her he wanted it too. Gazing up at him, she felt decidedly liberated at his reaction and the softness of his gaze. "It could be part of the... lesson?"

He groaned as he shifted on his feet, his cock lifting as if to give its own consent to this scheme. "You know that no man can resist that, right?" He pursed his lips as if struggling to make a decision. He shook his head then, lowering their hands to where his cock was waiting impatiently.

"If this is what you want, hold on tight," he instructed. "I like it hard and fast in the mornings."

He didn't let go but continued to guide her hand, clasping his over hers. At their slow, deliberate rocking his cock hardened even more, lengthening, and she looked down as he built up speed. He breathed in short snatches, but suddenly he paused and cupped her chin in his free hand. His eyes looked drugged as he studied her face through half-mast lids. He ran his thumb savagely over her lips, spreading them open. "This would be more comfortable for your hand if you were on your knees," he whispered.

To her, going on her knees meant something different. She shuddered at what it could imply. She couldn't do it, not now, not like this—the connotation was too religious, and as if he read her mind he let go with a groan and reached for her other hand instead.

"Cup me," he said between gritted teeth, as he settled her hand to his balls.

One hand palmed his sack, which was heavy. He adjusted their grip on his cock with the other and resumed their stroking, this time with more vigor as he stabilized them by pressing against the wall with his free hand. She glanced down at their hands, desire swelling between her legs at the image, knowing she was part of it. Her body swerved with her own unreleased tension, which was becoming more powerful as she watched his need building up.

"Tighter, baby," he said with a curse, his hips undulating with each push and pull. "You can do it." He sped up even more, his fingers now hovering over hers, only guiding her rhythm.

She was in awe, feeling him surrendering to her movements alone as he relaxed his grip. It would be her that would send him over the cusp. At the thought she clenched him, and the rush of release as his semen ran through his erection, to the tip, rippled up the inside of her hand. He moaned, holding onto her as his seed squirted over her, spurts of male paint recklessly splattering her breasts and stomach.

He drew in a sharp breath as he ejaculated, and fisted his hand over hers again, making sure she couldn't let go. Her heart was pounding, her arousal seeping to her thighs. Only a minute later, finally spent, did he unfurl his steel grip from her fingers and pull her hands to his chest. When he dropped his chin to her head, wrapping her in his arms, she had to steady herself at his unexpected weight. She pressed flush to him but inside she was floating, weightless, and with his heart beating under her palms, she felt more liberated and empowered than she'd ever felt in her entire life.

"Sweet baby," he murmured as he kissed the tip of her shoulder, nipping gently to the slope of her neck.

"My hands—" She stretched her fingers over his pecs to ease the strain in her hands. The pursuit of his release had been almost savage. She was clearly not jerking fit.

A giggle bubbled up but her breathing stalled as he brought her hands to his lips, kissing her fingers, one by one, slipping his tongue over them, his eyes closed.

"Your hands are very precious... and very handy," he said when he finally looked into her eyes. He let go and pushed her a small step away. Her hands dropped to her sides. She felt empty and dejected at the sudden distance between them.

"Was that it?" The question popped out. He was spent. But what about her? Her body had been begging for him to touch her, to take her where he'd promised. And now... the disappointment crashed through her. Surely he wouldn't be that selfish?

Touch me.

His gaze dropped to her breasts and the semen that slowly gravitated down, aided by the trickle of water that occasionally drizzled over her as he moved.

"That was just leveling the playing field, Mila."

She didn't understand and gazed up at him.

"Since Marl—" He broke off and shrugged as if to say *never mind.* "I have a pile of orgasms." He grinned now. "Each one waiting its turn. It would be unfair to you to open the door and gush them all into your sweet, virginal pussy, don't you agree?"

Heat rushed to her cheeks. The image he'd conjured was weird... and worrying. *A pile of orgasms.*

She swallowed at the thought. She'd enjoyed his lesson, but from the start she'd planned for this whole sex-thing to happen only once, to know what it felt like... but already she was at it for a second time with James. With his confession, the danger of her own moral decay while spending a week in his apartment—with him *alone*—suddenly seemed inevitable. Why did she sense that once sexual desire and need was switched on, it wasn't so easy to switch off?

But his words also implied that he hadn't been around the block as she'd thought. He hadn't been messing around much if she'd understood him correctly. There was relief in knowing this. Mila hoped that she wouldn't be one of so many that she'd just become a number to him.

"You're thinking too much, Mila," he murmured. "All I meant was that I'd be able to go on for longer the second time around, making sure you orgasm that little voice out of your mind."

That little voice—the one she hated—she'd do anything to be rid of it.

He raised his hands to her hips, splayed his fingers over her and traced a burning web of heat up her belly. Reaching his semen, he idly spread it over her ribcage and massaged it into her breasts, into her areolas and nipples. At his slow, calculated touch she quivered, her nipples going painfully taut, bolts of desire shooting to her core.

He was marking her, spreading his scent over her, making her his territory. She wished he'd mark her with his mouth, with his tongue, blending with her in what she deemed the first token of love.

"James," she murmured, "why don't you kiss me?"

He shot a glance at her eyes, then dropped his gaze back to her breasts, his ministrations slowing, becoming even more titillating as he squeezed her nipples. "I have been kissing you."

She licked her lips. "Real kissing. French kissing."

"I haven't shaved." He didn't meet her gaze. "You'd be raw around that gorgeous mouth if I started kissing you now... in the way you should be kissed."

He hadn't shaved, but it wasn't the whole truth. He was lying and she knew it. This wasn't love or being in love. This was just raw sex. And yet... she wanted him to kiss her. *Just once.*

"Turn around," he said, dismissive of her question as he nudged her around, propping her arms on the wall. He stroked her arms, cupped her elbows and kissed her shoulder tenderly. He gathered her wet hair, twisted it and piled it on her head in a knot. His hands eased down her back, one letting go as he picked up the soap.

The smooth, slippery bar ran from her lower back up to her neck, and she shuddered at the feel of it against her skin. It was cooler than his hands, gliding, and with the little pressure he applied the sensation was totally erotic. He ran his hand with the soap over her hip, her ribcage and higher to her breasts, lathering them one by one. His other hand joined in, rubbing the soap over her chest and breasts. She'd never known her skin to be so sensitive. Every trace of his touch drew a map of roads that were only leading south where she tightened more with each stroke. She was melting under his tender touch, similar to last night, every gesture aimed to reduce her to a begging mess of sexual desire.

He turned the water on again, and it gushed over her back. He drew her into his arms then, kissing the back of her neck and her shoulder whilst he rinsed the soap off her breasts with his hands. She could feel his arousal against the small of her back and the cheeks of her butt. Every muscle in her contracted at the thought of making love with him. Yet she had to control the urge to turn around in his embrace, circle her arms around his neck and kiss him, as she'd wanted to from the first moment. Something in his actions told her not to do that. He had this boundary, one that she'd never imagined could exist, and one he wouldn't allow her to cross.

This was not love. This was just sex. Just once.

Chapter 13

JAMES TURNED THE FAUCET OFF, having washed off everything except the guilt. It had been eating into him since he'd realized that he'd taken her virginity. But now, after her innocent question and his hypocritical answer, he felt even more.

He had to get his mind on board, or he would go down the same spiral that had floored him for the past eight months. Not that the two issues were the same—no, they were as opposite as fire and ice—but still, it annoyed the hell out of him that he'd managed to develop a conscience. His moral limits had never been tested, not until those last months with Marlène when she'd asked him to cross a boundary he hadn't known he had. Now Mila was testing him again, on the opposite side of the spectrum. How far could he take her without one of them—or both of them—getting more deeply involved?

Stepping out of the shower he reached for a towel and held his hand out to her. Mila took it, carefully stepping out onto the bathmat. He hunched down, taking the towel to her feet. They had a slight sandal tan and her toenails were painted flamingo pink.

Each toe was straight and in perfect alignment with the others, in perfect proportion, like the rest of her. He swept the towel higher, over each of her calves, knees and to her thighs. She wobbled and groped his shoulder for balance. Instinctively he went slower, for she was quivering under his touch. As he reached her glistening pubic hair, he rubbed over her pelvic bone with both his thumbs. A moan escaped her lips as she raked her fingers into his hair, anchoring herself against his slow onslaught.

When he looked up to meet her gaze she'd closed her eyes, and his lips broke into a quiet grin. If he weren't careful, sassy Miss Johnson was going to come all by herself.

As he rubbed her dry, working his way up her stomach to her breasts, he stared at her lips. She licked them, bit them, and now they were slightly apart as she inhaled through her mouth, her chest heaving under his gentle rubbing. Now would be the time to kiss her, when she least expected it. Explore her mouth with his tongue and *taste* her.

Kissing would bring a new layer of intimacy, a deeper emotional layer to what they were doing. He couldn't go there with her; she'd get hurt and had nobody to fall back on. Kissing was the no-go zone for a reason.

He bit down on his tongue and straightened. Instead of kissing her, he focused on untying the knot of twisted hair piled on her head and drying it. But his mind wouldn't let go of the notion of their lips melding because his own craved the connection. When he looked down at her flushed face again, her gaze rested on his mouth. She raised her hand, touching his chin, tracing his bottom lip with such longing that James knew he should pull away. He almost succumbed to her hesitant touch as he let his stubble scrub her palm and fingers. He had to be the stronger one—he knew what was best. Her trembling slowed as he clasped her hand with his and kissed her palm, the rise of her thumb and her wrist.

He dropped the towel and pulled her by the hand. "Come."

He went slowly, wanting to build her anticipation and to get a grip on his thoughts. She followed. Why did it seem so hard to do this without kissing her? Last night it hadn't been an issue. Kissing would never have entered his mind with someone else—it had always been easy. His deal with Marlène had been that they could do whatever they'd wanted with other people—as long as they'd been going for it together as a couple and it hadn't involved any kissing. And now he found it hard to slip out of that "no kissing" frame of mind.

He shoved the thought away, unwilling to let the presence of his ex in any form intrude on this moment, which should be Mila's. The fact that he'd even thought of Marlène was messed up. It had been eight months and he still hadn't been able to move on. What was up with that?

That nagging voice had been whining in his head, telling him he needed to sort out his shit. Yeah, it was still there. That echo just wouldn't shut up. He couldn't move on because the situation had been about more than Marlène. She'd only embodied his whole screwed-up life until she'd technically gone off and cheated on him, crossing the boundary he hadn't wanted to cross, doing so *alone* with another man.

Clearly, neither their open lifestyle nor their swinging had precluded him from being cheated on. He'd been such a fucking idiot.

He hadn't been hurt; he'd been irate about Marlène's backhanded duplicity. Had she really thought he wouldn't find out?

Breaking up with Marlène and stepping away from the club had been the right thing to do. But the lapse of time had been worthless if he still couldn't get his head around such a simple thing as kissing the sweet girl whose hand now rested on his back.

Mila was waiting for his lead. He inhaled slowly, trying to sort his rambling thoughts into some kind of order.

Mila was pure, uncharted territory. She was only here for a short time, and he'd promised her this would only happen once. Inexperienced as she was, kissing would lead her on, making her think they could be more.

He stopped in front of the freshly-made bed, reached for her hands and circled her arms around his waist.

Just once.

Images of the night before ran through his mind. He would have done so many things differently. She'd been quite bold, taking his every initiative in her stride, walking into his fantasy as if she owned it. It would be a lucky man who'd get to make Mila his in every sense of the word. Someone worthy of her. Someone who wanted to explore being in love together and wanting to please each other for that reason. Someone younger, less experienced and willing to take a risk with his heart.

His cynical heart had never been at stake, even with Marlène. He'd made sure of that.

If nothing else, he should respect her beliefs and stick to his promise of just once. Beyond now, there wouldn't—couldn't—be any more. Mila might be in Paris, rebelling against her religious background and upbringing, but she'd never be able to swallow the idea of having multiple sexual partners, of opening the door to an intimate sexual relationship to strangers. Already he'd sensed that, for her, this sexual encounter had meant more than a satisfying lay. He'd been her first. He swallowed as her hands spread over his stomach, reached up to his chest, feeling for his heart, which was beating too fast.

"You've made the bed," she whispered into his back, where her forehead pressed between his shoulder blades.

He hadn't needed any physical reminder of last night's fiasco. He grunted. "Try not to think, Mila, only feel. Can you do that?"

She didn't answer and for a second he thought he should blindfold her so that her senses could take over her mind. But it would be too much for her. She craved a deeper connection with him, and the least he could do was give her something to remember. Wasn't the plan to make up for his previous fuck-up?

He turned around and cupped her face in his hands, stroking her cheeks with his thumbs as he gazed into her eyes. "Repeat after me. No thinking, just feeling."

She nodded. "No thinking. Just feeling." Her voice was soft, pleasing him.

And so obedient.

She was driving him fucking wild.

"Come," he said, guiding her onto the bed where he made her kneel.

Her hair hung in thick damp strands around her face, some water still finding its way down and gathering on the tips, hovering before dropping to her breasts where it lay like raindrops on the deeper rose of her nipples. He knelt on the side of the bed and rested his hands on her hips. He licked the drops, one by one, catching them with slow, warm brushes of his tongue as they eased downwards, from the underside of her breast to the tip.

When he caught her nipple in his mouth and sucked it gently, she gasped and dug her fingers into his hair. "James."

He let go to look at her, wondering if she felt that sweet feeling when a simple kiss blazed its way down to her clit. "Feel that?"

"Yes."

"More?" She was so sensitive, upping his need to satisfy her. "Yes… please."

He suppressed a grin and paid the same attention to her other breast; her reaction was more intense this time, her legs slowly lowering as her chest heaved, her knees edging sideways just as he'd wanted her to open for him.

He cupped her pussy, slipping a finger into the slit, finding her clit that was hard and swollen, her lips moist with her arousal and begging for his penetration. She moaned as he circled her entrance and dipped a finger into her, all the time teasing her nipple with his tongue. She clenched at the movement and he exhaled, her reaction to him more passionate than he'd expected.

As he retracted his hand, she pushed her pelvis forward, trying to keep the contact with his hand. "James," she murmured, almost helplessly.

He gave her two fingers this time, going deeper and letting his thumb slide off the ridge of her clit.

"Ride my hand, Mila," he murmured. He looked up, and she opened her dazed eyes, her bottom lip glistening and slipping from between her teeth. She breathed and for a moment he thought he'd lost her. "Hold on to me," he said, and with a nod, she slipped her hands from his hair to his shoulders.

He steadied her with a hand on her hip, his other entering and exiting in a leisurely rhythm, his thumb teasing her clit with each penetration. With a surrendering moan, her hips pressed harder and he let her set the pace, for he had her at a point where her body and mind were in sync.

He sucked her nipple again, feeling her contract each time he laved her nipple. She'd started to gasp, her breaths more labored with each penetration, which he pushed deeper and deeper, catching her g-spot with the tips of his fingers on each thrust.

For a moment he gazed at her, giving her breasts a moment of reprieve. Her face wasn't schooled, she wasn't trying to hide what she was feeling as he touched her harder, his thrusts making up for the absence of his lips on her skin. As he studied the rapture on her face, a part of his past split off and disintegrated. Here there was no need for a barrier of other people between him and her. There was no one else in the room but him and her and her sexual experience, which he felt as profoundly as she did. It was a deep arousal, not sitting on the surface for all to see.

When he latched onto her breast again her inner walls pressed closer, contracting around his fingers. "Come," he whispered on her skin, scraping his teeth over her nipple as he held his fingers deep and still. At his soft instruction, the wave of her orgasm crashed over her body and she gripped his shoulders tight, her hips pushing against him, as she tried to take him as deep as she could.

"James…" she moaned, her nails digging into his skin.

Still, she came and he slowly drove his fingers in and out of her pussy, extending her pleasure as long as possible. Her hands lifted and she wrapped them around his head, pulling him to her chest where the fast beats of her heart whispered to him. Her hair curtained around them as he looked up into her eyes, which were shining, her lips so temptingly split in a Mona Lisa smile. He wanted to kiss her so badly, it dried his throat and tongue.

Be stronger. They were okay. She didn't want more than this. She wouldn't want more… she wouldn't want *him* if she knew about his lifestyle. Her innocence should be protected. His chest tightened and his breathing stalled. He'd do anything to shield her from his real world, where swapping and swinging was the only way he could cope with any type of intimate relationship because it made him feel in control and… safe.

The first step was to not let her any closer.

He swallowed and tried to be as resolved as he knew he should be. He reached for the nape of her neck, stroking her lovingly. "Feeling better?"

She smothered a chuckle, and when she dropped her head back with a heavy sigh her cheeks shone red with her release. He slipped his fingers from her, wet and shining with her spent arousal.

"Taste," he murmured, offering his fingers to her.

For a split second, she hesitated, then closed her lips over the tip of his finger and swirled her tongue around it, sucking off the taste of her own juices, pulling him deeper into her mouth before letting go with an appreciative moan. Inside him, desire pooled, and his erect cock stiffened even more.

"Your hands are very precious… and very handy," she murmured, echoing his earlier words.

"Touché, baby," he said with a grin, and got up, allowing her to see the full effect she had on him.

She shifted from her knees and sat down, straightened her legs, and leaned back on her arms. She eyed him at leisure. "Does that thing come in any other setting?" she asked, then bit her lip as she peeked up at him.

"Nope, this seems to be the standard setting around you." He grinned as he took his cock in hand, slowly stroking it for her viewing. "And you may refer to it as my cock, Miss Sassy."

Would it be rude to ask her to suck him off? Those sweet lips were pleading to be stretched around his cock, to tighten and pull in a slow mimic of what he was doing with his hand.

"You enjoyed that?" he asked, wanting to be sure they were on the same page. She'd mellowed with the heat of her release, her body no longer rigid and shy like she'd been in the shower.

"More than I should have," she whispered, her gaze still glued to his hand and its ministrations. She was avoiding his gaze. He knew in her head things were spinning in a direction they shouldn't be going.

"Look at me, Mila," he said, letting go of his cock as he knelt on the bed, straddling her, stroking her legs up to her thighs.

Her eyes, wide and bright, gazed up at him.

"We're not done."

"No?" she breathed, almost inaudibly.

"No." He leaned closer as he brushed a kiss on her temple, his lips against her ear. "No thinking, just feeling."

She nodded, locking gazes with him as he stared back into her eyes.

If he weren't mistaken she wouldn't mind spending the whole day right where they were. If only he could keep her there, but it was against his better judgment. Mila wouldn't allow it, and her conscience was going to be his saving grace. *Just Once* didn't morph into *Just One Day* like that. Not with Mila. He was already pushing his luck by telling her they weren't done.

With a grunt, he dropped to her belly, licking and kissing the little mole, dipping his tongue into her belly button and then tracing a line to her hipbone. She stirred under his lips and arched her back as he softened his kisses to the dip between her thigh and pubic bone, her hands messing with his hair, guiding his head lower. He shifted so he could lift her leg, splaying it to the side.

Reading his intention, she opened up for him.

Learning too fast.

He wanted to slow down. He wanted to slow *her* down. Instead of heading where he intended, he softly brushed her inner thigh with his chin, retracing his kisses back to her belly.

He could almost feel her deflation as she relaxed her hips, stilling. He'd given her a taste of his tongue on her clit last night; it would serve her right to keep her wondering what he could do with it when he got serious about oral sex.

Hell knows… He wanted to spend the whole week with her, exploring every inch of her skin, to see how many ways he could take her. This was not helping his already flailing resolve.

But if there was to be only one last time, he needed her to feel every inch of him. He wanted to bury into her and get lost. He gazed up from her hip to find her eyes fixed on him, lids half closed, lips begging to be ravaged. He straightened, took her box of condoms from the bedside table, and handed it to her with a nudge of his head.

She fiddled with the box, her fingers trembling as she finally took a condom out and held it out to him.

"Your turn," he murmured, enjoying the two spots of red spreading on her cheeks.

"I don't know how."

Of course you don't. He couldn't send her out into the wide world without this basic knowledge. What if she ended up with some asshole who abused her innocence and went bare on her?

A rise of protectiveness ripped through his chest at the image of Mila with someone else.

Fuck. He hadn't seen that sensation coming. It was a bolt of awareness, sharp and blinding. Trying to disguise his reaction to the image that flashed through his mind he took the condom from her and tore the package open. "Look at me, Mila."

Her gaze locked with his, and he had to fight against the need to kiss her and pull her into his arms right then. "Like this," he murmured hoarsely, wanting to get it on with her already, wanting to link her to him.

"You're going too fast," she whispered as her gaze dipped to his cock, but already he'd pinched the condom at the top and rolled it on.

He swallowed. *Next time, baby.*

Except there wasn't going to be a next time.

He breathed in deeply and closed his eyes. Why did it suddenly matter? He shouldn't think; he should only feel as he'd instructed her. It was too darn difficult.

He shot her a glance but found he couldn't look at her with the protective and almost possessive emotions tearing inside him. And there was something else too—something softer that had settled in his chest that made his heart beat faster and his stomach stir. Better to ignore those unknown feelings. Instead, he gripped her legs and edged his hands down to her knees to split her open. He reached down and stroked through her wetness, knowing she was ready. He tuned into her breathing that had become stilted and leaned in, gliding the tip up her slit, lubricating himself with her arousal. With each move her breathing became heavier, fueling his desire. He positioned his cock at her entrance, wanting to delve into her with one thrust and make her gasp with the force of his need. He couldn't recall ever feeling like this before.

Fuck it.

This was Mila.

He felt for her breast, her shoulder, and propped over her, finding his way around her body.

When she gripped his thighs and reached for his buttocks, urging him closer, he thrust into her pussy, inch by inch, trying to feel if there was still a barrier between them. The one he hadn't sensed the night before. There was none.

He went at it carefully, gently, each penetration measured and dragged out. Every beat of her body collided with his as it doubled, tripled. She was tight, virginal still, clenching. He had to slow down but he couldn't. Inside him, he revved up, the urge to claim her anew—as his only—overwhelming him.

"Oh, God," she moaned, her fingers digging into him, her legs hooking him closer as she rolled her hips to meet him halfway, encouraging him deeper.

The slow ripple of a fist-like grip around his cock caught him off guard. It was surely too soon for her to come again, but her hand was on his face, gentle and warm as she nudged at him. "Look at me, James."

It was a barely audible command, but he had to open his eyes. Only to stare into hers as she tipped over the crest and came. Her gaze was mystical, her eyes dark pools, shimmering with desire's fulfillment, and something he'd never seen in a woman's eyes before.

Purity of soul.

He blinked. What he saw in her gaze couldn't mirror in his own. He couldn't let her peer into his darkness, for it would swallow and destroy her.

He closed his eyes and dropped his forehead to hers, an intense orgasm bursting from him.

I'm so thoroughly fucked.

Chapter 14

MILA STARED AT THE CEILING, the rush of the most incredible orgasm she'd ever experienced ebbing in her limbs. The world spun back into focus and she turned to James. He had slumped down next to her, his palms to his eyes, his chest still heaving. For a split second his sculpted body looked vulnerable as he covered his face. It was a minute before he drew his hands down to his mouth and breathed into them.

A chuckle bubbled up. "A man-made orgasm is much better than a handmade orgasm."

He rolled onto his side and pinned her down with his gaze. His lips split into a slow, lazy grin, and all she wanted to do was lean into him and kiss him.

He laughed. "I must be losing my touch."

"Not at all," she murmured, the heat of a blush rising to her face under his unwavering scrutiny. It was having him inside her, the connection she'd had with him, much more than anything else that made her think that. It had been pure bliss.

"You're something else, Mila. I didn't feel it coming."

Her face was burning. "Well, I hope you felt *me* coming this time around."

"I surely did," he chuckled, still staring at her.

Her second orgasm had surprised her too. She hadn't thought she had it in her, but with him, everything seemed possible. His open perusal became too much, and she dropped her gaze. "What time is it?" she asked.

James turned and looked at his bedside clock. "Just past eight."

"Already?" She needed to get on with the day; she couldn't waste one day in Paris. Her body surged with a rush of energy. "Don't you have to be at work?"

"No, not today. I was booked for Brussels but will take leave to sort out some admin."

"Oh." She had the whole day ahead of her, and so did he. With nothing to do. But admin.

A whole list of things they could explore together, rather than admin, popped up in her mind. None of them included the tourist attractions in Paris. *Dear Lord.* They wouldn't have to leave the bed, never mind the apartment.

She turned her face into the pillow, hiding her smile and the filthy ideas that were flittering through her mind. Less than a day in his company and already she was thoroughly debauched.

"I have to work later this week. Meetings, conference calls. The usual."

She glanced at him to find him staring at her. "I've got to go." She sat up, reaching for something to put on. There was nothing. *Nada.*

"Where to?" His voice was laced with a devilish laugh as if he understood her consternation.

"The Louvre opens at nine. If I go now I might still meet up with a short queue."

James pulled her back down and into his arms. "You mean you're not going to waste the day in bed with me?"

He'd read her mind.

"You won't need any clothes, so you can stop fidgeting," he teased.

She laughed, but his comment was sobering, even if her body begged her to relax against the hard warmth of his chest; her mind was rising in slow revolt.

This was supposed to happen only once... For a moment she absorbed the heat of his skin, the brush of his lips on her temple, the sweet scrub of his stubble on her skin. "You're on your own."

She shifted in his arms and he let go with a chuckle, leaning back with his hands behind his head. He was casually observing her, and she bit down on her lip. She could hardly feel shy now. Not after everything that they'd done. She couldn't will the heat on her skin away, but she got up and strode around the bed to the bathroom as if she was on a catwalk, breaking out in a laugh as he gave her an encouraging low wolf whistle. So freaking sexist, but so pleasing, to have it coming from him.

Plus, she'd never had one of those blown her way before.

When Mila came out of the en suite twenty minutes later the bed was made again and the bedroom empty.

She walked into the kitchen and James was there, dressed in jeans and a T-shirt, his hair still rumpled. He placed croissants, layered with cheese and ham, and coffee on the counter.

"You can't attempt the Louvre on an empty stomach," he

said, giving her the once-over.

"Just attempt?" she asked with a chuckle, pushing her glasses higher up her nose. Her protective gear was back on; she didn't feel quite herself yet but was satisfied with this little barrier in the bigger wall she now needed to construct between herself and James Sinclair.

"A week won't be enough for a first round of the Louvre," he said and grinned as he pushed a plate towards her.

"You went to buy this?" The fridge had been empty when she'd arrived, and her meager purchases hadn't done much to change the situation. The croissants smelled divine and she was ravenous.

"There's a *boulangerie* across the street."

"Thank you." It had been sweet of him to think of breakfast and rush off to get it. No man had ever made her a meal of any sort. She was usually in charge, cooking for her family. She brought a croissant to her mouth, biting through the outer layer of crispy crust. She closed her eyes as the first wave of buttery sweetness hit her tongue and groaned. "This is the best croissant I've ever had," she murmured between bites.

"Worth the flight here, isn't it?"

She nodded, but when she looked up at him, James's gaze was on her lips. He reached out and with the pad of his thumb brushed something from her bottom lip.

The touch was so sudden and intimate that it sent a wave of longing through her. He tipped back, retracting his hand, and a small crumb clung to his thumb. She wanted to lean into his hand and lick the crumb off, but he did it himself, not taking his eyes off her.

So much for that wall. This wasn't part of their deal. The same thought hovered in his gaze.

James said nothing, but raised his coffee and took a long sip, still staring at her. She looked away. He busied himself with his own breakfast, and they ate in silence.

"I'll make a plan." He looked up as she finished her coffee. "About the bed."

She didn't want to think about the bed. She would have stopped time if she could have, but everything was hauling them in separate directions, as it should be.

"I should make a plan." She was the intruder in *his* space.

"Don't worry about it." His tone told her to drop the subject. "If I'm not here tonight, don't worry about me." He set his cup on the table, and it clanged in the moment of weighty silence.

"You're going to sleep somewhere else?" She swallowed at the croissant that clogged in her throat. She had no intention of ousting him from his apartment.

He shrugged, non-committal. "There are a few friends that will put me up until I get a couch sorted."

"I've noticed the furniture is a bit sparse." She meant it as a joke, but he didn't laugh. She'd also noticed half the apartment was locked up, but it wasn't her place to probe. "I can find space in a youth hostel."

He said nothing as he took his empty plate and cup to the sink. "You'll be okay here tonight, alone?"

He'd totally ignored her last words.

"Sure." The atmosphere had shifted and she blamed herself. All she wanted to do was get back to the playful banter of before. It was her zone; this sticky discomfort with him was not where she wanted to be. Not after everything they'd shared. "Unless someone barges in on me. Again."

"That won't happen. Again." His voice was steady, his back towards her as he rinsed the dishes.

No. It wouldn't and it shouldn't.

She gathered her plate and cup. "I'll deal with this when I get back." The air between them was laden with something she didn't understand.

"I'll catch you later." He didn't turn around to face her as he said it.

Which could mean anything. One thing was clear—she'd been dismissed. She might not see him again. Maybe she'd managed a hit and run. The notion tore through her chest, and she couldn't get away quickly enough, because a knot constricted her throat, tears stinging behind her eyes.

Chapter 15

JAMES LEANED OVER THE SINK. In the lounge, Mila was gathering her things, and seconds later the apartment keys jingled. The front door shut, echoing through the empty lounge to the kitchen.

He should never have touched her after she'd bitten into that croissant. What the hell had he been thinking? But those lips… and the emotions he'd felt earlier, which had been off his usual radar, had triggered him into stepping out of line.

He gripped the sink, containing the urge to rush after her and explain why the mood between them had polarized within a matter of seconds after he'd touched her. He couldn't give her more than what they'd had that morning, and she wouldn't want more. Not when she knew. And at that point in his thought process, Marlène might just as well have waltzed into the room. The question about the two locked rooms and the lack of furniture, which had hovered unspoken, had hung between them.

It hadn't been Mila; it had been him. He'd been responsible for the shift between them. Anything that Mila knew about him and

Marlène would have come from Stacey, and that couldn't have been much. He'd been careful not to let his sister see too deeply into his life.

He should have pressed Marlène a lot harder when he'd offered to buy her share of the apartment months ago. If he hadn't been so busy… but now Marlène's locked rooms and silent presence had become like a tumor, quietly killing anything good around him.

The sudden strain had been unfair towards Mila, and with her thoughts going places, as he knew they did—with that little voice preaching away in her head—she'd be analyzing how their morning had concluded for the rest of the day, feeling shitty about everything by the end of it. That was the last thing she needed and the last thing he'd wanted for her.

He cursed as he tossed the tea towel to the side, leaving the kitchen as it was and rushing to his en suite.

He showered in double time, not wanting to lose her in the crowds that would stream to the Louvre that morning. If Mila thought she would get a shorter queue by getting there half an hour earlier, he had bad news for her.

The Louvre was close to his apartment, but the building was vast and the pyramid entrance took longer to reach. He lengthened his steps, noticing the queue as he rounded the corner into the court. He stopped short; she didn't need to do it like this. He had connections at the Louvre. Someone could get her in first thing in the morning and take her on a tour if she wanted. At least get her in and let her make the most of her time, instead of wasting it like this.

He dug his cell phone out of his jeans pocket, making the call as he started stalking the queue, looking for her. She'd dressed in capri jeans with the legs rolled up, and a white T-shirt.

It didn't take long to spot her near the end of the line; it was as if he was drawn to her, to her hair that was tumbling down her back, her butt, sweetly hugged in her tight jeans, and her bare arms, which he wanted circled around his neck. He recognized her body, its impression stamped on his, and he groaned as he stepped up to her.

"Mila." He reached for her elbow, cupping it in his hand.

She looked up at his touch. "James." She was pale, drained, with her eyes wide as she took him in.

"Are you all right?"

"I think your coffee was too strong this morning."

He took her hand and tugged her out of the line. He'd served her decaffeinated coffee; it was the only stuff left in the apartment. He leaned over to whisper in her ear, "One doesn't have two orgasms in a row and rush off like that. One stays put, preferably in the arms of the man who took you there."

Her eyes widened and she licked her lips as a blush rose deliciously to her cheeks.

"That brought back some color." He grinned. "Come on."

"Are you abducting me from the Louvre queue?" She was starting to resist by pulling him back towards her now-empty spot, where people were already shuffling to close the space.

"I know someone who works here as a curator. Clea is happy to let you jump the queue tomorrow."

"Really? You're that connected?" She dropped her gaze. "You can't let me take advantage of your friends like that."

Clea was hardly a *friend*-friend. But that didn't matter much right now and he wasn't going to explain any of it to Mila. "It's just a favor. She'll get you in first thing and you can go around the whole day by yourself."

He guided her past the buzzing queue to the closest restaurant on the Rue Rivoli. On the sidewalk, the tables were packed with tourists and instead of finding a seat in the sunshine he took her inside, where it was darker and cooler. A waiter pointed from afar for them to sit down at a small rounded table, squeezed in close to a window.

As they sat down she avoided his gaze. "Thank you. I need some sugar or something."

He searched her face. She needed more than a sugar high. She needed a debrief. "I shouldn't have let you run from me this morning."

"I didn't run—" She broke off, fiddling with the saltshaker on the table.

You were so running, baby.

He sighed. Best get this explanation out smoothly. "Marlène—my ex—moved to New York when we broke up. She hasn't had time yet to collect her things. I suspect she doesn't have space for them in her New York apartment. All her furniture used to fill most of this apartment. Her stuff is locked up in the two other rooms."

"Oh." She glanced up at him but quickly looked away again. "You don't need to explain your situation to me, James."

No, he didn't. But he wanted her to understand. "With all my travelling, it has been hard to resolve our household issues. Marlène's busy too, working as beauty editor for American *Vogue*."

"Stacey's dream job."

She was redirecting the conversation, and he was grateful she didn't probe deeper... although, for the first time, he felt like he'd dealt someone an undeserved hand. He shrugged a non-committal yes. Marlène had somehow managed to get under Stacey's skin in the dream-job department.

"Is it a hectic career? I mean... if she is so busy? Would Stacey be able to maintain a career like that?" Mila glanced at him.

"I don't know. She first has to finish her studies."

"She's having a hard time. Finance isn't going to get her a gig in beauty editing. I'm not sure if she really likes her courses… unless she pulls herself together it isn't going to happen."

"I know." He kept a closer watch over Stacey nowadays, but nothing seemed to improve the situation.

"The amount of freedom your dad allows her doesn't help. She's messing around, failing, starting again, just for the sake of it."

He frowned and looked at her. "Just for the sake of it?"

She hunched her shoulders up and dropped her gaze as if she'd spoken out of line. "Comes across as spoilt, to be honest, and such a waste of time and money."

He cursed inwardly. Their dad had stopped paying for Stacey's studies after she'd started failing subjects twice in a row. His dad had been lenient, but he'd drawn the line for Stacey there. James had picked up the tab, telling Stacey that he wouldn't do more for her than lend the money, which she should pay back. But he'd written the money off.

"Our dad only wants Stacey to be happy," he said defensively, wanting to justify his own actions.

"She'd be happier if someone made her stop messing around. It only makes her feel… uncared for."

He stared at her. Uncared for? He'd do anything to make Stacey feel *cared for*—not like the unwanted after-effect of a night of misplaced passion between their father and mother. He could hardly see how paying for Stacey's studies had anything to do with her messing around or feeling cared for.

Or had it? It was an unwanted reality he'd never considered. Stacey hadn't been the same since their mom's death and he didn't know how to deal with her.

Hopelessness twined with an irrational loathing and yanked at his guts. Was he being weak? Like his dad? That Mila was right about Stacey needing a firmer hand was something he couldn't admit. What if he had been adding fuel to the fire?

A waiter approached them and James took the menus from him, wanting desperately to change the conversation. "What do you usually have for breakfast?"

"A kale smoothie. And poached eggs." The disgust in her voice sat shallow and he chuckled.

"Not a high-fat, high-protein butter bomb like the one you had this morning? With caffeine to chip away at the cholesterol in your veins?"

She laughed. "I wish, but that's not in my brothers' diet prescriptions."

He hitched his eyebrows at her. "Your brothers? You live with one of them?"

"I live with most of them. Still at home."

She still lived with her folks? Mila was the squashed sandwich filling between four brothers. Two older, two younger. No doubt all of them kept an eye on her, making sure no unsavory elements came close to their beautiful sister. No wonder she'd still been a virgin. And at twenty-four she was still under her parents' roof, probably being the perfect little housewife to a bunch of bullies.

"And how does that work out for you?" he rasped, not knowing what else to say.

She gazed into his eyes as her hands stopped fiddling, but they were trembling as she dropped her gaze.

"No need to sugarcoat it for me, Mila."

"I hate it."

He shifted in his chair as the waiter approached their table. In true French style, the waiter swiftly corrected Mila's rearrangement of the salt and pepper pots, impatient to take their order.

101

James ordered two espressos and some pastries to get rid of the man.

She was gazing at him when he let go of the menus, but when he met her eyes his heart, which had started to speed up, banged on the wall of his chest. She'd been opening up to him, and now... her eyes were too moist. She'd been on the verge of crying before the waiter had interrupted them. He squashed the urge to cover her hands with his.

"You speak French." She didn't contain her shocked admiration.

"It rubs off on you, eventually. I've been living in Paris for more than seven years." He didn't want to talk about himself. Her comment about his father and Stacey had already been too much, too spot-on, but he'd made it worse by digging into the truth of it. Stacey should stop messing around, and his dad was doing nothing about it, only wanting his little girl to be happy. And somehow he'd ended up doing the same. Nothing they could do or give would ever make up for losing their mom.

It was slippery ground, especially with Mila's eyes that didn't hide anything from him as they silently sought the truth from him. She was as open in her mind as she'd been with her body earlier that day. He raked his hands through his hair, mentally shrugging her comments off.

"Why do you still live at home?" Such a situation would drive him nuts.

"It's practical." She didn't elaborate.

He could just imagine how practical that would be—money-wise. "But suffocating?"

She swallowed but made no comment.

He had to change the topic. "Jake and Joshua still play for the Springboks?"

"Johnson and Johnson," she said with a smirk but took up the saltshaker again.

The famous front rowers of the South African rugby team, Jake and Joshua had not been battered and beaten yet. He'd lost track of the rugby world since getting out of the game years ago. He still watched the occasional match but it wasn't his sole existence anymore. Something he'd been secretly thankful for. There had been more to life for him than an obsession with a sport. He would have made the most of a career had it taken him on that path, but the broken bodies most of his older rugby cronies lived with made him relieved that he'd gotten out early with a good excuse of two messed-up knees.

"The other two?"

"Ruben and Ben are both playing provincial and trying to break into the squad."

"I'm not sure the sports commentators can deal with two more Johnsons on the team."

"Neither can I." Her voice broke and her hand wiped at a wisp of her hair, tucking it behind her ear. On her cheek, her swift movement had left the trail of a tear.

She was crying. His stomach tightened at the sight.

"Fuck it, Mila," he said softly. "What's this?" He shouldn't hug her, but he reached out and pulled her to him. She belonged in his arms, right now, nowhere else. "Ssh," he tried to soothe her, but now that the gates were open, the tears were flowing.

The morning had been too much, and he suppressed a sigh as he shifted to gather her even closer to him. He'd been an asshole for not making her stay in bed with him, for not forcing her to let him take care of her as he should have after their intense sexual experience. He'd needed to be with her, but between their jokes, her urge to be gone, and their little *just once* deal, he'd let her go. He'd thought it for the best but it had been another fail. She wasn't a one-night stand going home and she hadn't known what she was signing up for. When was he going to get it right with her?

He grazed his lips against her temple, ignoring the waiter as he placed their order on their table. Her hand sidled up to his chest, and he pressed his own over hers, letting her feel the erratic beating of his heart, which for some reason didn't want to find its regular rhythm that day.

Eventually, she looked up at him, clearly wanting to let go, but he held on to her hand.

"I promise you I never cry this much." She swallowed. "In fact, I *never* cry."

He stroked strands of her hair from her face. "Not allowed to, are you?" he murmured. She was pretty when she cried, her lips plumped even more, her nose tinged red only on the tip, and her dark eyes were like black pebbles wet by the rain.

Her expression said it all. He was right. Little Mila Johnson had needed to toughen up pretty fast to survive her four rugby-obsessed brothers and fanatical religious family.

"You bring out the worst in me."

"I bring out the best of you," he reflected. She was sassy, sweet, sexy—not like the younger Mila, who'd been tucked deeply away in her shell, quiet and awkward. She'd showed him her vulnerability, a side of her that others weren't allowed to see. He lifted her hand to his lips and pressed a soft kiss to her thumb. "You can tell me anything, Mila. It won't go any further."

She blinked at his words and shook her head. "I didn't come to Paris to find a shrink."

That might not be entirely true, but she needed to download. "Good thing I'm not one then."

Chapter 16

MILA GAZED AT JAMES'S FEATURES, which had softened in the dark light of the restaurant. His gaze searched her own, without haste, prompting her to trust him. He still held her hand tenderly. She trusted him. She'd trusted him with her body. But to trust someone with what had been going on her head for years would be different. But James would understand, he knew how she'd grown up.

It was a fresh experience to be with someone who didn't immediately hone in on her connection to the famous Johnson and Johnson brothers, who didn't plunge into a conversation about the latest rugby match within a minute of meeting her. If she hadn't brought up her living situation, it might never have crossed his mind to talk rugby with her.

He leaned back and placed his arm on the backrest of her chair, not letting go of her hand. She'd felt so rotten standing alone in that line earlier, with intense emotions she couldn't pinpoint ballooning in her chest, threatening to push to her throat and constricting her breathing. The sensation had meant only one thing—

tears. But she'd learned long ago to close *that tap*, as her mother called it, on the first drop.

The soft touch of his hand on her elbow had tugged her back from the abyss of her thoughts just in time, and when he'd taken her hand in his she couldn't pull away. Being in his arms was what she'd needed, even if her conscience hissed that it was wrong, that she was pushing the boundaries of their deal. And yet his hand was still covering hers, and his heart was thumping strongly under her palm.

Why did she sense that her mind and body were never going to be in sync again? After the morning her body was light, almost flying, until she had to pause and stand in a queue with her damning thoughts creeping up on her. That little voice hammering at her that every thought, every sensation was incongruous with what she'd been taught growing up.

He squeezed her hand and lowered it to rest on his thigh. "Tell me."

"Is it wrong that I couldn't care less?" she blurted out. "I honestly don't care if they make the team, whether one of them scores or if the Springboks win or lose. My whole life seems to be one long haul between rugby fields, awful poached chicken breasts, and sport vision exercises."

She took a deep breath. "Sweaty shirts and shorts and socks and mouth guards. The permanent locker room stench." She pulled away from him and forced him to let go of her hand. "The constant focus on their stupid injuries. Of course they're going to get injured! Look at what they're doing with a bunch of other idiots on the field!" She gulped. "Sorry. They're not all idiots." She shook her head. "But you would know about this, all of it."

The pressure had huffed out of her, and she fell back against her chair, took her glasses off and rubbed her eyes.

"Yeah, I get it." He held a paper napkin out to her. She took it with a soft "thank you" and wiped her nose.

"It's like I'm chained to a treadmill I can't switch off—it doesn't take me anywhere, but I must run along like some support vehicle. Ready to wipe up the blood afterward. And each freaking season it's back to the start." She exhaled, her breath escaping in short quivering huffs. "With all four of them in the game, there is almost no off-season… it's become one long continuous drag."

She shook her head with a groan. "The worst is that I feel so disloyal. I should be supportive, but it's all fake, every minute of it."

When she met his gaze, her body trembled. "My whole life is one long pretense, and I haven't got the energy to keep it up any-more. Every man I meet only wants to talk rugby. Every girlfriend I make thinks I'm the shortcut to one of my brothers." God help her, it was awful to admit it to him, but it was the truth. "Every-body except Stacey, who was around before any of it. I can't seem to meet anybody out of that circle."

And then there was the church and her parents with their expectations.

She dropped back against the chair, exhausted. He didn't say anything but his hand came to rest on her shoulder. "I'm sorry," she murmured as she closed her eyes. "My parents don't understand. They are so immensely proud of my brothers I can't even start to tell them how I feel."

He squeezed her shoulder, running his hand down her arm, and hugged her to his chest. "This is your life, Mila. You can be supportive while you're living it for yourself."

He hadn't judged her brothers or her parents. He hadn't judged *her*. He'd said nothing but those few simple words and relief washed over her. Maybe it was okay to feel the way she'd been feeling.

When he let go he reached for their coffees. "Do you want to ruin this perfect espresso with sugar?"

"Yes, please." She needed a bit of a rush which didn't include James's body next to hers, or his hands and fingers, which reminded her of that morning.

He spooned some sugar into her black espresso and stirred it. "Here you go. Butter bomb?" he asked as he shifted the plate with pastries closer to her.

"If I have to." She licked her lips, her mouth watering just looking at the picture-perfect pastries. Her mind could list a hundred reasons why she shouldn't, health-conscious as she'd been forced to be. But this… she wasn't going to resist.

He smiled at her. "You have to. You're in Paris."

Caving in, she took a bite with a soft moan. "They're sinful."

A soft smile tugged at his lips as he gazed at her, but he said nothing as he ate his own. When he tossed his coffee back and put the cup down, he looked at her, serious now. "What do you want for your life, Mila?"

She blinked. As if anybody had ever cared. "I want to see the world, and not only from its rugby stadiums."

"There's much more to it, I agree."

"I want to find my niche in art. I've been floundering lately. I need some visual… inspiration, to find my way back to what I love doing."

"And this is why you are in Paris?"

"The primary reason."

He hitched his eyebrows. "I see." A smile sparkled in his eyes. "You want to elaborate on the secondary… and tertiary reasons?"

108

Heat shot to her cheeks. How did he know? Stacey's freaking to-do list. "Already accomplished."

He leaned into her, the warmth of his body enveloping hers, making her clench her legs together, overly aware of their thighs that had been rubbing against each other for the past half hour. His lips were at her ear, grazing softly from the top to the soft bud of her earlobe. "I'm glad I could be of service."

The sensation of his intimate whisper shot to her core, making her innards pool. "Don't go there," she murmured. She wanted to sink and hide under the table. Did he think that she'd used him? Had she? The thought was too much, overridden by that very familiar tingling inside her lower belly. There was a buzz in her body that demanded attention—his attention—as a memory or two of that morning flitted in her mind's eye. There was only one way to switch this feeling off. By giving in to it.

Oh no no no. She shifted in her chair, breaking the connection between their thighs.

He laughed and leaned back, his hands cupped behind his head. Totally relaxed, his gaze rested on her—soft, but containing something she couldn't place.

Had she told him too much? She'd never been so straightforward with anyone and the trust she'd put in him chilled her hands and rippled down her back in sudden unease. It was disturbing that he already knew her body and its needs. But now... "You now know my dark soul," she whispered. "My pretense."

Clamping down on her wandering mind she knew she should apologize, should make him understand that she'd be okay when she went back home. This break was doing her a world of good. She only needed to refuel so that she could carry on with the facade once back home.

"Your soul is hardly dark, Mila." He chuckled. "It's the purest I've ever seen."

She bit down on the surge of emotion that rushed through her at his words. This was going to be much harder than anticipated. "Stop toying with me, James Sinclair."

Unabashedly his gaze dropped to her breasts, pausing there a second, before his eyes slowly grazed higher, to the wide neckline of her T-shirt and the column of her neck. The heat of his perusal warmed her skin and its residual tingle burned down to the apex of her thighs. He was caressing her with his eyes alone and with undisguised desire; her nipples pebbled as a deep-seated longing settled in her core.

"That's going to be a tough one," he murmured.

The most annoying heat she'd ever experienced built up in her cheeks and she groaned inwardly.

He sighed and stood, his chair scraping on the floor. "Wait here a minute," he said and walked to the bar. She studied him at leisure, trying to ignore her racing pulse. His T-shirt was not exactly tight-fitting, but there was no mistaking the muscles that bulged underneath the fabric, stretching over his biceps. He narrowed at his waist, but not much as his legs were solid pillars of strength. Despite not having an ounce of fat on him he was a hunk and she suppressed the wave of fresh desire as she recalled how agile he'd been in and around the bed.

There was a flash of euros in his hand, and she flinched. He was actually paying the bill behind her back. She could be a lot of things right now, but she wasn't a charity case or a girl that could be bought with dinner.

When he returned to the table she had her bag on her lap. "How much do I owe you?"

"It's on me."

"Ugh, please."

"I see you are feeling all sugared up. Please choose not to pick a fight with me." He held his hand out to her. "Let me show you my favorite parts of Paris?"

"I—" She broke off. He'd taken the wind out of her sails—it was her choice.

A wickedly innocent smile played on his lips. And he wanted to show her his favorite parts of Paris.

She'd love to see Paris through his eyes.

"These museums are on your to-do list. Or they should be," he said as she made a conscious effort to ignore his hand, dropping her wallet back into her bag. "They're less intense than the Louvre and you can do both in one day. I promise you short queues."

She rose to her feet, her diluted resolve evaporating. She hooked her bag over her shoulder and scooted out of the corner. "What about your admin?"

"Torture I can put off for another day."

She closed her eyes a moment, praying that spending time with this man wasn't a massive mistake. He made her laugh too easily. He was easy to talk with, and that was maybe a bigger danger. "You promise this isn't going to go any further?" She opened her eyes and gave him an unwavering stare.

"I've already made that promise for today," he murmured. "Earlier." He didn't break their locked gazes.

He wasn't going to be there tonight. He hadn't spoken the words but she heard them anyway.

She didn't really want to be alone in Paris. She wanted to enjoy this with someone who understood art. From the collection on his wall and the books on the shelf in the apartment's corridor, he seemed to have a love for art, and it was hard to resist.

"Okay." She took his hand with a broken smile. "Only because I love every piece of art you have hanging on your lounge wall. And of course your art book collection."

His eyebrows raised a stitch, then he narrowed his eyes. "Remember that watercolor you are working on is mine."

She smiled. "Thank you for the subtle reminder."

They walked out of the restaurant and he hailed a taxi. "First, I'm going to get you some flowers."

A taxi stopped and he opened the door for her. She clambered in, sliding over the leather seat to make space for him next to her. He gave brisk instructions to the taxi driver and the car pulled away into the traffic.

"Then we'll do lunch at this nice little place I know not far from here," James continued. "And then—"

"You don't need to smooch up to a girl you've already slept with." The words spilt forth from her unchecked tongue. She had no idea what he was talking about. She didn't need flowers or fancy lunches. The deed had been done.

"I'm not trying to ease you into my bed, Mila."

No need, she was there already.

He frowned at her, hand fisting where it rested on the seat between them. "And I hope you never fall into bed with a guy after just having dinner with him."

Nope. Dinner was totally superfluous with her. She'd been the ultimate cheap date. The idea made Mila cringe and she turned to look out of the taxi's window to hide her face.

"Just enjoy the day, okay? And yes, I'm going to force some flowers on you. So be polite, as I know you can be, and accept them gracefully."

"Okay," she murmured, feeling flustered, but there was a naughty sparkle in his eyes, which she couldn't place.

After a couple of minutes, the taxi pulled up and they got out.

"This way," he said, leading the way to a tree-lined gravel pathway. When the building came into view between the trunks and leaves, she drew in a sharp breath. She'd seen it so many times in art books she would have recognized it from a mile away.

"L'Orangerie!" She broke out in a laugh and grabbed his hand. "Your flowers?"

He grinned, almost childlike in his joy. "You like Monet?"

Her pulse raced in excitement, and she quickened her steps, and he kept up, not letting go of her hand, although she was trying to tug free. "I love Monet!"

He smiled at her, and inside her, everything melted. Overnight James had crawled into her heart, and now he was staking his claim.

There was hardly a queue, as he'd predicted. They were later than the opening time and the first rush of visitors had already been admitted. Soon they were walking into the great oval room and she held her breath, awed by the beauty of the water lily landscape that encircled them.

"Can we stay?" she murmured, trying hard not to beg.

"As long as you want. This is one of my favorites too."

She wanted to hug him so much. Kiss him even more.

Instead, they walked the ovals slowly, commenting and pointing things out to each other. Eventually, they sat down on the seat in the middle and she pulled out a watercolor palette and pad.

"I was wondering what you were lugging along in that bag of yours." James smiled at her. "Feeling inspired?"

She nodded. "I'm all jittery inside." She hadn't been so inspired about painting anything in months. But being surrounded by this magnificent Monet had her fingers trembling with excitement.

"Good. As long as you have a steady hand," he chuckled. "But that we know you have."

With a tug of her lips into a whisper of a smile, she muttered. "Don't go there, James Sinclair."

He just laughed as he dug his phone from his pocket. "I'll have to check the markets, so take your time."

Chapter 17

JAMES UNLOCKED HIS PHONE, GLAD it was on silent because a barrage of messages popped up as he looked at the screen. He scanned through them, only to realize with irritation that most of them were from Marlène.

Missed call. Times five.

Pick up your phone. Times three.

I'm coming home earlier. One godforsaken message.

He swallowed, suppressing the hard *fuck* that wanted to burst from him. *Home.* She had some nerve. Marlène had added no more details, and he bet she wouldn't have shared them with him if she'd known them. It was likely that she hadn't had her exact arrival date at that stage. She had a tight schedule, but sometimes things panned out differently and she lost or gained a day. *Shit happens.*

And the shit was going to fly while Mila was staying in his apartment. He shot up, pacing around in the oval, gathering his thoughts. Marlène and Mila. The one was going to destroy the other.

When he came full circle he sat down next to Mila again.

She'd been busy painting a cropped detail of the massive mural onto the watercolor paper, her movements easy and flowing. Nothing broke her concentration and he had to clear his throat to get her attention.

"I'm stepping outside to make some calls."

Her hand paused and she glanced at him, then searched his face. "Everything good at work?"

"Yes. All good. Just some calls I have to make."

"Okay."

"I'll be back, so don't go anywhere."

She smiled. "No problem."

She bent over her work again, and he curled his fingers into his palm, keeping in check the need to stroke her hair and gather the cascading tendrils behind her ear. She was beautiful sitting there, transfixed by her work, oblivious to the rest of the passing world. She radiated inner peace, and seeing her there he knew he'd never tasted inner peace and at the current rate, he never would.

He strode out of the gallery and into the sunshine, which wanted to force itself into his sudden dark mood. He dialed Marlène's number and listened as her phone rang and rang unanswered before it clicked over to voice mail. "Let me know when you're arriving. I'd like to be at the apartment."

As he killed the call, he rubbed his eyebrows with his thumb and forefinger, trying to get a grip on the anger and irritation that battled in him. Without a doubt, Marlène would respond with a message along the lines of "With a bottle of champagne on ice?"

He knew her too well. They might have broken up, but Marlène wasn't a woman who'd let go easily, especially not with their relationship having been what it had been. He couldn't blame her with the lifestyle they'd led; they'd been fantastic together in bed, even if that was all that it had ever been.

He sat down on a bench some meters away from the entrance of the gallery, so that Mila could easily see him should she decide to come outside. He scrolled through the rest of his email and messages. There was nothing significant, except the reminders of the meetings he had scheduled for the week. There was one at the club the next evening. His finger hovered over the details. Seven o'clock, followed by dinner and the rest of the evening at the club.

His stomach tightened. He'd successfully managed to avoid these quarterly management meetings for the past eight months, being either in New York or Singapore at the time. Had he unconsciously scheduled it like that? The devil only knew how he was going to get out of this one.

He sighed and leaned back as his phone started ringing. He glanced at the screen. Jean-Pierre Costeau. Thinking of the bloody devil.

"Jean-Pierre," he answered, knowing he couldn't avoid the other partners any longer.

"You answer your phone for a change," the other man laughed. "You've become very good at this disappearing act."

"Just busy at work. Traveling a lot."

"I know, I know. But you are here now, right?"

He wasn't going to get out of it. "Yes, for a week or so."

"You're coming to our management meeting tomorrow night?"

"I—" He broke off, looking at the trees that rustled as a slight breeze traveled through them. Who was he kidding? Help was not going to come from the heavens. Not for him, at any rate.

"James, we really need you there tomorrow night. The figures are looking good but we need your input, your ideas. That head of yours with the number-crunching. You know if it weren't for you, the club would never have taken off as it has. You owe it to your-self, my friend. And to your financial investment."

He swallowed. He'd only footed some cash to start the busi-ness, but now, going to the club, hanging out with his old cronies just didn't appeal to him anymore. The money was ticking over and things were running smoothly. He should leave it at that.

"James?" Jean-Pierre's voice drilled through to him. "You need to be there. Serge is out of town. If you're not there we don't have a quorum."

"Yes, yes. I'll be there," he caved in, despite knowing that they didn't really need him for anything but being a number to re-place one of the other, more consistent, partners.

"Super." An awkward pause followed. "You're good?" Jean-Pierre asked.

"Yes." He'd answered too quickly.

"Marlène let me know she'll be in Paris soon."

Fuck Marlène.

"I know." *I'm trying to avoid her.*

"You two should talk things out, my friend. This thing with you and her… it's unhealthy."

He wanted to laugh. Had any of it ever been healthy? That wouldn't have been his exact word choice. "We're okay. We resolved our issues when we broke up."

Again a quiet silence from the other side. Respectful of his answer, but blandly stating that *yeah, whatever, we all know you're still pretty much fucked up.*

"Listen, I've got to go. I'll see you tomorrow night." He'd do anything to cut the conversation right now. It felt as if he'd weaned himself of the club over the past eight months, but Jean-Pierre was a smooth-talking lawyer, known for his skill in talking anybody into anything.

"Sure. See you tomorrow."

He rang off, his fingers quivering as he shoved the phone back into his pocket. He cupped his face in his hands and breathed into them, rubbing his eyes with his fingers. When he'd contained himself he reentered L'Orangerie and found Mila still sitting where he'd left her.

She was engrossed in her work, lifting her gaze every half minute or so to look at the water lilies on the wall, then back to where her watercolor palette rested beside her. Occasionally she brushed her hair from her face, tucking it behind her ear, revealing her profile. Whenever she looked up, she'd lean towards the mural, narrowing her eyes.

She must have felt his gaze on her because after five minutes she looked around. He started walking, not wanting her to know that he'd been surreptitiously studying her.

"That's looking good," he said as he sat next to her. What she'd created in the time he'd been gone resembled in miniature Monet's masterpiece, but it held a stamp of her own style.

"It's rough." She smiled as she held the pad at arm's length. "I'll add some details later with pastels, to create the same effect as Monet's brush strokes." She sighed, a deep breath of contentedness slipping from her as she lowered the pad to her lap. "Thank you for bringing me here." She glanced at him, and for a second he thought she would lean in and kiss him, if only a peck on the cheek.

He checked his watch to tear his gaze away from hers. "It's been two hours. You've had enough?"

"Can you ever have enough?" she asked, but packed her materials into her bag, leaving the pad open on the seat to dry.

He chuckled. "For some things, a lifetime won't be enough."

"Agreed," she murmured, glancing around as if she'd never see the murals again.

"One last turn," he said, sensing her regret at having to leave.

They strolled the gallery one last time and she checked her watercolor paper to see if the paint had dried. Satisfied, she folded the pad closed and carefully slid it into her bag.

"Where to now, Mr. Tour Guide?" she asked as they stepped outside.

"Are you hungry?" He searched her gaze. He was ravenous, despite the pile of pastries he'd consumed, something he never did. Some habits were hard to shake, and he found that even after years, he still followed the dietary rules laid down when he'd had a potential international career in rugby.

"I—" She blushed.

"You are?" He grinned with a wink. "All that activity this morning."

Her blush turned deeper and he suppressed a laugh as he pulled his phone from his pocket. He'd love to surprise her with more than just an ordinary lunch if he could pull it off. It was a joy to observe her reaction to things, seeing everything fresh through her eyes as she experienced it for the first time.

He scrolled down his contact list for Etienne's number. Etienne would curse and probably ignore his call mid-lunch service, but for Mila it was worth the scolding. The phone rang while she stood with arms folded, studying him guardedly. As Etienne answered he turned away, speaking in hushed tones over the phone.

Two minutes later he rang off with a satisfied smirk. He turned back to Mila and nudged with his head in the direction of the Seine. "This way. The place I have in mind is not far from here."

They walked a while in silence, only the crunching of gravel answering their footsteps, and arrived at an intersection where they had to wait for a red light. On the other side, there were a few restaurants and already people were tightly packed on the sidewalk, sitting around the typical small circular French tables, with their bodies facing the never-ending traffic. He'd never understood the French obsession with sitting in car fumes, cramped together outside, inhaling each other's second-hand smoke. But then there were a lot of things he'd never understood about the French, even after living in Paris and being with Marlène.

As the light turned green he took Mila's hand, guiding her across the street, not wanting to be separated from her in the crowd of tourists and lunch–goers who hastened along with them. He didn't let go when they reached the other side, and in him a small victory dance made his heart pound faster as she squeezed his fingers and held on tight. It was a novel feeling to hold her hand in his with no other intention but connecting with her, subtly drawing her closer to his body when the sidewalk narrowed with tables and diners. The little rush he got from these small things was new to him.

"In here," James said, leading her up to a restaurant's entrance, which was so understated, the average tourist was likely to miss it.

The maître d'hôtel welcomed James and Mila and led them into the restaurant.

Mila's grasp clenched his hand tightly.

"Relax," he said, realizing too late that she might be intimidated by the businessmen and elegantly-dressed women who sat at the other tables, their conversations soft and low.

"I'm not dressed for this place, James," she whispered to his back.

"Doesn't matter, it's just lunch," he whispered over his shoulder.

They reached their table, which was tucked away in a private corner, with starched white tablecloths and crystal wine glasses that caught the light.

"You know the owner?"

"The chef-owner, actually. What gave it away?"

"It looks like the type of place that needs a reservation months in advance."

He shrugged.

"I already know that I can't afford to eat off this menu!" Mila mouthed to James as the waiter pulled out her chair. She hesitated.

James inclined his head, indicating that she should sit down. "It's my favorite lunch stop in Paris so I had to bring you here. As my treat."

She rolled her eyes. "Conniving. A sandwich would have been more than sufficient. Preferably a homemade one." But she sat down, chewing her lip as the waiter, with a bit of flair, draped her napkin over her lap.

"The French live in horror of *ze sangwich*," James mocked as he sat down. "And they always eat a proper lunch. You may broil me a tough chicken breast tonight to return the favor," he added with a grin.

"Fine," she murmured, fiddling with her napkin as the waiter poured them water, whilst describing the day's lunch menu.

"It's a shortened version of their tasting menu," James said. "Three courses. You'll love it."

She sighed. "You're too kind to me."

"Impossible."

When the waiter walked off she glared at him. "Where in your Paris exploits did you meet a chef-owner of a Michelin-starred restaurant?"

Sassy Miss Johnson hadn't missed the plaque outside the door then.

"Don't these types of people work all hours and have no social life whatsoever?" she asked, staring at him.

He shifted in his seat. Where did these questions come from? It was as if she was in on all his secrets, digging deep with a sharp shovel. "I met him at a club. About a year after I moved here."

"A club?" She scrunched her nose up. "I'm not the clubbing type," she said casually. "The music's too loud, suffocating cigarette fumes, bad lighting, drunk students' bodies crashing into each other on the dance floor, slippery vomit in the corners. Yuck."

"Hmm." He couldn't quite meet her gaze. His club and her club were poles apart. "This club is different. Definitely not aimed at the student market. And no vomit allowed."

"Maybe I'd like it better. You should take me there."

His stomach clenched as if a fist were crunching it into a tight ball of paper.

She laughed. "I wonder if I'll be allowed in."

Fuck no.

He was intensely grateful for the waiter, who was approaching them with two plates in his hands. He had to change the direction of this conversation.

"The last time I went clubbing with Stacey they questioned if my ID was a fake at the door," Mila said as she rolled her eyes with a grin.

She looked up at the waiter, who'd almost reached their table.

"That was before I had glasses. They make me look older, don't you think? Old enough to get into your club?"

He inhaled, a sudden shortness of breath almost overpowering him. There was no way in hell Mila would ever put a foot in the club. The image of her in that place... the other men—

Fuck no. They'd be all over her like a bunch of blood-sucking leeches if she gave half an indication that she was keen.

He couldn't let his mind even probe in that direction. *She's mine.* The idea made him feel worse, handcuffed and derailed.

The sweet smell of the scallops he'd ordered wafted under his nose in sharp contrast with the sour swamp that had settled in the pit of his stomach.

Mila pulled in a sharp breath as the waiter placed their entrées in front of them. It was one of James's favorites, with its bright green pea mousse, sweet and soft, flowing over the saltiness of the scallops, crunched up with micro greens and delicate flowers.

"Oh my word... this is gorgeous! The smell... oh—look at the little flowers!" She met his gaze, her eyes so full of sparkle and life. "Oh James... I've never eaten something so breathtakingly beautiful before."

His heart was jolting, his pulse irregular as his eyes glimmered at her, taking in her beautiful face, the even complexion of her untainted skin, her eyes big and wide, accentuated by the dark-rimmed glasses that she wore. Those eyes were something else, and the way she looked at him he wanted to tug off her glasses, lean over the table and kiss her lips. Mark her.

She's mine.

She took up her knife and fork, gingerly cutting into the tower of scallops, lifting a delicate bite to her mouth. She closed her eyes, chewing, her lips so tempting. "This is heaven," she moaned as she forked up another bite.

No. This was hell. Or a chamber of hell, which he hadn't known existed.

Ridiculous.

But he liquefied inside, as every cell in his body reminded him that this hell was the one he'd been intimate with most of his life. That quiet, surrendering way in which his dad observed his mom as she flirted with other men, eventually going off with them, fucking them all. Never objecting to her actions, letting her be because he'd rather have what she'd had left over for him than nothing at all.

He'd never wanted to tag anybody as only his, but then, this thing he was starting to feel for Mila... was he falling in love?

Fuck no. Not if he could help it. He'd never been in love. Never wanted to be in love. His dad's misery had cured him of love, prematurely. But with everything that had happened between his parents, and then with Marlène—hell, he'd been grateful for the heads up.

He clenched his jaw, watching as Mila ate on in silence, probably confused at his indifference towards the food.

Mine. There was no such thing.

"You look like you're about to pass out, James," she said softly. "Better eat something, there is no way I can haul you back to your apartment on my own."

Chapter 18

Mila's heart thudded in her chest when an hour later the taxi stopped at the Rodin Museum. This was high up on her to-do list and this time she insisted on buying their admission tickets.

Once inside the grounds, James smiled at her. "Do you want to do the gardens first, or the house?"

"The house." She itched to see all the sculptures she'd only seen in art books. "Do you have any idea what immense skill it takes to be a sculptor?"

"I've no idea," he laughed. "I'm more for paintings. They're easier to manage in the space I have."

She shot him a smile. "You need a special nook for sculptures. And lighting. It makes them come to life." Her breath stalled as they walked into the building, where the light from the outside beamed through the tall French windows. "Wow," she whispered, in awe of the exhibition, which was covered in strokes of light, falling on Rodin's masterpieces. The room was big and airy, but the space seemed intimate at the same time.

"I know." He leaned toward her. "Go at your own pace, I have my favorites. This museum is small enough that we won't lose each other."

"Thank you."

They set off in the same direction, but soon she noticed James had moved on from the pieces at which she'd lingered. She was a mess inside, overwhelmed by James's presence, which was as deeply unsettling as everything else. He didn't follow her, but she sensed him looking for her, making sure they were sticking close.

She'd been herself with him, and it had been easy, less stressful than always being on her guard, which she'd had to be at home for some years. She might have pretended last night when he'd stumbled upon her in his bedroom, but since this morning, she'd laid bare to him her true self.

During lunch, he'd turned strangely quiet at intervals, which had nothing to do with chewing his food. She couldn't shrug off the notion that something else had been on his mind, something that had been triggered by a phone call, or that something had happened when he'd stepped out of L'Orangerie.

She'd tried to shrug it off, but already she cared more for James Sinclair than she'd ever bargained on. She'd always cared for him. It was hard not to care when a man like him started taking care of you. She swallowed and chewed her lip, having reached the highlight of the museum's collection: *The Kiss*.

The sculpture stood center stage in one room, the light from the windows caressing the white marble figures of a man and a woman, shadows accentuating the muscles and the curves of their bodies. It was disarmingly beautiful and innocently erotic.

She circled the sculpture slowly, taking in every detail—the faces, the man's hand, which rested hesitatingly on the woman's thigh. When she looked up, James stood on the other side, and her heart skipped a beat on finding his gaze on her. Instinctively she knew he'd been observing her almost as intensely as she'd been taking in the details of the image in front of her.

"Do you like it?" he asked quietly.

"Of course," she whispered back, stepping towards him. "It's moving, don't you think?"

"It was intended to be part of The Gates of Hell."

She blinked. "I haven't seen The Gates yet."

"It's outside in the garden."

She nodded. "Why do you think The Kiss is part of the Gates of Hell?" She bit her thumb, taking a closer look. "Besides that he's a reluctant kisser," she mused. Much like James.

"Reluctant? Why do you say so?" The weight of his gaze rested on her, and she shrugged.

"His body. The way she urges him down, embracing him, and yet his back is so straight, tight, too tense. And his hands—" She leaned closer, taking in more details of the sculpture. "It's almost as if he caved in."

"He has."

"Not Adam and Eve again? Apple and Snake?" She raised her eyebrows at him. The sculpture had nothing to do with original sin, she was certain of that much. The Gates were based on Dante's Inferno as far as she could recall from her art history classes.

"It's because he just read this little book." James pointed to the man's other hand, which was resting to the side, not touching the woman at all. An uncarved, unrefined object seemed to slip from the man's fingers. "Dante's Paulo and Francesca. They were reading about Lancelot and Guinevere. It's a cross-reference. They're about to be caught out for their little liaison."

"Well, that's depressing." She gathered her hair over her shoulders with a frown. "I can't remember much of the details. Did she seduce him?"

"Does it matter who seduced whom?" James asked. "He fell in love with her against his better judgment."

"And she cheated on her husband, didn't she? To be with him."

He didn't answer her directly but his jaw tightened, as he ground down on his teeth. "And what do you think about that?"

It was as if shards of glass had shattered to the floor, surrounding their feet and her way out. He was referring to his mom and her heart contracted at the pain he was trying to hide. She had to pick her way out carefully. "Besides the obvious wrongness of it all, she must have been miserable and hated herself, for hurting her husband. Because it must have hurt."

"You think so? You are too kind towards the lady."

"Probably, but her husband must have hurt even more. But I can hardly judge, can I? I've never been in such a situation." Their eyes held across the sculpture, and when he looked away she shrugged off the heavy weight of his comments. She circled the sculpture and met up with him again. "Studying art has given me a much broader view of life. I've become much less judgmental, which has been a blessing, coming from... where I come from."

He nodded, and she sensed he knew exactly what she meant. He chuckled as he took her hand, nudging her to a point where they could see the laps of the lovers in the sculpture. He leaned to her ear. "I believe in the original version the man had a full-blown hard-on."

The intense moment had passed and she struggled to smother a laugh, trying to keep quiet in the gallery where voices were hushed undertones to feet shuffling on the floors. "Seriously? The things they censure out of our school art history books!"

"Yep."

"It must have been a hard sell on a nineteenth-century crowd."

"No pun intended."

They chuckled together. He let go of her hand and rested his hand on her lower back. "We're done in here. Let me lead you to the Gates of Hell."

"That sounds so ominous." She bit her lip to contain the laugh that still wouldn't settle.

He directed her outside into the gardens and she lifted her face to the sunlight as he dropped his hand from her back, leaving a heated spot on her skin. Everything felt very far from hell right now. This was the closest she'd been to heaven.

Her gaze roamed the gardens as he urged her in the direction they should take. Flowers in full bloom stood thick in the hedges, their sweet summer scent compounded by the sun.

A minute later she spotted the Gates where they stood against a wall of the garden. It was a massive sculpture in the shape of a double door, cast in bronze. From afar, it looked disordered, as human figures were pulled and sucked into a wave, which only wanted to spit them out. The sculpture gave off a sense of chaos and angst, even more so the closer they got.

"Well, the Gates are closed. That's gratifying." She laughed as they walked closer and she could distinguish individual human figures, some contorted and in pain, others seemingly caught in the lava-like casting without their knowledge. "With all the misery going on on the outside, who needs hell, in any case?" She studied the individual parts of the doors more closely, and he stood back to give her space.

"What are these people doing?" she whispered in a low voice, pointing to some bodies contorted awkwardly, limbs protruding.

He bent over, closer to her and the door. "That, to me, looks like an orgy."

She burst out laughing. "What? Really?"

"Rodin style." He grinned at her.

Her laughter subsided, but her chest still rose and dropped with the joy of it. "I can tell you this much, my dad will never preach about orgies taking you straight to hell."

She didn't turn to look at James and he made no comment. Mila had to remember not everybody had been squashed into a box like her.

Eventually, she stepped back. "Where are the murderers and rapists? The child abusers. The wife beaters? Those are the real sins. And this Thinker at the top, is he even considering all of the other sins?"

"So you don't seriously think it is a sin? Having sex? Outside of marriage?" He peered into her eyes from underneath furrowed brows.

Heat rushed to her face. The little nagging voice, which took on either the sober reprimanding tones of her dad or the more menacing pitch of her mom, had been deadly quiet for a few glorious hours. Had James needed to bring that issue up? "No. Yes. Sometimes."

"Interesting." He blinked and cocked his head. "If you can't make up your mind you'll have to give those answers some context."

"People are all different. It's not wrong to make someone happy, is it? To feel loved and wanted? To show love... physically?" She swallowed, dropping her gaze.

That morning hadn't quite been that, had it? Showing love physically. That morning had been more in line with quenching a thirst. Now that James had taken her virginity, she wasn't sure she would be able to drink from just any old tap, like some people tended to do. Having sex when and where and with whomever they pleased, like Stacey did. It was so out of her mental frame of reference, and now, having experienced the physical side of it, she knew it would be impossible for her. She needed more than sex; she needed soul too. She was glad James had been her first. Not a stranger she'd never see again. How messed up would that have been?

She looked to the trimmed hedges and the path that led to some trees.

He stepped away from the Gates. "Let's walk the gardens."

She nodded and followed him, finding her inner equilibrium again after walking for some time under the flickering shade of the trees.

"I honestly don't care what other people get up to, but for me—" she started softly, and he lowered his head to her. "It's when sex is unwanted, whether in marriage or not, or forced on one party." She looked up at him. "And when it leads to other issues…" She broke off. She didn't want to think about those other issues.

"What issues?" he asked softly.

"Unwanted pregnancies."

He was studying her face, then shrugged. "Usually avoidable with contraception." He scanned her eyes, but as if the agonized turning in her gut had mirrored in her eyes he said, "What's happened to make you say that, Mila?"

She groaned, wishing the tightness in her throat would retreat. "My younger brother Ruben has asked his girlfriend to have an abortion." She blinked. "I'm not supposed to know. They thought they were alone, but they got to the heart of their heated argument so quickly, it was too late for me to tell them I was there and I was forced to eavesdrop."

She was supposed to be in church. Listening to her dad's Sunday morning sermon. But she'd played the truant that morning, and ever since Mila had been paying for it. She'd wished so many times that she hadn't been there, standing in the laundry, folding some clothes, when Ruben and Stella had barged into the adjoining kitchen, already quarrelling. They hadn't seen her, and soon words like "sex," "broken condom," and "pregnant" had been tossed around.

Mila and James came to a standstill under a shady cluster of trees and she hooked her thumbs in her jeans' front pockets. James was studying her face, and the heat on her cheeks had become a permanent sensation.

"The worst of all was," she spluttered, when he said nothing, "that Ruben said he doubted the baby was his, and that she was trying to trap him into marriage. He said she must have an abortion." Her throat tightened more, and she bit on the inside of her mouth to divert her focus to some sort of pain. She was *not* going to cry in front of James again today.

"He didn't suggest a paternity test?" James asked, his voice dry and scratchy.

"No, how cruel is that?" She swallowed hard, letting her anger at her brother overrun her disillusionment. "To just bark at her to go have an abortion?" Her brother's actions had come as a shock, but worse had been his attitude towards the situation, which had left her stone cold and in doubt whether she knew her own brother. "You can imagine if my parents found out... if my dad found out... Good Lord. If his congregation found out!"

He still said nothing, but his hands rose to her shoulders and he drew her towards him. He hugged her tight, and for the umpteenth time that day she felt the stress seep from her as she melded her body against his.

James rested his chin on Mila's head, her body flush to his. He couldn't hold her any closer and heaved out a breath as he felt her relax. He pressed a soothing kiss to her hair, not knowing what to say. She'd reached the point where everything got an awkward type of transparency, where she realized things had another side to them, that what she'd thought was two dimensional was actually in three dimensions, and beliefs she'd held to all her life were being exposed as frauds.

James had been born into that phase; he'd skipped the entire coming of age part. It had sucked to know that all things were broken and that way of thinking had influenced his way of life. But it had been for the better because until now he'd come through life unscathed, or so he'd thought.

Eventually, she turned her face and leaned back to look at James, and reluctantly he let her go, reaching for her hands.

"What does my shrink say I should do about that?" she whispered.

His chest tightened at her honest question. She wanted advice and he had no idea what to say to her. He shook his head. "I can't really say, never having been in such a situation before."

She shot him a woeful smile. "A situation where someone tells you such a shitty story or having a pregnant girlfriend who demands marriage, knowing you'd cave in because your family is a bunch of holier-than-thou churchgoers?"

"Both, actually," he answered with an empty chuckle. He wanted to get her mind off her worries, but it wouldn't be easy to let go of her brother's perceived sins. He understood why, and he would have hated to land in such a situation. Lucky for him, Marlène had been more neurotic than him regarding pregnancy, the horror of a baby ruining her body, and then the years of dealing with a snot-nosed kid having put her off having children for life. "Take your own advice, Mila. Don't judge. It's usually the only thing you can do."

"You have no idea how hard I'm trying." She bit her lip and turned her head towards the avenue of trees. "But it irritates me to hell and beyond that my brothers can go around and do what they want, and I'm to be as holy as the Virgin Mary until I get married."

My sassy little rebel. God, what he would give to see her totally unleashed.

"Let's walk this way," he said, letting go of her hands, knowing that with each touch he was building up physical anticipation in himself. Was she even aware if it? Of the pile-up of tiny touches, each one more intimate, stretching their mutual boundary bit by bit, to a point where there was only one way to release the pressure.

They'd reached a bench in the park which overlooked the freshly-mowed lawn, with the view of the house at an angle. The late afternoon sun blazed the greens into fluorescent brightness.

"Can we sit here a while?" Mila asked.

He glanced at his watch. "Sure." He'd be able to check in with the closing of the European financial markets as he did every day, if he could get his head to concentrate while sitting next to her.

She sat down and dug her paint and paper pad out of her bag, then looked up and stared at the scene in front of them for a few minutes. She exhaled a pent-up sigh, and as if sinking into a deep inner peace she started to draw. He leaned back, watching as the blank paper came to life under her fingers.

A tremor ran through him. Unscathed? How had he ever thought that? He was in it deep—for the first time. Had he waited his entire life for Mila Johnson to grow up, so that she could come and scar him with her innocence?

Chapter 19

"I'm done," Mila said with a grin, turning towards James and lifting her drawing so he could see.

The sun enveloped her face and she squinted to see him against the rays. He'd been watching her for a long time, the weight of his gaze shifting occasionally, sliding over her body. She didn't mind him observing her. It made her feel warm inside, with a glow that she couldn't quite define, having never felt it before.

He took the pad from her, studying it for a second, then gazed back at her. "It's beautiful. Will you paint it later?"

She took out her phone and took some photos of the building and the garden from where she was seated. "Yes, I'll use these photos as reference. Unless I have time to come back and it's another gorgeous day with the light as it is now."

"We can stay longer?"

"I promised to broil you a chicken breast."

"You did." His face split into a slow grin. "But I hope to convince you otherwise."

"You are way too conniving for your own good." She stretched lazily. "After that lunch, we should only eat a broiled chicken breast." She checked her phone and gasped. "It's already five thirty! Aren't they going to throw us out soon?"

He got up and picked up her bag for her. "Yes, it's closing time, but it was nice not having to rush you."

Her heart swelled at his comment. He had such patience, sitting with her, not interfering or being chatty. She'd liked the quiet companionship he'd selflessly offered, and if she'd dared, she would've leaned back against him for a cuddle. Oh Lord. A cuddle? With James Sinclair? Of all things, he didn't appear to be the cuddling type. Although each time in his arms had been just perfect.

With fumbling fingers, she collected her things and slipped them into the bag he held open for her. "Thank you," she murmured, avoiding his all-seeing gaze.

"Why so shy, Mila?" he asked softly.

"Just tired." Her little prayer for forgiveness was taking on mammoth proportions at the rate she was throwing white lies around.

"Let's amble over to the bookshop for a coffee."

She nodded absentmindedly and walked abreast of him to the museum's exit, where he hailed a taxi.

"Where's the coffee shop?" She'd thought it was part of the museum.

"Not far from here, but we'll catch a ride. Your feet will take enough of a beating tomorrow in the Louvre."

Her pulse sped up at his words. She couldn't wait to explore the Louvre, and yet, today had been pure perfection. "I really enjoyed spending the day with you."

A taxi pulled up and he opened the door for her. "And I enjoyed spending it with you."

She clambered in, and when he got in next to her he gave her a mischievous smile. "We are not done."

His words dropped like a warm water balloon in her belly, letting desire, which had been taking a much-deserved nap whilst they were in the garden, raise its head with a slow stretch and a "what were you saying?" yawn. Earlier that morning, she'd come a second time after hearing those words. As the memory of every ripple of that intense orgasm spread through her body, she held her breath, her core muscles tightening of their own volition. The things he could do to her by just hinting… she bit her lip, restraining the unsettling urge to straddle him and kiss him, hard.

She turned her burning face away to look through the window, deciding with a tense exhale, which she tried to hide from him, that she shouldn't reply.

When the taxi pulled up to the sidewalk ten minutes later he got out and waited for her to get out of the car. He reached out to her and she hesitantly put her hand in his. His fingers were warm, firm as he pulled her out and towards him, his lips to her ear. "Stop fretting, Mila—a promise I make, is a promise I keep."

"Then stop toying with me, James Sinclair."

"Why? It's fun to see you blush."

As if on cue heat rushed to the roots of her hair and she looked away. "Because—" She bit her own tongue to stop the words from slipping off her tongue. Because she might not want to keep that promise they made.

How could she even feel like that? She was not one to go against her better judgment, moral or otherwise. She shrugged and stepped away from him, taking in the rectangular tables on the sidewalk—so not French—and the people sitting outside reading and chatting. Looking up at the shop's sign, she read, "Shakespeare and Company?"

"My favorite bookstore in Paris. They have everything in English."

They crossed over the pavement to the entrance. "I haven't brought anything to read." And nights were going to be lonely until Stacey got there. She might as well browse and get something to take her mind off James.

"They have a good art book selection if you're looking for something you can't find at home."

"Those are addictive and expensive." She'd seen his collection. It was to die for. Most of them had probably come from here.

The door closed behind them and she took in the store, the low hush of patrons murmuring, the intense smell of printed books hanging in the room, laced with a dash of aged and faded paper.

"I'll be on that side," he said and pointed to the art book section at the far end of the shop.

Good. She needed some distance from him. The day had almost rolled on too easily, like a date she wanted to be on, with a friend she'd known for years, someone she'd secretly had a crush on and who'd finally come to the party.

She wandered through the store, not in any particular direction, picking up a book here and there, but really wanting to be where he was, browsing art books with him by her side. When she got to the classic English literature she paused and picked up *Tess of the D'Urbervilles*. It was thick, and after reading the back cover she popped it back into its slot.

Her hand hovered over *Jane Eyre*. She'd never read it before, and for a moment felt almost uncultured. Did watching the movie count?

A tickle ran down her spine and she turned to see James meters from her, waiting. She'd felt his gaze on her before she'd even looked up.

"Found anything you like?" he asked as he closed the gap between them.

"I'm looking for something to read." She tugged *Jane Eyre* from its slot on the shelf and gazed at the cover. "Can't go wrong with a classic, can I?"

"A book about a man with a secret in his tower, seducing a sweet, innocent girl?"

"He doesn't seduce her." She playfully swatted him on the arm with the book. "She loves him so much that she comes back for him despite everything that has happened. Despite all his secrets." She looked up at him, finding his jaw set and twitching.

He dropped his gaze first, turning towards the bookshelf. After a quick inspection, he took *Jane Eyre* from her, holding out another book. "You should read something French while you're in Paris. Here, *Madame Bovary*. The ultimate French classic."

The cover didn't pull her in, with its impressionist painting of a woman, who turned away from the onlooker and looked distracted. "What's it about?"

"A wife who slowly destroys herself, because she is bored, firstly by having a lover... or was it lovers? Then by becoming a total shopping maniac and ruining her husband financially. In the end she—"

"Say no more! If that just doesn't cheer us right up," she said, laughing at the monotonous tone he'd used. She shoved the book back and retrieved her copy of *Jane Eyre*. "Now I'm going to browse the art section."

He chuckled as she edged past him, and he didn't follow her immediately.

Two hours later they were back in the apartment with their purchases. They'd stopped at a supermarket on their way home and she'd bought some turkey and salad essentials. She was digging in the food cupboard to see what James had in his pantry for a salad dressing when there was a knock on the front door.

She strained to listen, not sure she'd heard a knock. But someone knocked again. James was in his bedroom, packing his things for the evening. "James?" she called.

"Just a minute!"

She went to the front door, looking through the peephole. A man stood in front of the door, waiting, with a bottle of champagne in his hand. Why hadn't he rung the bell from the intercom on the street as she'd had to? She shrugged, wondering if he was a neighbor who lived in the same building.

James hadn't mentioned a friend coming over, but the man looked about his age. She opened the door an inch, and he cocked his head and smiled even wider.

"Hi," he said in English. "I'm here for Stacey? And her friend Mila?" His gaze swept over her face and her hair that she'd bundled together and tied on her head as she usually did when cooking.

Mila took in his face, liking his tall frame and dark, slightly unkempt hair. He wore a tailored shirt, tight fitting over his slender muscles, slim-fit trousers and shoes that Stacey would swoon over. She'd have to let her know what she'd missed out on. Her heart skipped a beat. Was this the friend Stacey had wanted to introduce her to?

"Stacey's not here," she replied, not sure if she should open the door as wide as it could go and let him in, or subtly make him go away. She didn't want a fifth wheel during dinner with James. The way the man was peeking past her into the apartment made her wonder where James was. Surely he hadn't missed the loud knock on the door or their voices in the entrance hall.

"Ah, *dommage*. Sorry for Stacey." He looked at her, still smiling, the white tips of his teeth peeking through his perfect lips. "You must be… Mila? Did I say that right?"

She grinned. "Yes, Mila." The way he said it made her simple name sound so seductive.

He leaned in towards her, pressing a soft kiss to her cheek, then turned and kissed her on the other cheek. "I'm Damien. *Enchanté*. And welcome to Paris."

The kissing had happened so fast, his sudden, unexpected proximity intense. He'd pushed right into her personal space, and for a split second, she was disoriented, as this intrusion wasn't exactly welcome. When he pulled back she laughed, shifting on her feet. "Sorry, I'm not French. That was a first."

"Got you there," he laughed back. "I can see you're not French," he said as his eyes dropped to her body, probably studying her cheap clothes.

Nope, those weren't French and her whole outfit possibly cost the same as his left sock. She smiled knowingly. Only Stacey could pull a man like this out of her magician's hat in Paris. From where did Stacey know him?

He pulled his fingers through his hair, messing it up more. "That's how we French say hi." He had a bone-melting French accent, and it only added to his allure.

"How do you know Stacey?" She didn't want to ask him in, not until James was there to hint that it would be okay.

"Ah." He paused, looking past her into the apartment. His eyes hooded over, and he pursed his lips as footsteps sounded on the parquet floor.

James put his hand on Mila's hip, his chest not touching her back, but his body's warmth almost scalding as he made his presence known.

"James." Damien pronounced the J so softly, letting the rest of the word ooze into a negligent S. A second passed, in which she was certain he wanted to lean in and kiss James too. How weird. Instead, he held out his hand. "I didn't know you were in Paris."

She wanted to shift to make space in the doorway for James to shake Damien's hand, but James hadn't moved. His hand weighed on her hip as he ignored the handshake that should be happening. Tension pulsated between the men, and she was like the glass wall that held them apart. They obviously knew each other, because after a moment James said, his voice so cold, it made a shiver speed down her spine, "Damien."

"I came to see Stacey... and Mila, of course." Damien's gaze dropped to hers, then lower, to the hand that rested on her hip, the fingers flexing, then tightening again.

"I see. Stacey's not here. Neither is Marlène."

Mila swallowed at the mention of James's ex-girlfriend's name. Damien's gaze darted between hers and James's, and she sensed a silent, unspoken feud battled between the men.

She shifted on her feet, uncomfortable in the tense atmosphere. James pulled her closer so that her back rested against his chest and his arm circled around her waist. His posture was stiff as a plank, yet he leaned in and pressed a kiss to her temple. She closed her eyes, not sure what to make of this sudden move. Her hands moved up to his arm that possessively held her close.

Damien laughed, a dry, throaty smirk that broke free from somewhere in his gut. "Not wasting your time either, Sinclair." He stepped away from the door. With a grin and a wink to her, he raised the champagne bottle in a mock cheer. "*Bonne nuit.* Enjoy."

He was gone in a second, his swift rush down the stairs echoing in the corridor. When James's arm didn't loosen its grip she realized she could hardly breathe.

"Let go, James, you're holding me too tight."

"Didn't your parents teach you not to open the door to strangers?" he hissed, but his grip loosened and with a soft stroke over her belly he dropped his hand. He stepped away and waited for her to retreat from the door.

"He didn't seem to be a stranger, knowing Stacey, and clearly knowing you," she said as she pushed past him. "He didn't buzz from the street intercom, I thought he was a friend of yours."

He gripped her wrist. "Don't ever let him into this apartment. You understand?"

A cold stone settled in her stomach at his tone and his harsh words. He let go with a tight sigh but didn't say anything.

"It's none of my business," she whispered as she walked off. A second later the door banged, and she closed her eyes as the keys clanged. James had locked the door behind Damien.

Chapter 20

J AMES CURSED UNDER HIS BREATH as he rested his forehead against the door for a second. He'd shut the door too hard, had turned the key too harshly. It was none of her business for now, but soon it would be her business. He sensed it in his gut, where the past few minutes had twisted him tighter than a cord.

With Damien on his doorstep, it had felt as if his whole world had closed in on Mila, and as if he could do nothing to prevent her from getting burnt.

He knew Damien—too well. Damien liked to fuck a woman's ass while she was blowing another guy at the same time. And yeah, he'd been that guy. And Marlène had been that woman. Numerous times. Things didn't get more intimate than that. The things Marlène had wanted would be way off Mila's radar. Mila was different, untainted and still exploring herself, wandering in the foothills of her own sexuality. But most confusing of all was how he felt different when he was with her.

He pushed off the door and scrubbed his face to get a grip.

How the hell had Damien known that Stacey was going to be there? And where the *fuck* had he gotten his sister's number?

He threaded his fingers through his hair, cursing as he stalked across the carpeted floor of the lounge. Mila was in the kitchen, eyes downcast as she chopped some tomatoes. So freaking innocent, so unaware.

He paused. He shouldn't get any closer to her; he shouldn't let her in.

It's a little too late for that, an inner voice whispered. The lid had been opened and with certainty, he knew that she would see his whole sordid world for what it was before she left Paris.

She swept the chopped tomatoes into the salad bowl and looked up to meet his eyes. Her gaze was unwavering, and he could do nothing but to look away with an ill-suppressed sigh.

There was an easy way out of this, a way that would explain everything and would stop her wondering. It would also make her stay the hell away from Damien, with his double dose of dick and suave French charm. He swallowed, huffing out a breath. If he told her the truth, then everything would stop right there.

"Marlène cheated on me with Damien." He hated bringing his ex into any conversation with her for it soiled Mila, indirectly. But she would understand cheating in the normal sense of the word, for what it was worth.

She lowered the chopping board, her eyes widening. "I'm sorry. I didn't know."

"Of course you didn't. No need to be sorry." Maybe it had been the best thing that had happened to him. Because if not for what had happened, he'd still be with Marlène and wouldn't have met Mila. He inhaled sharply, shaking his head against the notion that sprung up in his mind.

He broke away from her intense stare, in which he found no pity, but only incredulity. The expression would've made him chuckle any other time. Yep. He'd been cheated on. He continued to the bedroom where he was still unpacking his suitcase from Singapore, flinging his dirty clothes with heated resolve into the laundry basket.

When she called him for dinner twenty minutes later he had his things sorted. Washing for Madame Leborgne to deal with, a cabin bag packed with his things and the suit he'd need for the next day's work meetings hanging on the door. He'd dressed in his gym clothes and a superficial sense of calm settled over him as he rolled the suitcase to the front door.

In the kitchen, Mila was quiet as she dished up. He wasn't hungry. The anger at Damien and at seeing his shitface staring down at his Mila had closed any gaps in his stomach.

"Are you going to be okay here tonight? Alone?" he asked between bites, finding the food hard to swallow. They'd had this discussion before, but now… who the fuck else was going to bypass the street code and knock on his door with her here alone? Who the hell else had Marlène given the door code to? He wanted to punch something to shreds.

"Are you going to be okay? Alone?" she shot straight back.

His gaze met hers over the short stretch of the kitchen island.

"You look all pumped up," she said softly.

He couldn't look at her. Not with the sincere concern ringing in her voice, her eyes searching his with such worry—it pained him. He pushed his plate away, his fingers trembling with the need to dig into her hair and pull her towards him. He wanted to kiss her mouth, slide his lips over hers, taste the vinegar of the dressing she'd made on her tongue, while digging into her mouth with his own until she moaned. He wanted to make her think of anything but Damien and what had passed. He wanted to take this restless energy that had amplified in his body and fuck it out into her pussy. Claiming her, again and again. *Mine.*

Did she find Damien attractive? Most women did. Most men did. And Damien knew how to play his game. He'd been staring at Mila with that gaze that could make a woman come on command. What would have happened if he hadn't been there? Would Mila have let him in? Would she have slept with Damien? His gut contracted, bile rising to his mouth.

He'd seen that look in Damien's eyes and had known he'd been interpreting his words correctly. *Not wasting your time either, Sinclair.* Damien thought he was fucking her just for the piss of it. Had gotten there ahead of him. That Mila was fair game. Had that been true, at first? He couldn't get his head around it now, not with his body in this tightly strung state. "I need to go to the gym. Get rid of this cagey feeling."

Her eyes widened at his words. "Oh, okay."

He relaxed his fingers, which had curled into fists. "I'm sorry." He raised his hands, dropped them on the table.

"I get it, James. He upset you." She shook her head. "I'd be upset too."

She gathered their half-empty plates. "I'm wondering how Stacey knows him. It's cruel of her to have invited Damien here, knowing he's the reason you broke up with Marlène."

That was not exactly how it had gone down. And Stacey would know squat about it. Unless...

"I'm going to go," he said before the conversation went any further. There was only one mutual acquaintance between Stacey and Damien who could have introduced them to each other. Marlène. "You have my number. Call me, if you need to." He walked off, not waiting for further comment, in case he couldn't hold himself back anymore.

Two hours later he hit the shower at the gym. He'd worked himself into a frenzy, drenched with sweat as he pummeled the heavy boxing bag, but he hadn't been able to get enough. Not even the thirty-minute sprint he'd done on the treadmill afterward or the weights he'd lifted had helped.

All he could think of was Damien and Mila, and what could have happened if he hadn't been there. And then of Marlène, and what would happen if she arrived and he wasn't at the apartment.

He'd already decided he'd go sleep at a hotel, not being in the mood for any of his usual crowd, or for the explanations that might be needed. Mila didn't need to know that he opted for a hotel, but as he took his suitcase and walked out of the gym into the last wink of twilight, he didn't turn to the Regina, as he'd planned. He found himself retracing his steps, going home.

He entered the lobby, leaning against the wall close to the elevator for a minute. To gather his thoughts, to herd his scattered resolve back to where it belonged. He wouldn't touch her; it would be sleeping. The bed was big enough for both of them with space for a third to spare. Intentionally. King size, extra length, extra depth. He groaned as he took the stairs, at last feeling the exhaustion rise in his body from the overdose of exercise. With his jet-lag still biting, he could slip quietly under the covers and fall asleep. She'd slept so deeply in his arms last night, not stirring until that morning. Hopefully, it would be the same tonight.

He turned the key softly, opening the apartment door with a

careful turn of the knob. The entrance hall and lounge were dark, lit up only by the city glow penetrating the windows. He left his things by the door, took off his shoes and padded through the lounge to the master bedroom. The door was ajar, the air conditioning buzzing. For the rest, it was déjà vu.

Mila, with the covers half over her, a leg lazily hooked over the duvet, was asleep. The bedside lamp doused the room in a faint light, but she had her back turned to it as she slept on her side. *Jane Eyre* had slipped from her relaxed grip on his side of the bed. In her other hand, she held her glasses. She looked so at peace, angelic, sinless, having fallen asleep mid-reading. Ignoring the rise of his pulse, the slow heat that ran down his back to his balls, he edged closer on her side of the bed, wanting to switch off the lamp.

He glanced up her body, her Hello Kitty nightshirt having scrunched up to her hip. His gaze jolted to a halt when he saw her butt peeking back at him.

She had no underwear on. Fuck. He leaned closer as his already half-mast erection jerked to full salute, and he swallowed. Her leg was lifted just high enough for him to see how the lips of her sex grazed the duvet.

He should have known. Hadn't he told her *no panties* in his bed? He grinned, his pulse dancing. She had no idea that he would be there right now... If he hadn't known that he would have thought his Sassy Miss Johnson was a cock tease.

Chapter 21

MILA WOKE SLOWLY, AT FIRST wanting to snuggle deeper into the covers as the air conditioning had cooled the room more than she could bear. And there was no James to keep her warm like he had the previous night. She stirred, stretching her arms, only to feel warm skin under her touch.

She opened her eyes as her fingers unfurled only to be trapped in a gentle grip. James was on the other side of the bed, lying on his side, his arm reaching out and his pinky playing with hers, a minuscule connection of heat. She must be dreaming and stirred to wake up, but he caught her hand.

There was nothing frightening about the situation, nothing strange, and she turned to him and smiled. "You're here."

He wore a white T-shirt and boxer shorts; his hair was rumpled and a pillow wrinkle streaked down his cheek.

"Hope you don't mind."

He'd spoken, so it must be true that he was there, and inside her, a bubble of joy drifted up, just as the slow stir of lust woke in her belly. He hadn't stayed away; maybe he couldn't stay away. Or so she hoped.

"What happened?" She figured he might just as well shatter her illusions now.

"I'm not sure who else has access to the apartment. I—" He broke off, weaving his fingers with hers, letting her melt with the sweet gesture. "I didn't want to leave you alone and exposed. Strangers bursting in on you…"

She licked her lips, not sure what to make of his statement, but inside a slow grin was spreading. "Damien did knock, you know. He didn't just let himself in."

His expression changed from sleepy-serious to guarded and she extracted her hand from his to rub her eyes. Did he really think she would have succumbed to Damien's charms? Would have invited him in and let him have his way with her. God. Would she have? After a bottle of champagne? Skunk drunk, sleeping with a guy who trampled on other people's relationships? Not that she would have known about that.

He said nothing.

"My parents did teach me not to open the door to strangers, James," she whispered as she peered at him again. She wouldn't have let Damien in, no matter what. She wouldn't even have opened the door.

For a moment it was quiet, James's jaw ticking in the light that fell through the gap where she hadn't closed the shutter.

"Did you like him?"

"Who? Damien?"

He blinked with a groan. "It doesn't matter."

But it did, otherwise he wouldn't have asked. "He's good looking. Very French, I suppose," she murmured, wanting to turn the conversation around, get that insecure look out of his gaze. Who would have thought that James Sinclair could feel insecure? But now that she knew about Marlène and Damien, she understood why that look was there. Who cheated on a man like James? He was handsome, clever, funny, engaging, caring... and a generous lover. Why would a woman cheat on a man like him?

After last night's episode, it had been clear that James wasn't over Marlène and their breakup yet. It had stung because deep down Mila was falling deeper for him with every passing day. She blinked and forced herself to put her feelings aside and joke around to lighten the mood.

"He's way too scrawny for me. I can't possibly date a guy whose butt is half the size of mine." She suppressed a laugh. Damien's ass had been tight, low-slung, with no muscles at all. The image of him rushing off was as clear in her mind as if he'd strode away a second ago.

"Is that so?" He rose on his elbow, resting his head in his hand, studying her. "I didn't know size mattered... in that department." He chuckled then. "So you like a rugby body, as long as there is no actual rugby involved."

"I suppose so," she said and bit her lip to keep herself from smiling. James was hot as hell, and feelings aside, she didn't mind burning.

"Dangerous ground, Miss Johnson." His gaze traveled her face, paused at her lips and eased to her neck and breasts.

Under his gaze, she became too hot, and an urgency to kick off the stifling covers swamped her. She shifted the duvet, hooking her leg over it, halting with surprise. The soft lick of silk on her sex reminded her that she wore no panties. Per his instruction, she had, with a bit of mischief, tossed them to the side when she'd gone to bed. If it weren't for the air conditioning, she would have ditched the rest too. She inhaled a sharp breath with the realization that her nightshirt had scrunched up to her middle. The silk duvet cover was rubbing over her sex, delicious, teasing, and she froze when under his blazing gaze she wanted to roll her hips to get more friction.

"No panties," he murmured, his gaze shooting back to hers. "Good girl."

The way he said those last little words made her core pull tight, increasing the undercurrent of need that lingered. She was so not a good girl. Her body craved his touch, it was as simple as that. Her hand slipped forward and he shifted his so their fingertips caressed in small kisses, tip to tip, sending a tide of heat through her body.

"What else did you do last night? After I left?" he asked softly. He stilled her with the slight pressure of his fingertips on hers and then traced a slow path down her forefinger with his own.

"I—" she started, but caught her breath as his finger dipped to her thumb, taking a turn around the cuticle of her nail, then retracing its path. The caress was so soft, so subtle, but it sent a sensation down her hand, all the way to where her sex was heating up.

"Were these fingers busy, Mila?" he asked, his voice deeper, quietly inquiring.

"Busy?" she whispered.

"Did you touch yourself?" His eyelids had dropped, hooding his gaze, which was no longer sleepy.

The rush of heat was unmistakable as it drenched her cheeks. He was actually asking her if she'd masturbated.

"Did you think of me as you got off?" he continued, his gentle tracing of her fingers still ongoing, unaffected by his own words. "Miss me?"

Her breathing had paused, every cell in her body intent on his touch, while his soft murmurs were creating havoc in her lower belly.

"Were you very wet?" he quizzed. Her body had molded into the mattress, weighed down with desire. A drop of liquid seeped between her thighs.

"No," she barely whispered, needing to break the intense look between them, which James was holding as if he had her hypnotized.

"No?" He was shifting closer, trailing his hand up her arm to her shoulder, but slipping to her naked hip.

Her nipples were hard and begging, the heat of his palm on the curve of her hip grounding her.

"Are you sure?"

"No." Did she have to sound so helpless?

"So it's a yes?" he teased.

She could reply but gnawed her bottom lip instead. This was only going to end one way. She should stop this, but he was mesmerizing her with his soothing voice and gentle hands.

"Which is it, Mila?" he commanded quietly, his gaze fixing hers, willing her to spill the truth.

"I'm soaked right now."

There was a barely perceptible lifting of his lips at the corners of his mouth. A somewhat triumphant gleam shone from his eyes.

"But I—" She broke off, the words unwilling to slip from her tongue. That little voice cleared its throat.

"But what?"

"I don't do that." She dropped her gaze, too embarrassed to keep staring into his eyes, her ears burning, her whole body flushing.

"And why not?" His hand, which had been stroking circles on her hip, stilled for a second before it slipped lower, to the apex of her thighs.

She zoned in on his arm, then on his hand and fingers, which were putting pressure on her pubic bone, making her want to curve into him, give him access to her sex.

"Because I'm a good girl." Did she have to sound so apologetic? Did she have to feel so wanton, wanting to widen her legs, and let him finger her until she came?

"That you are. No going solo in my bed, understood?" he said, his tone soft, yet firm. A finger slid to her swollen wet sex, feeling what his words had done to her. His finger grazed her pleading clit, stopping short of entering her, gliding back on its tracks. Once. Twice.

She closed her eyes. The build-up was there, her pelvic floor clenching and moisture seeping from her. Her hips rolled, begging him not to stop.

His breathing had become stilted, labored. She opened for him, but instead of stroking deeper, giving in to the friction her hips demanded, he extracted his hand and left her hanging on the edge.

Unhinged, she opened her eyes. He stared at her, a somber light in his eyes, flushed, with lips pursed. He lifted his finger to his mouth, licking the taste of her from his fingers. She closed her eyes at the erotic image of his tongue and lips on his fingers, her pussy gushing more for him to taste, to lick and claim.

"James," she murmured helplessly, not sure why he'd stopped. She'd been so close.

Please.

She shouldn't beg him, knowing how wrong it would be. Knowing that this was not their *deal.* They were just a casual coincidence. If there had been something deeper, maybe she would have let him play with her, and she would have played back. But right now, this type of game was wrong.

Why would he want her when he could have any other woman out there? Serious, career-focused women who could meet him head-on in every aspect of his life and who had seen the world. Editors of *Vogue* magazine. Not an overprotected, religious girl who'd hardly left home and had never traveled beyond her own confined borders.

Opening her eyes, she met his gaze head-on. His eyes had turned stark and sober.

"I'm going to be late for work. And you're going to be late for the Louvre," he said as he turned around and put his feet on the floor. He tossed the duvet to the side and stalked to the bathroom.

Chapter 22

GET A SHOWER. GET TO work. Get some distance.

James turned his face to the beating onslaught of ice-cold water, letting it seep over his heated skin, willing his cock into submission. He was not going to jerk off at the thought of her, and leave a shower scented with his semen, only to tease her.

Fuck. How much had he wanted to tease her?

What had just happened had been too close and too wrong. Had he really lived under the illusion that he could be next to Mila and not touch her?

The night before, instead of falling asleep as he'd hoped, he'd stared at her, had taken in every one of her fine-boned features and memorized them. She was a beauty with her dark hair and long lashes that threw curved shadows over her cheeks. Her full lips had lured him to kiss her. She was a contradiction to everything that usually attracted him. She was too young, too inexperienced; he'd always preferred older blondes, who talked business, whether normal or sexual, as smoothly as he did.

Even in the art world, which he'd frequented as an investor, his acquaintances were into the money side of art and not the making of it. Yet her hands that had held a pencil and paintbrush like a magic quill had captivated him. She was talented, though he knew she didn't believe in herself.

He showered slowly, trying to get a grip on himself—a grip, which did not involve his dick—so he could actually figure out a plan B.

Ten minutes later he hung his head over the hand basin, having washed the last of the shaving cream off his face. The situation was unbearable and the only solution was to get some distance between him and Mila.

With cold resolve, he opened the door to the bedroom only to find it empty. He listened to the sounds coming from the kitchen and closed his eyes. There was nothing more dramatic than the happy gurgle of the coffee machine. Where had she gone?

For a moment he panicked, then he forced himself to shrug the concern off. He dressed at speed in a tailored gray suit and white shirt and hooked an unfolded tie around his neck to deal with in the taxi on his way to work.

When he stepped into the kitchen, Mila was there, no longer in her nightshirt, but in shorts and a tight tank top, clearly braless as she turned to him, slightly out of breath, her eyes sparkling and her cheeks rosy.

"I'm—" He paused. She looked orgasm-flushed. He clenched his jaw, knowing he hadn't been involved in that one. Had she gone against his specific instructions? Something stirred in him and he pursed his lips. But then... he could hardly blame her, the way he had left her earlier on, but he forced himself not to give a damn.

"I'm off to work. I have a business dinner tonight and won't

159

be here. I—" He conjured a grin as her gaze grew blank. "I won't sleep here tonight, so…" He rubbed the back of his neck with his hand. He'd never felt such a coward, or so coldheartedly stupid in his life.

"That's fine." Her voice was toneless. "Coffee? Before you go?"

"No, thank you. I'll grab some at the office."

"Croissant?"

Too late he noticed the croissants from the bakery across the street. He dropped his gaze for a second. She must have run over to the *boulangerie* to buy croissants while he was showering. She hadn't helped herself as he'd thought but instead had gone to reciprocate the breakfast he'd made for her the day before.

Good girl.

Bad boy. His stomach tightened and he clenched his jaw. He had to focus on distance. "No thanks. Take it for lunch. You're going to get hungry."

He strode to the kitchen island and squatted to open the bottom drawer. He rummaged through a stack of leaflets until he found his well-worn map of Paris and a pen.

He straightened with a fake smile. "This is a bit old but won't be dated," he said as he unfolded the map on the countertop. "Some of my favorite haunts are still around. Most of them are legendary."

He pored over the map while trying to avoid Mila, who'd leaned against the counter, her fingers inches from his, distracting as hell. "There's a wine bar here called The Sommelier, a seventies disco-themed club here, and here you have an English pub." He pinpointed the locations on the map. "All frequented by the expat crowd, English-speaking students. The lingo won't be an issue for you." He gazed up at her, but her eyes were downcast, following his ministrations on the map.

"Go out tonight, meet some other people." *Get laid by someone normal, forget about me.*

She met his gaze. "Don't you dare add 'people my own age'."

"Okay, I won't." He blinked. "Go have some fun."

They were quiet, measuring each other up. She'd said she wasn't the clubbing type. "There are also classical music concerts at Sainte-Chapelle, but I don't have info on that."

"Don't worry about me. Business dinner tonight?" she asked after an infinite minute, her hand reaching towards him.

He didn't have it in him to move away, but she only took both ends of his tie and pulled him closer, the silk slipping between her fingers. She tied it quickly, expertly, whilst her gaze stayed on her hands. She lifted his collar, her knuckles grazing the sensitive skin along his hairline and his neck, sending sparks down his spine. He inhaled softly at the touch.

"There," she murmured. "Four brothers. If nothing else, I know how to tie a tie."

This was the moment where she would pull him closer, and he would lean in for a kiss. His mouth went dry, his lips whispering their willingness, eager for him to cave in and have her. She smelt of coffee and sleep and Mila, a heady mix of something he should never have inhaled in the first place.

"Mila." He groaned.

She adjusted his collar, straightening his lapels, softly brushing her hands over his chest. "All good." She stepped away and gave him a once-over. "Off you go."

He turned on his heel and walked out, grabbing his suitcase, which still stood at the front door where he'd left it the night before.

As he got into the lift he paused. That had been wrong on so many levels. And exactly who had dismissed whom?

Chapter 23

MILA STARED AT THE TWO croissants on the table and sighed. It had been as if James couldn't get out fast enough, and his random scribbles on the street map of Paris gave a clear message: *This is it. From now on, you're on your own, baby.*

He'd actually stopped calling her baby after the first night. With a groan, she gathered her hair over her shoulders. She was frustrated and confused because that morning had been a mess of mixed signals. Whilst they'd been in bed everything had slipped into something sensual and sexy, and yet he'd withdrawn from her, had gone cold, leaving her itching for release. And now her frustration was going to keep her edgy for the rest of the day.

Her phone rang, pulling her out of her fog, and she scrambled for her bag to dig it out. *James Sinclair.* Did her heart have to skip a beat at seeing his name?

She hesitated, because hearing his voice right now, promising a myriad of things he would do to her, was not going to help her pull herself from the pit he'd left her in.

Act grown-up, dearest, she chided herself and pressed the answer button.

"Hi."

"Listen, I just spoke to Clea. She'd rather meet you at the Porte de Lions entrance at twenty to nine." His tone was all business.

"Okay." She closed her eyes. Why did she hope for something more here?

"Do you know where that gate is?"

"No, but I'll figure it out." What was she waiting for? An apology? A promise? A rude wake-up call? That was what she needed.

"It will be on the map. Or Google it. It's less busy than the pyramid entrance."

"Sure."

"You can't miss Clea. She's tall, has long blonde hair, and always wears a black suit to work."

Ugh. She should have known about the tall and blonde part.

"I have a meeting at eight," he said, almost apologetically.

"Stop worrying about me, James." Did her voice have to catch on his name? She cleared her throat and took a sip of coffee, cold and bitter. "I'll be fine."

There were a few seconds of silence on the other side and then he said, "Enjoy the Louvre. I hope it is everything you've imagined it to be."

"Thank you."

He rang off and she clutched the phone in her hand. He'd dealt with everything so lightly. Did he even feel any of the confusion she felt now? He deserved to be feeling some of her pain. He was driving her mad, almost intentionally. She'd love to give him a bit of his own back.

For a moment she hesitated, then she opened the messages

on her phone. She'd never been into sexting, never had anyone to sext with, but James had this one coming.

You, Sir, are a pussy tease.

She pressed send, closed her eyes, and exhaled some of the tension that had been sitting on her chest since he'd marched out earlier.

Minutes passed, and she decided to help herself to a fresh cup of coffee. When her phone beeped a message back, her stomach clutched tight.

I'm only a pussy tease to Good Girls.

She grinned as her pulse sped up. Her fingers flew over the keys.

Just my luck!

He messaged back after a few seconds.

This morning was not part of our deal, Mila.

She wanted to forget about the deal. She wanted to forget about the shadow of Marlène and Damien hanging over him and his anger the night before. She wanted to be with him, and be thoroughly fucked like he had fucked her the previous morning. She wanted that connection to him, but this time even deeper. They'd been sharing secrets, and she was feeling more connected with him than she'd ever felt with another human being.

Her fingers trembled; she had no witty reply ready for him.

Then her phone beeped.

Rub one out, I give you permission to do so and solemnly promise you won't burn in hell for it. ;-)

Good Lord. Of course he'd recommend that. Hell and all.

I don't believe in hell. You're way too cocky for your own good. But I bet you know that.

She pressed send and put her phone down to take up a croissant and bite into it. Her phone beeped.

You have no idea how cocky I am right now. It's hell, to be honest.

164

She smiled. She had him right where she'd wanted him. Served him right. She licked some crumbs off her lip. Could she really ask him… should she dare? She took another bite and tossed caution to the wind.

Are you going to be at the apartment tonight? After your business dinner?

There was no quick response and time ticked-ticked-ticked. She kept staring at her phone, holding her breath. When it finally beeped she inhaled sharply.

No.

Her heart dropped and her stomach tensed. That morning he'd told her he'd been worried about her being alone at the apartment, with French models like Damien knocking on the door, chilled champagne in their hands.

Did this mean he had somewhere else to sleep? With someone else?

Why did it have to feel so horrible? She closed her eyes trying to ignore the agonizing churn of half-chewed croissant in her stomach. It was time.

Ok. Bye James. xxxxxxxxx

She could send him as many kisses as she wanted over text, he wouldn't care for one of them. She closed her eyes and prayed that he would be as horny as she was for the rest of the day.

And, dear Lord, let him think only of me.

Chapter 24

JAMES READ THROUGH THEIR CONVERSATION again. It was past six in the evening and his whole day had been a bloody waste of time. His ability to concentrate had reached sub-zero levels because all he could think about was Mila.

Sir. Pussy. Tease. He tossed his phone to the side.

Calling him *Sir* like a little submissive, luring him to her with that innocent question whether he'd be back at the apartment after his meeting.

The meeting got him thinking about the club and invariably his thoughts drifted to the issue of Marlène. There had been no more messages from her and he hadn't bothered to contact her again. He had no desire to talk to her. What he wanted was for her to take her stuff and fuck off out of his apartment and his life.

And that thought brought him right back to the club. He didn't want to go to the meeting, he didn't want to see the place. He hadn't wanted to go there for eight months. But now, the need for distance was even more intense, and for this, he could only blame

Mila. Above everything else, he wanted to spend time with her. He didn't want her to go out on her own in Paris, irrespective of the fine selection of innocent joints he'd jotted down for her earlier on.

Fuck it.

He picked up his phone and scrolled his contacts for Jean-Pierre Costeau. He dialed and raked through his hair while his phone rang.

"James," Jean-Pierre answered. "Why do I know this is not good?"

"I won't make the meeting tonight." He almost groaned at the non-response on the other side. "Something's come up at work."

"Aha." Jean-Pierre smirked. "What's been crashing? Frankfurt? Paris? It's too late for Tokyo. Don't tell me I've already lost millions."

"Nothing's crashing," he said, rolling his eyes. "Only an un-foreseen… emergency."

"I see." Jean-Pierre was quiet for a second then he chuckled. "Cut to the chase, James. Who is she?"

He loosened his tie and unbuttoned the first two buttons of his shirt, stopping the incredulous chuckle that wanted to break from his throat. "What do you mean?"

"Ha, I spoke to Etienne last night. He said you brought a charming girl with you for lunch at his place. He wanted to send some champagne over but—"

"Just a family friend," he interrupted. Bloody hell.

"Hands-off territory?" Jean-Pierre mused.

He didn't answer. Why was it so hard to talk around things with Jean-Pierre? Probably because they'd known each other for ages, were practically best friends in a way.

"You didn't keep your hands to yourself, did you, James?" Jean-Pierre laughed. "I'll drink to that! Why don't you bring her to the club tonight? After the meeting, we can meet her."

A fine spray of prickles rushed over his skin, from his forehead down to his abdomen. "No."

There was no response. "Not sharing yet, are you?"

He wanted to curse but took a stiff breath. "I called to let you know I can't make the meeting. I read through the agenda and there is nothing in there that requires me to be there."

Jean-Pierre sighed into the phone. "I hoped to see you, in person. Never mind. I'll forward you the minutes."

He rang off, a lightness settling over him as if his ball and chain had been separated and he could actually walk without dragging the load. As he packed up for the day he checked his watch. It was almost seven and with traffic, it would take him at least another twenty minutes to get home.

For a second he gathered his thoughts. It might be that he got to the apartment and she wouldn't be there. Maybe she would have taken his instructions and gone out alone. Then he'd go stalk her down, but his hunt would start at the apartment.

Mila dropped her bag next to the wingback chair, flopped into it and kicked her shoes off. She rolled her neck and groaned as she pulled the side table in front of her legs and settled her feet on it. She sat for five minutes, digesting her day.

It had been wonderful but intensely emotional to see so many pieces of art that she'd studied for years. Her feet were killing her, but she'd stayed until the last minute, and already knew that she'd go back the next day. She had hardly scraped the surface of the Louvre, as James had predicted.

He'd been on her mind the whole day, and she'd found that she was having conversations with him about art as she'd moved from one painting to the next. She had missed his sharp comments.

She'd switched her phone to silent because she was in the museum, but also because she didn't want to have moments of useless hope about any further messages from him.

She reached into her bag and took out her phone. Bar letting Ruben know she'd arrived in one piece she'd hardly used her phone. Her friends and family thought she was completely out of reach and she rather enjoyed the quiet reprieve her lies had bought her. There was going to be consequences… she'd deal with them later.

Only a few messages from Stacey stared at her from the screen.

How is Paris!?!?!?

Apartment all good???

My rewrite was horrible. Not sure why I'm bothering.

Was Damien there last night?

She took a deep breath at the onslaught and read through it again.

She had no idea how much she should reveal to Stacey. James's private life was his to deal with and share, not hers. She'd had the whole day to dissect the situation and she'd come to the conclusion that Stacey had no idea about what had caused the break-up of James and Marlène.

Paris is beautiful. Thank you! Went to the Louvre today. My feet!!!!! Killing me!! Damien was here but didn't stay long.

She bit her lip and inhaled. Would Stacey plague her now? She hadn't mentioned James, but neither had Stacey. She was going to keep it like that for now.

Pressing send, she prayed that Stacey would have neither the time nor be in the mood to dig into why Damien had left so soon.

Minutes later her phone beeped.

Sounds fantastic. Apartment is cool, right? Louvre on his freaking doorstep and all.

His. James. It was the only reference Stacey had made to her brother. She swiftly replied that it was *amaaaazing*, hoping that Stacey would back off.

Then the message came through: *Why didn't Damien stay?*

She sighed. The best would be to create a diversion. *Because he wanted to see you and not me.*

Stacey's reply popped over in seconds. *Awww... that's sweet. I haven't met him yet. I'm really pissed off at not being there right now.*

He was Stacey's type too, his looks, the clothes he'd worn, his easy manner, they all fitted right into Stacey's usual tall, lanky but handsome agenda. *You'd love him, but I really hope you don't.* She typed the words, but then deleted them. There was no way she was going to push Stacey in Damien's direction. Maybe once she was in Paris they could go to Versailles for the weekend to make sure they missed Damien. From James's reaction last night, he'd be furious if they went out with Damien and she wouldn't blame him.

Next week you'll be here! Now go study so that you can have a guiltless trip. She sent it off, knowing she sounded twice her age and that Stacey was going to have some snarky reply.

YES MOM. XXX

Mila grinned at the caps. She might be mothering Stacey, but someone had to.

She tossed her phone back into her bag, took her shoes and went to the bedroom. She needed to relax her tired legs and sore feet. A long warm bath would soothe her aches.

After soaking in the hot water for some time she washed her hair. When she got out of the bath she dressed in a loose-fitting diaphanous top and some panties. She padded barefoot to the

170

kitchen for a glass of her red wine, which hadn't tasted half as bad as the price had predicted.

Walking back into the lounge she looked out of the windows and took in the view of Paris. The light was right, as it was almost the same time as she'd painted on the evening of her arrival.

She returned to the kitchen and fetched some cups with water and kitchen towels. Back at the wingback, she settled her brushes and paint on the side table and got comfortable in the chair with James's painting. She was committed to finishing it so she could leave it for him when she left. Even if she didn't see him again, he would have this something of her, something that would remind him of more than just sex.

As she got busy she lost track of time. In Paris, summer afternoons oozed slowly into evening, and she figured she'd have at least an hour to paint before she'd need artificial lighting.

When metal sounded against metal as someone inserted a key into the front door, she frowned and looked up, startled and confused. Her shoulders cramped from where she'd bent over the pad to paint, her eyes tired of the intense concentration.

James appeared in the entrance hall and her heart skipped a beat at seeing him. He looked ruffled, his tie loose around his neck and his hair disheveled as if he'd dragged his fingers through it too many times.

She sat straighter, brushing the tendrils of hair from her face. "Hi."

He dropped his laptop bag at the entrance and tossed his keys into the bowl at the front door. "Hi." He closed in on her, and with each step he took, her heartbeat edged up a notch. By the time he stood at her feet and she had to lean back to see his face, her pulse was racing.

"Rough day at the office?" she breathed, their earlier sexting running on repeat in her mind.

"You could say that."

She looked down so that he couldn't see her grin, but her eyes came level with a budding bulge in his trousers and she had to look even lower. There was a rustle of fabric and with a sigh, he dropped his jacket to the floor. She looked up to see him tugging at his tie. He unknotted it slowly, intentionally, and her stomach did a slow turn at seeing his fingers, the memory of him licking her juices off them earlier as vivid as if he'd done so a second ago. The tie landed on top of his jacket.

"We have unfinished business." He stared down at her as he started to roll up his sleeves.

She shifted in the chair, sudden heat crashing through her at the look in his eyes. *Yes, we do.*

"Your business dinner?" she whispered. She was in it deep this time.

He took his time to finish rolling up his sleeves. Every cell in her beat in a frantic tick-tock. She had no idea what he was getting up to, but within her, there was an unruly reawakening of this morning's unfulfilled desire.

"Cancelled." He placed his hands on the armrests and bent over her. She wanted to lean back, to get away from his gaze that didn't break with hers, but she was trapped. His lips were inches from hers, and hers felt dry in anticipation that he might kiss her.

She ran her tongue across her lips, her breathing stalling as he bent over to run his lips across her temple. At any moment he could slip lower, to her lips.

But instead of searching for her mouth, he grazed her ear. "But that's a good thing because now I can take care of other... issues."

She closed her eyes as a heated wetness gushed between her legs. "What issues?"

"Someone called me a pussy tease." He nibbled her earlobe and she dropped her head to the side to give him access to her neck. "What does that even mean, Mila?"

Her skin broke out in goose bumps at the slow, feather-light tease of his lips on her neck. "It's the male version of a cock tease."

"And what are you, Mila, if not a cock tease, sleeping half-naked in my bed?" His voice had gone a tone lower, deeper, with even more promise of some sweetly wicked intention than before.

"You weren't supposed to have been here." She had nothing but moaned words to defend herself.

"I find I rather like you in my bed. I'm not supposed to be here now, and yet, I find I can't stay away." He'd reached her collarbone, his lips trailing a path down the slope of a breast. "Against my better judgment."

At his last words she bit her lip, trying to contain the flood of emotion that rattled her. *He couldn't stay away.* And yes, this was wrong, because he was toying with her just for the pleasure of it. Already it was more for her.

She kept her eyes closed, not ready to read what was in his gaze. Half a minute later, when she'd gotten a grip, she opened them again. He'd dropped to his knees, his hands placed next to hers on the chair's armrests. He'd stopped touching her and had pulled away. He was waiting.

"I don't want you to stay away," she whispered. "Against my better judgment."

He reached for her paintbrush and pad, which she'd been clinging to during the rush of his sweet onslaught, and put them aside.

His hands were on her shoulders and he brushed her hair

from her chest and breasts. When his palms grazed her hardened nipples, heated sparks shot down to her sex and she moaned. She touched his face, cupping his cheeks in her hands, wanting to pull him to her lips and to bury her fingers in his hair, but he stilled her hands with his.

"Hold on with both hands to the back of the chair," he instructed. Their gazes clashed. "Don't touch anything else, or else I'm going to tie you up, understand?"

Her body shivered at the promise of things going kinky, but she nodded, her weight sinking deeper into the chair. She gripped the back of the chair and his hands stroked up her thighs and reached for her panties, which he tugged at. She shimmied her hips forward.

"What are you doing?" she asked, dosed with desire.

"Just showing you what I understood by pussy tease, Mila," he said as he slipped her panties off and flung them to the side.

Her pulse danced as he hooked her legs over each of the wingback's armrests and with her sex exposed, all focus drained to her pussy. Things were going only one place, and her delayed orgasm from that morning was threatening to explode just at the thought of his mouth on her clit.

He gripped her knees, immobilizing her in the chair, his tongue and lips on her skin. His mouth made its way slowly up her inner thigh to her sex. Her nails dug into the backrest as she held tighter, trying not to squirm under his delicate ministrations.

"James," she whispered, feeling drugged. "I'm going to come."

"I hope so," he murmured. His tongue grazed the lips of her sex, and she bucked against his mouth. "But not without a bit of teasing."

With his hands on her knees, there was not much scope for movement. Her hands begged to break free, to take hold of his head and get some control over what he was doing, but instead of letting go, she held on tighter, lifting her pelvis to his mouth.

He licked her then, rolling his tongue over her clit. The feeling was almost too intense, but she had nowhere to go and could find reprieve only in a deep moan that caught in her throat. He licked her again, his tongue sparking to life every last nerve in her body. Every muscle tightened and a ghostly ripple of pleasure rushed through her. If this was how he started she wouldn't be able to take much more.

He reassured her by smoothing his hand down her thigh and slipping it under her shirt, never letting his tongue stop its torturous and languid licks. His hand edged higher, so slowly; she caught her breath. The tension in her sex was wound tight, pulsing to the shattering point. When he ran his thumb over her puckered over-sensitive nipple, the caress shot to her core. She whimpered, craving more, unable to resist anymore. When his thumb and fingers tightened around her nipple the sudden pressure was too much. A ripple of contractions burst through her, one by one, from her innermost core to her clit. She cried out as her orgasm exploded against his tongue. His lips closed over her clit and he sucked gently, extending her release.

Her breathing had broken into ragged pants, and when he eventually let go she dropped her tired arms. He shifted and rested his head on her chest, his hands clasping her hips. She threaded her fingers through his hair, wanting to anchor him to her.

After a moment he lifted his head and searched her eyes. "This has been the only thing I've had on my mind since this morning."

"Pussy teasing?" she breathed, her body still adrift. "It was rather rude to leave me the way you did."

He smiled, a naughty grin. "Wasn't it worth the wait?"

Oh yes. Heat rushed to her cheeks.

"I'll take that as a yes," he murmured, stroking his hands to her knees, lifting her legs over the armrest and placing them back on the seat. "You've eaten?"

"No." Surely it would be her turn to return the favor. The prospect made her swallow nervously. She'd never given a man a blowjob and would hate to disappoint him.

"I'm talking real food, Mila," he said, with a slow smile.

A mix of relief and disappointment floated through her at his words. She'd been hungry early on but had wanted to paint while the light was right. Her glass of wine stood on the side table, untouched. She shook her head. "I've been painting."

He glanced at the pad on the floor. He picked it up and studied it keenly. "I love it," he murmured as he put the pad down and touched her legs again. "Let's go for dinner. There's a nice place up the road and we can talk—" He broke off, looking toward the window.

A man who wanted to talk? She held her breath; it was too good to be true.

"Chat about your day at the Louvre," he finished, not meeting her gaze.

She should have known. They were not going to talk about what had just happened. About her coming in his mouth within minutes of him walking into the apartment. Or about why he was there in the first place—business dinner cancelled or not. Or about their mutual better judgments.

But she wanted to have dinner with him and talk about her day. She could steer clear of every exhausting emotion, focusing only on art. "I'd love to but I don't think I can walk right now. Not even up the street."

He got up. "Come on, I need to shower first, so you can put your feet up a bit." He held his hand out to her and she eased out of the chair, feeling stiff and weak.

She'd hardly straightened when he scooped her up in his arms as if she was feather-light. "James!" she shrieked but enjoyed the sudden romantic gesture as he pressed a kiss to her head.

"Why do you always smell so delicious?" he murmured in her hair as he carried her to the bedroom.

She nestled to his chest, taking the moment for what it was, forcing herself not to wish for more.

He settled her down on the bed and extracted his arms from around her back. "Give me five minutes," he said as he stroked some wisps of hair from her face. "And don't fall asleep," he warned as he handed her *Jane Eyre*.

She chuckled as he disappeared into the bathroom, closing the door behind him. She clutched the book to her chest. There was no way she could fall asleep now. In the bathroom, her lover, possibly the sexiest guy on the planet, had turned on the shower. In her mind's eye, he was stripping, and the mere idea made her ache to have him inside her again.

But he hadn't gone there, didn't take it any further beyond pleasing her. And he hadn't expected her to reciprocate the favor. Why? Her body felt empty, with a new need that she never before knew existed. She wanted *him*.

But then... he still hadn't kissed her. That fact was like a pause button, forcing her to stop, step back and take stock. She was delusional to think that he actually cared for her.

Chapter 25

JAMES CONGRATULATED HIMSELF ON HIS self-control as they walked down Rue Saint Honoré half an hour later. He'd actually managed to go down on Mila without ripping her flimsy shirt off and taking her as every cell in his body had begged him to do. Cold showers had become *de rigueur*, as had a worrying craving for making something, which he suspected resembled *love,* with Mila, and not only giving in to mutual sexual desire.

He glanced at her. She looked gorgeous in a strapless summer dress, dark blue with little red roses scattered all over the fabric. The skirt fell from her narrow waist and grazed her knees, with the bodice of the dress clinging to her curves. Her bare shoulders were driving him nuts and he groaned inwardly. She was so goddamn sexy and was totally unconscious of it. When James had finished his shower Mila had already dressed, depriving him of any pleasure in watching her put on that little number. He had no idea which part of her had had this foresight, but if he'd found her waiting still semi-naked on his bed, it would have been a very delayed dinner.

He'd made peace with his uncontrollable attraction to her but what raged a war inside him was that hopeless knowledge that she deserved better than him. She deserved more than what he could give her.

A block down from the apartment they passed the narrow street in which the club was situated. He saw the club's door from afar and cringed as the black door blinked back at him. The only indication of the club's existence was a silver plaque on the door, so small it was hardly noticeable. The plaque only gave the house number and in cursive said *Club Privé*. A security camera was mounted at the right-hand upper corner of the door. There was another secret camera mounted a bit higher up to take footage of would-be visitors. There was a single buzzer intercom. Nothing on the outside gave a hint of the luxury and opulence that awaited members on the inside.

His entire body shuddered as he looked away. Mila had been quiet since he'd met up with her in the kitchen after having dressed. She'd been reading at the kitchen counter, and the wine glass, which had still been full when he'd come home, had been emptied. Dutch courage.

He felt disconnected from her and every time his gaze had met hers, she'd flushed a deep red. He wanted to know what was going on in her head. He'd hate to be wrong, but morals aside, he suspected that Mila was starting to enjoy her French sexcapade.

He reached for her hand and led her into the restaurant where he'd made a reservation after his call with Jean-Pierre. It had been a cocksure and arrogant move on his part, and he wasn't sure what he would have done if she'd said no to dinner.

The waiter seated them at a corner table, in an intimate and private area. As they sat down her leg brushed against his and he shifted away, just to find his leg gravitating back to her naked knee again and again.

She was still unnaturally quiet after they'd ordered. He was used to her being chirpy, vibrant and full of jokes. He hoped he was not to blame for her stillness. "Are you tired?" he asked.

"No." She blinked. "Yes."

"So very pensive, Mila," he murmured. Had he made her orgasm into another orbit? The idea made him grin. "Did you enjoy the Louvre?"

This question lured her out of her shell, and soon they were chatting, the earlier tension seeping away as he piqued her with rude comments about art, and she made him laugh with a snide comment to put him in his place.

"Why do you know so much about art?" she asked when the waiter collected their empty main course plates.

He hovered over the question, but Mila probably knew something of his family's bumpy road to riches. His dad had a snakes-and-ladders type of luck with his businesses, and his mom's whims didn't help.

"During one of my parents' lows, my mom nearly bankrupted my dad. I was in the last years of high school at the time. To make ends meet I had to step in." He bit the inside of his lip. Those days had been far from rosy. "My mom had invested, or splurged rather, in random pieces of art during one of my dad's ups. Turned out some of the pieces she'd purchased had an excellent return." He smiled, a bit pessimistic. "I got hooked. It's a nice egg to have in my array of baskets."

She looked at him with such tenderness it made him melt. "Stacey never talks about things like that. She doesn't know much about that time, does she?"

"She was too young to remember much." Stacey had been a little girl who'd only wanted to wear princess dresses and fairy wings. He'd wanted to keep her in that dream world for as long as possible.

"And you still look out for your family? For Stacey?"

"My dad is doing well now. He actually listens to me nowadays." He met her gaze. "But yes, I look out for what is mine." *And you are mine.*

She didn't look away but searched his eyes. As if she'd read his mind she shifted uncomfortably and stood. "Excuse me."

He watched her as she descended the stairs to the underground restrooms. Something was off with Mila and he couldn't figure out what it was. He didn't like seeing her like this, distracted as if she was bored of him already. He groaned at the thought.

She returned five minutes later and as she sat down he asked, "Were you planning to go out tonight?"

"Where to?" she asked, staring at him blankly.

"To one of the places I recommended?"

She shook her head. "No, I—" She broke off.

Relief swept through him at her answer. And triumph, but he didn't want to probe deeper. "Do you want dessert?"

"I want—" She broke off, averting her eyes, fingers fiddling with the napkin.

"What would you like?" he asked softly.

"I want—" Her gaze met his and her eyes shimmered.

His heart pumped faster, his pulse rushing. "Just say it, Mila."

"I want to scrap the *just once* deal." She blushed a deep red, her voice such a soft murmur he had to lean in to hear her. "I want you," she whispered, her lips brushing his ear, sending a bolt of lust to his groin.

He hadn't realized how much he'd hoped that scrapping their

deal would be on her mind. He'd actually prayed for it.

Still, he braked against the notion. "It's not a good idea, Mila."

He wanted her that moment, on the table, her legs wrapped around him, moaning in ecstasy as he fucked her until all the remaining crockery had crashed to the floor. But not in front of the other diners. Never.

He might be used to having sex with like-minded people and then letting go, but Mila... he'd been her first. And now, things were going deeper between the two of them. He was already more involved than he'd planned to become, and with her asking for more... her feelings were getting too involved as well.

And that was only scratching the surface. Underneath it all was his past that threatened to bubble up like some poisonous gas. Of course, it might never come to that, with her going home. He was flying to New York the following week. But if it did, he wouldn't be there to pick up the pieces. The last thing he wanted was for Mila to leave shattered.

"I know I'm not Marlène, I can't—" Mila whispered, "I don't want to replace her—"

It felt as if the earth caved in under him, sliding him into a boiling pit of fury. "Fuck Marlène," he growled. "Don't you ever, *ever* compare yourself with Marlène."

Her face drained of color and she glanced to the side, where the diners at a neighboring table shot curious looks at them.

He huffed out a breath, but it didn't help to soften the bolt of anger and possessiveness that shot through him.

He reached for her cheek, palmed in it his hand and made her look at him. His fingers quivered as he stroked her hairline. Touching her hardly eased his anger at her comment, and he exhaled again, fighting for control over the absurd emotions that pummeled him.

Mila was this world, Marlène was the one he'd left behind. Out of choice. For the first time, the realization hit him. It had been a conscious choice. He knew that he didn't want to go back there. It was a type of hell he'd only recognized for what it was once he was out of it. It had been fun. It had been safe. It had been a place where he'd had control. But James had never felt as alive as he did now.

With Marlène it had been motions—manageable, an act that played out time and again, the script well known. With Mila it was emotions, and he had no idea how to control anything he was feeling.

"I'm so confused, James," she murmured, tears teetering in her voice. "It's been so intense with you, I—"

Jesus, she was going to be the end of him. "Mila, what's happening between us has nothing to do with Marlène."

He leaned closer, pinning her down with his eyes, searching hers. Her lips were trembling, moist from the tip of her tongue and from little nervous bites she'd been worrying them with.

Fuck this shit.

He leaned in and kissed her.

Chapter 26

HER LIPS WERE SO SOFT, so willing as he captured her mouth and pressed deeper. *God*, he groaned internally. She opened for him and he roamed with his tongue, mating with hers in a slow dance. She kissed him back, gently, almost in reverence of their passion that threatened to boil over. He slipped his hand around her neck, pulling her towards him, and as her hand settled on his chest he caressed the soft skin between her neck and her naked shoulder. He should have known it would be like this. Hot and tasting of sweet promises, of everything he had sidestepped for too long.

Eventually, he pulled away, but cupped her chin in his hand, his thumb stroking her plump bottom lip. With her flushed face inches from his, he murmured, "Let's take this somewhere private." The need to be alone with her, to experience her without an audience, was overwhelming.

She nodded. He pulled some euros from his wallet to cover the bill, tossed them on the table and reached for her hand. They got up and he guided her out of the restaurant, his hand resting on her lower back. Once outside, they headed to the apartment, hand in hand.

He was clinging to her, almost desperately, with lengthy steps rushing the short walk back to the apartment. He wanted to break into a run, to get her home as quickly as he could. The weight of her gaze rested on him every few steps. It took all he had in him not to pause and claim her mouth again, in the middle of the sidewalk, surrounded by tourists and other Parisians going about their business.

They got to the apartment and he punched in the front door's code. Once in the small lobby, he pressed the call button for the lift. He crowded her to the wall, kissing her, his stubble brushing against her chin. She moaned and he broke away.

Softer. Slower. He wanted to step away but she circled her arms around his neck.

"Don't," she whispered, "Don't pull away like that." She pressed her body flush against his, every curve a tease in its own right. The softness of her breasts succumbing to his harder chest; her smaller frame against his awakening his need to protect her.

Her supple middle gave way under the pressure of his erection. *God*, he was hard. A deep groan rumbled from his chest as their tongues twined together and she moaned. When the lift pinged open he urged them inside, still kissing, his hands firmly on her butt keeping her glued to him.

He felt for the uppermost button, pressing it hard, hoping the lift would by some miracle take them where they wanted to go. They kissed during the ride to the top floor, and when the lift opened they let go. He let her walk out first, resting his hand on her lower back, steering her ahead. When they came to the apartment door he paused. She stared at him, expectantly. He lifted her hand to his lips, teasing her skin with soft kisses from her palm to her wrist, and higher to her shoulder.

"The whole evening, this little spot," he whispered against her skin, "right here," he pressed a kiss on the tip of her shoulder, "has been driving me crazy."

His tongue trailed over her collarbone to her neck as his hands caressed her sides, up to her breasts, which were way too pert in that distracting little dress. He sucked gently at her skin, and with satisfaction felt the rush of goose bumps crawling down her arm, puckering her nipples into hard little pebbles against his palms.

He shifted to look at her. She'd closed her eyes but a smile played on her lips. If he guessed right she rather enjoyed driving him somewhat crazy.

He cupped her cheeks in both hands, letting his lips find their way to her temple and her eyes, where he kissed her closed eyelids, his touch feather-light.

"What else drives you, um... crazy?" she murmured against his lips, as her hands circled his waist, resting on the curve of his butt. She pulled him closer.

He kissed her softly. "You, in general." Everything had been a blurry state of confusion since he'd walked into his apartment and found her in his bed a few nights ago.

She laughed. "And just how do I do that?"

He kissed her softly on the lips. "Hmm." He smiled as he lifted his gaze to meet hers. "Let me count the ways."

He trapped her between his body and the door, tugged his apartment key from his trouser pocket and slipped it into its slot. "It drives me crazy that you're here. Waiting." He opened the door, circling his arms around her waist, pulling her into the apartment. "For me. Alone."

"Mere coincidence," she murmured against his cheek. "I

wouldn't read too much into it if I were you."

"Maybe," he chuckled as he closed the door. "But I'd like to read everything I want into it." She *was* everything he'd wanted. Her purity and disinterest in other men… maybe he could trust her. Not once had she been into any other man in the time they'd spent together. She never looked, never stared at anyone else. There had been no admiration in her voice when Damien had stood at the doorstep, nothing afterward that hinted that she would rather be with Damien than with him.

He kissed her again, his hands back on her butt, gently kneading before scooping her up and lifting her to his groin, her dress falling like silk over his hands. Her feet dangled and she broke out in giggles as she clasped her arms around his neck. With swift strides, he covered the distance to the bedroom.

He didn't put her down as he'd intended but raised her higher and she looked down at him. His cock pressed against her sex and the feeling sent a cascade of desire through his body. He was going to make her come again, so slowly this time, it would classify as torture. He stared into her eyes as he murmured, "It drives me crazy that you're all I need."

The look in her eyes tugged at his heart. "You're all I need too," she admitted softly.

Her words tore at him. He'd never expected to hear from any woman that he was all she needed. What Mila didn't know was that they'd inherently admitted to two different things. She wouldn't know, wouldn't understand, but he felt safe with her. His heart felt safe with her. He closed his eyes, breathing, feeling the rise and drop of her chest against his as he slowly let her slip from his grip, making her stand again.

His lifestyle had always protected him from the feelings he

was developing for Mila. Now he understood how his dad loved his mother. Worse was that this feeling, this obsession, was only going to get deeper, grow stronger.

But the worst was that, at some point, he would have to be honest with her. He would have to tell her about his past, and then *this* would end as abruptly as it had started.

"Don't," she whispered as she stroked the tip of her nose against the line of his chin, "get that look on your face."

He blinked. Had she been reading his mind? "Which look?" Did he really need to know?

"That look that tells me you don't want this to go any further." Her fingers got busy with his shirt's buttons.

He swallowed. It wasn't that he didn't want to go further. He was scared shitless of what was happening between them. Being such a fucking dick didn't help. It was time he was honest with her. "Mila…"

"I get it, James. This can't be more. It's not going anywhere." She pressed a kiss on his chest. "In any case, what are we going to do, with you going all over the world and with me stuck in church or some rugby stadium?"

"Mila—" Her words gave him a physical ache at the tip of his heart. He couldn't think beyond anything but now.

"Don't—" She broke off. For a moment she looked away. She closed her eyes and swallowed. "Don't overanalyze and think this is anything more than… what it is. We're both adults."

It was his own logic and she spoke it like a pro, using it against him. Worst thing was, she was right. She was giving him every reason why they could have sex and then walk away as if nothing had happened—like he had countless times. She was saving him from the fuck-up that hung over his head, threatening to come down in a shitstorm.

And yet, he wanted to pull her towards him, to a level of intimacy he hadn't experienced before. "Stop telling me what I shouldn't do." His voice was stern and deeper than usual as he tried to get a grip. He couldn't help it. It was as if she had the upper hand, more control in this situation where he should be the one in charge. Being in charge was the only way to walk away unscathed, but it was too late for that, wasn't it?

She leaned in, her lips pressing a kiss under his ear. "Then stop talking nonsense and fuck me," she whispered. "You know how I need to be fucked."

Her words were like hot wax over his skin. A shock coming from her, too much, but totally arousing. Need rippled down his back, bringing his erection back in full force. "Is my good girl talking dirty now?"

"Hmm," she murmured softly.

"Good girls don't talk like that," he reprimanded playfully, wanting to shift the conversation away from the dangerous precipice they'd been hovering at a minute ago. "That mouth of yours is going to be in serious trouble if you carry on like that, Mila."

She'd finished unbuttoning his shirt and let him slip it off. Her fingers ghosted over his pecs, hardening his nipples, sending waves of heated desire over his body.

"Maybe my mouth wants to be in trouble," she said innocently, then licked her lips. The thin layer of moisture glossed her mouth, plumping her rosy lips.

The desire to have her go down on him had been vivid and topmost in his mind since he'd seen those lips days ago. He groaned. "You're driving me crazy."

She tugged at his belt and slipped the leather from the buckle. She shot him a small smile. "You were still counting the ways."

She kissed his collarbone and trailed her lips over his chest, then closed her mouth over his nipple and sucked, extracting a desperate moan from him. If she started like this, he was going to be a mess in minutes. He gripped his fingers into her hair at the nape of her neck, guiding her head lower, making sure she understood where he needed this to go.

Already she was at the button of his trousers. "Have you done this before?"

Her hands stilled. She straightened as a blush stole over her cheeks. "No."

Sweet Jesus. He should have known. He would be the first man to claim her mouth. He dug his fingers deeper into her hair and brought her back to him. She opened for him in a deep kiss that made his cock squirm against the cramped space in his trousers. If she gave head the way she kissed, he was going to be a goner.

Chapter 27

Mila was lost in his kiss, but after a minute pulled away as her thoughts returned to his erection that teased her stomach. Her hands, which had rested on his chest, stroked over his six-pack and her fingertips brushed against the strip of hair that graced his lower abdomen.

Her fingers trembled but she worked at his trouser button. His gaze rested on her as he gently stroked her hair from her face and gathered it in a makeshift ponytail with his fingers.

"You don't need to do this if you don't want to." His voice was gruff but thick with desire.

"Too many don'ts," she whispered as she caught his gaze with hers. He was considerate, not pushing her into anything she didn't want. Had he no idea that this was what she wanted—to please him above anything else?

His hands slipped to her naked shoulders and down her bare arms in a touch that was so caring that she wanted to lean into him, force him to hold her and never let her go.

She'd been so condescending earlier, telling him that they were both adults in this situation. That she wanted nothing more than this moment of intense intimacy. But walking away as if nothing had happened... he seemed to be fooled, but her heart was bleeding.

She looked down, scared that he would read her thoughts in her eyes. She unzipped his trousers, and his erect penis jutted out above the rim of his jocks.

He clasped her arms tighter but then let go, fiddling with the zip on the side of her dress. "Take it off," he whispered.

She obliged, lowering the dress and stepping out of it. And then his hands were on her, cupping her naked breasts, stroking them with reverence, letting her nipples pop into hard buds under his touch and gaze.

"Beautiful," he murmured and his hands caressed her lower, to the rim of her standard white panties, which he traced with slow fingers. "Perfect."

Heat flushed her face. "It's nothing fancy."

"It's fucking sexy." His gaze bore into hers and her face burned. "Stop doubting yourself, Mila," he murmured as he raised a hand to stroke her cheek.

He looked worried and maybe he had the right to be. She wanted to go back to shower 101 because she needed his guidance.

She nodded and lowered herself to her knees, eye-level with his cock, which was still gift wrapped in too many layers of fabric. Her mouth went dry and she had to swallow at a scratch in her throat as she worked his trousers and jocks down his legs. He stepped out and kicked the clothes to the side.

As her gaze traveled up his legs, she tried not to be dazed by the muscles in his thighs, but when she got higher her breathing stalled. His cock was jutting upwards, tight, and was glistening at the tip with moisture. She looked higher, to his face, as her hands edged up to level with his cock. "That's a massive amount of trouble coming my way."

"Nothing you can't handle." His eyes were dark and his jaw twitched as he ground down on his teeth. "Just take it slow, soft." Her pulse sped up at his words, her body flushed with anticipation.

With one hand on her head, he steadied her and his cock twitched, raising a notch. He gripped it in his hand, offering it to her. She opened her mouth and closed her lips over the tip, tightening around him. She tasted him on her tongue. Salty and with an intense flavor of man that took hold of her taste buds.

He released a heavy groan and let go of his cock, allowing her mouth to travel the silken length of his shaft. She moved back and forth, intensely aware of his reaction to each movement. When she took him deeper, sucking slightly, he exhaled a slow *fuuuuck*, making her innards contract with desire. His grip on her head tightened, guiding her. His breathing grew heavier with each slow thrust that penetrated her deeper and deeper. His hips started to roll in her direction, driving her to take him so deep his tip brushed against the back of her throat. It was a slow, soft contact, but her throat closed up at the intrusion. For a moment she thought she would gag, but she closed tighter over him, paused and swallowed with him still filling her mouth.

"Mila," he grunted. "Good girl." He pushed deeper and the pressure on her throat slipped down her spine, to settle in her sex, the last place where she'd expected it. The sensation in her pussy urged her on and she kept going, extracting soft groans from him each time her lips rode up his cock. She tasted small gushes of his pre-cum on her tongue and let it slip down her throat. Having him like this was so intimate, pleasing him so empowering. She wanted him rougher and as far as he could go.

She tightened her lips again and took a long pull back to the tip. A tortured chuckle broke from his lips and his hand let go of her head. He pulled his cock from her mouth and she stared up at him, flustered, only to catch him studying her with drowsy, desire-drenched eyes.

"I knew those lips were magic," he murmured. He cupped her cheek in his hand, tugging a wisp of hair from the corner of her mouth with his thumb.

"You liked it?" She was begging for his affirmation.

He bent over to take hold of her shoulders, urging her up with a gentle tug.

"I loved it." He held out a hand for her.

Hesitantly she put her hand in his and rose to her feet. Why had he stopped then? Hadn't it been good enough?

"Sweet Mila. I could fuck that mouth all day long." He brushed her lips with his thumb, sliding it over the moisture that still lingered on her mouth. "I *want* to fuck your mouth all day long." He groaned, a sound that hovered between a nervous laugh and a contented sigh. "But what I want more than anything else, is this." He wrapped her in his arms and kissed her, with such tenderness her knees turned weak.

When he lowered her to the bed she threaded her fingers through his hair, a dance of joy racing through her heart. He was here with her, kissing her as if he owned her, wanting it more than anything else.

Their legs tangled as they kissed and after a long moment he groaned and urged her onto her back. Her legs splayed open, giving him space to settle. His cock nestled on her already-drenched sex, and she arched against it gently, relishing the sweet torment of each movement as she split open, her clit exposed against the fabric of her knickers.

"I'm going to have to slow you down," he murmured, but he was lazy to shift away from her mouth, his kisses lingering on her chin, running down the edge of her jaw and lower, down the column of her neck. His kisses made her core tremble, his hands on her skin were setting her alight, every nerve in her body responding to his touch.

He raised onto his arms, pinning her between them and breaking the connection of her sex against his. He dropped his head to her breasts, which he suckled slowly, stirring up the embers in her core, which never seem to go out when Mila was around him. The attention he paid to every part of her body made her wilt with desire, weakened to such an extent that she was willing to do anything he asked of her as long as he didn't stop. Already she felt that build-up of tension in her pussy, which he knew so well how to release.

He straightened then, kneeling between her legs, his penis large and prodding the air, bare and begging with his pre-cum glistening in the last light.

"Let me…" She closed her eyes, the flush of heat rushing over her body before it settled in her cheeks. She was begging. "Let me taste you again." She rose on her elbows, catching his gaze. She wanted to shift to accommodate him, but his hands on her chest stopped her and she dropped back.

"Not yet, Mila." A small smile played at the corners of his mouth. He ran his hands between the valley of her breasts, to her stomach and the apex of her thighs. "Close your eyes," he instructed, "And don't interfere."

She swallowed as his words sunk in but did as she was told and allowed him to guide her hands to rest above her head. *Oh*

Lord, she'd been here before.

His hands retraced their route down her chest and settled on her hips, his thumbs idly tracing circles on her pelvic bone, slipping slightly lower with each turn.

The pressure was divine and she moaned as he slowed on a downward sweep, which ran down and into her core, building the erotic sensation in her clit.

"James," she whispered as she arched her back, every nerve in her body zapping sensations to her sex.

"Just slowing you down, Mila," he murmured, but he didn't stop his ministrations. When, after a minute, he traced his thumbs even lower, to slip in under her panties, she gasped. He glided his thumbs down the lips of her sex, and then gently slipped them into her opening, together, into her tight center.

"This isn't slowing me down," she moaned, already feeling that certain tightness in her sex, which was only going to end one way.

"Not yet, Mila," he warned as he extracted his thumbs and tugged at her panties. When he got them off he tossed them to the floor and leaned over her to reach for a condom. As his body hovered over hers his cock rubbed over her stomach, and she reached for it, running her fingers over his firmly-strung balls and up the silk of his shaft.

"My sweet little cock tease," he murmured and lowered to kiss her, taking his time. She didn't let go, but closed her fingers around his cock, riding up and down until he groaned.

He pulled away and straightened to put on the condom. The last of the dusk light fell on his face and etched out each contour of his muscular chest. When his gaze met hers there was a warmth in his eyes she hadn't seen before. "My turn to do some teasing," he murmured as he lowered back on one arm, settling his cock at her entrance.

He dipped, only the tip, and slid out, and let his cock slide up to her clit and back, sinking into her pussy again. Each movement was the merest tease of the fullness that he promised, once he'd penetrated her completely. Still, he held back with control, and every nerve ending at her tight entrance was heaving with anticipation for him to plunge deeper.

The tension was tightening and she wanted to squirm, arch and push her hips up to him so that he could penetrate her, fuck her hard as her whole body wanted him to do. "James... Please."

"Not yet," he whispered back, but he let go of his cock and paused at her entrance, giving her a torturous moment to retract from the edge over which she was hovering.

"Please." Her voice had reduced to a helpless plea.

He kissed her, and as his tongue slipped between her lips his cock jammed into her, filling her to her core. She moaned in his mouth, but he didn't retreat. Instead, he lowered onto her, resting on his elbows to keep the bulk of his weight off her. They kept on kissing, his tongue playing cock in her mouth, as he rode her as she'd wished for. It was different from the other time she'd been with him. Every motion was loaded with something else, every penetration seemed deeper than where he'd been before.

She dug her fingers into his hair and he thrust, grinding deeper into her body. She was so close, with every part of her body gravitating towards the abyss.

He broke their kiss, his gaze dark and wild as he looked at her. "Come with me, Mila."

He'd hardly spoken when her orgasm ripped through her, seeming to tear from the top of her passage down to her clit, each contraction followed by a stronger one. It was too intense and she buried her face in his shoulder, clinging, aware of each gush of se-men as he came. He continued to push as if he would consume her.

When he eventually stilled she tuned into the frantic beating of his heart under the heel of her palm. He breathed haggardly, and with a sigh dropped his forehead to hers. Their bodies were hot and fused together with nothing to tear them apart. In her, every emotion of the past few days welled up. The pressure in her chest broke from her in a quiet sob, as tears, over which she had zero control, seeped from the corners of her eyes.

He rolled off her and she buried her face in her hands, swal-lowing at the cramping knot in her throat. She couldn't break in front of him. Not now. The tears were so quiet, but her breathing…

He was busy with the condom, opening a drawer, pulling something from it.

"Here," he murmured.

She peeked at him. He was holding a wad of tissues out to her. She took it with trembling fingers, not sure what to make of his half-turned back. She dabbed at her eyes just as he shifted, his weight denting the bed.

"What's this, Mila?" he asked softly, catching her wrist in his hand.

A sob broke from her chest. "I don't know."

"Shit, sweetheart." He nestled close to her, gathering her in his arms. "Mila." He kissed her eyes, kissed at her tears that were still flowing. "Did I hurt you?" His voice was heavy with concern and it gripped at her heart. But when he kissed her lips with such tenderness her heart caved in. It was his. Now. Forever.

"No," she murmured. She'd no idea what had overcome her. Did she have to be so weak? Such a mess? "No-no," she said again, wanting to make sure he understood it wasn't physical.

The weight of his gaze rested on her for a long second, then he unfurled her fingers from the wad of tissues she clutched like a lifeline.

"Those were meant to wipe," he murmured as she let go, "down there, not up here." He kissed her tears as he gently wiped the overflow of juices from her pussy. Dear Lord. That he could be so caring. That was probably the best sex ever and she was a mess.

He'd set the bar impossibly high. How would any man ever compare to this?

Chapter 28

J AMES SEARCHED MILA'S FACE. SHE'D closed her eyes, seeming asleep and almost angelic. In the little light, her tears seemed to have stopped, but the streaks on her temples and cheeks were still there. Those tearstains were working him like a shredder. He held her closer, trying to comfort her, but he felt helpless. There had been nothing wrong with the way they'd made love. It had been the most emotional sex he'd ever had. This was the first time he'd ever had a woman in tears afterward and he was hesitant to dissect what they meant.

But that was just it, wasn't it? Inwardly he cursed. With Mila, everything had become more. His sexfest had gone north, hitting him straight in the heart. He'd known it with every thrust. The deeper he went, the harder he was falling.

Exhaling, he settled on his back, making space for her to snuggle in the circle of his arm. Her hand eased up his chest and went to rest on his heart, which was still beating as if he'd run a marathon. She hooked a leg over him and he hugged her tight.

For a long moment, they were quiet, their bodies calming

down. But his mind was racing with so many jumbled thoughts that he couldn't get anything straight. Eventually, he swallowed. "Do you want to talk about… it?" he whispered against her hair.

"No," she murmured softly and pressed a kiss to his chest.

Too many nos.

"Mila—" *He* needed to talk about it. *For fuck's sake.* What was happening to him?

She perched on her elbow and peered at him in the dark. Her forefinger stroked from his forehead down the bridge of his nose to his lips, where it settled to make him hush. "Spare those lips for what they do best," she murmured and lowered her head to kiss him.

As she kissed him he couldn't think of anything but her lips and her soft warm body nestling against his. Eventually, she pulled away. She turned on her side to allow him to spoon her.

Again he pulled her close with his hand on her hip, not wanting to let go. With any other woman, he would have been more than happy to stop and step away as she was prompting him to do. To brush off any feelings they might have had for each other as simply as Mila had just hushed him. Hell, he wasn't innocent. He'd walked over a couple of women en route, but that was why the boundaries had always been drawn up in advance. Swinging worked until someone got emotionally involved. Sometimes it happened quicker than expected, before anybody could take stock and step away. The rules were to step away.

But with Mila… he couldn't do it. The mere idea that he could hurt her was suffocating him. He pressed his nose into her hair to inhale her sweet, intoxicating scent. To hurt her was the last thing he wanted.

He closed his eyes. "I have to tell you something." He spoke the words softly, hoping they would get lost in her thick tresses.

"Hmm? Now?" Already she sounded half asleep. Her body was still next to his.

"Marlène is coming." It was a start, wasn't it? The introduction to the shitty story that was his life.

Mila shifted but didn't turn around to face him. She took his hand and tugged it close to her stomach. "Oh." She paused. "Why?"

"To fetch her things." That was at least true. He hoped it would be the last time he saw her.

"When?"

"I'm not sure." Now he wished he knew exactly when Marlène was going to be there to spill her poison. He should've tried harder to find out her movements. Should have tracked her down at work. She had a personal assistant, didn't she? He bit down the curse hovering on his lips. "Probably late next week. But—"

She yawned, cupping his hand to her breast, making him hold on to the softest part of her. "Stacey will be here then."

He'd forgotten about Stacey. That was another pile of crap waiting to overflow.

"I don't want Stacey to know… about us."

He frowned. "What has Stacey got to do with any of this?"

She groaned like all she wanted to do was sleep. Like he was some idiot for not understanding. "Stacey would probably have a fit if she knew we were sleeping together. I'd much rather she didn't know."

"Why?" he quizzed. She was still lying quiet, but under his palm, her heart beat a notch faster.

"Don't mess with your little sister's best friend?" she offered. "Best friends don't come between older brothers and their perfect girlfriends? Ex or not."

What the fuck? "Really?"

She didn't reply.

"Mila?"

"She really likes Marlène. She's been idolizing her for years." She took a breath. "Stacey hopes you will get together again. She believes that work separated you, all the traveling you do... Stacey's convinced that long-distance caused your break up. She doesn't know about Damien."

He wanted to laugh, but instead, bile crept up his throat. If only he could claim that he'd broken up with Marlène because the long-distance relationship hadn't worked out for them. And Damien. Honestly, he should be grateful to him. Maybe next time he would thank him for taking Marlène places he'd refused to take her.

As for Stacey, he'd never thought he'd bare his life and secrets to his little sister. He'd deal with her when it came to it.

But it was more than all of that. Deeply rooted in her comment was something he recognized as inferiority. Mila didn't think she was worth squat in the bigger scheme of things. Pushed to the sidelines by her parents, she'd been trodden on by her herd of brothers. And she was tied to some old-fashioned religious code and had been too scared to tell her parents that she was going to Paris with her oldest—maybe only—true friend, to go and find herself and live a little.

"Stacey isn't entitled to an opinion here." He almost cursed. "Least of all one that goes along the lines of you not being good enough for me." The truth was the exact opposite. She was too good for him.

He huffed a sigh, louder than he'd intended. Having secrets had always been a burden, but a burden he'd carried with care. Now the pile was getting too heavy and he was trapped under the weight of all the secrets he'd kept over the years.

"It doesn't matter. I'll be gone by then if it is any later than next week," Mila said, the very tone of her voice spelling out that it was the end of the conversation.

She'd dismissed him. Again.

Just as he'd been gathering his guts to start the conversation about his past, she'd cut back as if it didn't matter, as if nothing affected her. He gritted his teeth. And it didn't matter, not if she didn't want more than what they had right now.

It was him who wanted more. And he had no idea how to go about it.

Swinger. Sex. Strangers. There had been a point where he couldn't have cared less. His inability to love at a deeper level had been a mere fact, like being left- or right-handed. Now every one of those words that summed up his life stood in his way. They were ready to burst from him but his guts floundered. He bit his tongue, letting the anger at the situation dry up and die instead of fueling something more.

For a long time, he stared at the skylight, knowing from her easy breathing that she'd fallen asleep.

For fuck's sake. He couldn't raise the topic of his past again. He wouldn't. He was such a coward.

He was falling for Mila, a younger woman who played him at his own game, and she was winning. He considered himself a no-commitment pro. Having sex and walking away was his niche. And here she was, not even aware of playing.

If nothing else, it probably served him bloody right.

Chapter 29

"DON'T MOVE," MILA MURMURED. ONLY a few more touches and she'd be done.

She suppressed a grin as James stirred next to her, his eyes opening with a soft murmur. He looked a bit worse for wear. From the dark circles under his eyes, he hadn't had a great night's rest.

Mila didn't feel rested either and had woken up at some crazy pre-dawn hour. Her conscience had wanted to psychoanalyze every moment of the past few days and make her pay. She'd refused to let her mind churn in some religious time warp and bow to some stupid feeling of guilt. Her parents would be so disappointed, yet again. She wasn't sure she could face more of that from them. And her brothers would probably tag her as a slut if they knew how quickly she'd slept with James.

What they didn't know wouldn't hurt them, right? And she wasn't planning to let anybody know about her and James. When she got on that plane to go home she'd be the only one in pain and she would keep it that way.

When she'd opened the roller blind three hours earlier the noise hadn't woken James. She'd tiptoed around the room to get her painting things and had managed to fabricate a type of easel out of the occasional chair in his room. She had drawn and then painted him while he was sleeping until all she had to do was some finishing touches. For those, she'd slipped back into bed.

He rubbed his face with his hands and yawned. "What are you doing?"

"Painting. Try to be still, please." It was way too late for that, but she'd already caught him on paper.

"What are you painting?"

"You." She bent over and gave him a little wake-up peck on the tip of his nose.

He grinned. "Let me see."

"It's not very flattering."

"Modern nudes rarely are, unless they're crap paintings," he joked and pushed up on his elbow to peer at her pad.

She handed him the watercolor pad and he fell back on the cushions studying it. She tried to read his face, anxious to know what he was thinking. His gaze rested on the painting a long time, hovering over the details. Inwardly she prayed he wouldn't make some snarky comment about it being a mix of an Egon Schiele nude and an attempt at a Rodin watercolor because for her it looked like a mishmash of the two.

"Except for my missing morning glory, it's a very accurate depiction of yours truly."

She laughed. True to form, his cock had risen to the occasion. "It's been nice to observe you in a more... eh... relaxed state."

He chuckled. "I should introduce you to a couple of gallery owners I know. They'd be interested in your work."

"Really?" In Paris? Her heart crash-burned into a sprint at the merest notion of having one of her pieces hanging in a Paris art gallery.

"Yes. The market here... this is something that will sell."

She couldn't exhibit this type of thing at home. Not with her parents' and brothers' eyes on every painting she ever did. They'd wonder who it was, whether she'd actually seen him naked, and never mind that it would be unacceptable to her father for the whole painting not to be draped in a giant loincloth.

She bit back the sting behind her eyes. James was such a darling. "This one is mine," she murmured. To remind her of him when she'd gone.

He placed the pad on the bedside table and turned on his side to slip his hand under the covers. He traced a slow path up her thigh and then rested his hand on her belly, stirring up every longing in her core.

"How're you feeling?"

"Good." But she could be feeling better. She eyed his erection that was nesting in the duvet as he shifted and nuzzled her naked hip with his nose. He pulled the duvet away from her body and she raised her hand, which still held a paintbrush, with a giggle, so as not to get paint on his white linen.

"Give me that," he teased as he sat up and reached for the paintbrush.

She handed it over with a bit of reluctance. "What are you up to, James Sinclair?"

"Just getting into a bit of painting myself." He dipped the brush into the cup of water and twirled it around the red paint in the palette.

"Slowly," she quipped. "That's a real kolinsky sable brush."

"Hmm," he hummed, "I wouldn't let anything else touch you, to be honest." And with that he gathered her hair away from her chest, exposing her breasts, which had been hiding under her hair.

She inhaled sharply at having his gaze on her, blatantly inspecting every inch of her curves, her nipples jutting out in hard points, eager for his mouth.

He hesitated, speculative. "Always so attentive," he murmured and his mouth closed on a nipple and sucked.

"James." She loved him when he was playful like this. Not serious and dark like last night, leaving her with flashes of weird images screwing with her dreams. The images were mostly of unknown women, all of whom she tagged as Marlène, without even knowing what this doyenne of Stacey's looked like.

"What a beautiful blank canvas," he speculated. He touched the tip of the brush to the middle of her chest and she bit down on a giggle as he swept a slow turn upward and then down over the inward valley of her breast.

"It's cold," she murmured, but inside she was warming up as her skin reacted to the light, intimate touch of the brush. Her nipples pebbled even more as he took the upward turn over her other breast, caressing the sensitive skin and brushing just shy of her nipple.

"Don't look," he whispered but she'd already closed her eyes as every nerve in her body focused on the sensation on her skin and his soft breathing as he manipulated the brush. It left her then, and he dipped it in the water, then more paint.

A second later the tip was back, tracing line after line, closing in on her sternum. Following the movement, she could guess what he was painting, and for all that she wanted to smile, inside her everything pulled tight together so as not to shatter into pieces.

"There," he murmured, a satisfied laugh edging into his

voice. "I suck at this."

She opened her eyes and stared down at her chest. He'd painted a red and pink heart over where her real one was, the curves going up the valley of her breasts, the tip of the heart closing under them in the middle.

She chuckled. "It's gorgeous." The paint was already running, drops forming on the edges and gravitating down her navel like red tears.

"Hmm," he hummed and caught the drops with his fingertip, leading them to follow the path he was tracing to her sex. Just above her pubic hairline, he drew another little heart, and the paint by default pooled together.

Under his tender ministrations, wetness had seeped between the lips of her sex.

He laughed as he reached towards the bedside table. He grabbed for some tissues but paused as he glanced at his phone. "Shit."

"What?"

"It's late." He dabbed the tissues at her chest, smudging his makeshift body art into a red blob.

"Thursday mornings. I've got a conference call with my team in Singapore. I can't be late." He leaned in and kissed her softly on the mouth as he cupped her breast and caressed her nipple with his thumb. Her body melted under his touch, feeling heavy and sunken as he deepened the kiss.

When he pulled away he whispered in her ear, "We'll have to work on my brush technique later."

He got off the bed, his erection leading the way to the bathroom.

"You're going to leave me again? After working me all up?" she teased. She wanted him… and the idea of what he could do with her set of kolinskies was enough to make her squirm and break into a small sweat of desire.

"I share your pain," he called back, "but there's nothing like a bit of anticipation."

She could attest to that and resisted the urge to walk into the shower and work on her own new skill set by going down on him again.

Instead, she studied the red smear on her chest and the tear trails his silent token of love had left on her belly and heart. God, it was going to hurt to leave James behind.

Chapter 30

By late afternoon Mila had had enough. Doing the Louvre back to back two days in a row might not have been the brightest idea. Her feet showed signs of new blisters and her eyes were dry and tired from staring at art the whole day.

She leaned against the wall by the door of the apartment to dig the keys out of her bag. When she inserted the key it wouldn't turn and she paused. She tested the door handle and the door swung open. James must be home. She bit her lip at the prospect of finding him here, waiting for her for a change. As she walked inside she reprimanded the butterflies in her stomach and told them to calm the heck down. She put her things down on the table in the entrance hall.

As she entered the lounge a slow chill crept down her spine. All the windows were open, letting the stuffy summer air into the apartment. The once-empty space was a jumble of gorgeous antique furniture. Sofas, lamps, side tables, dining room chairs and a table stood in disarray, filling the space. Above the roadside noises that rose through the windows, laughter traveled past the kitchen and into the lounge. She recognized one voice and her skin burst out in a spread of pricks, but the woman's voice made her stop in her tracks. Her laughter was husky, filled with such joy and teasing that Mila could, in her mind's eye, see her face, eyes sparkling as she looked up to her lover's face.

They were bickering in French, but between chuckles and scuffles, it was more playful than anything else.

There was a shriek and more laughter before the two piled out of the short corridor that led to the lounge. Mila wished she had something to clutch to her chest, something to shield her.

She had a few seconds to study the couple before they realized she was in the room. Damien was holding a red piece of clothing in his hand, just out of reach of a blonde, who was trying to grab it from him. She wore nothing but a matching bra and panties, made of delicate ruby-red lace and mesh. The underwear covered the essentials but revealed her nipples through the see-through bits. And they were pierced, little silver barbells peeking through the mesh of her bra.

The visual stirred a deeply erotic sensation in her lower belly, and Mila dropped her gaze in confusion. *Marlène.* Her body was breathtakingly beautiful. Every curve was in perfect proportion and toned. Her long hair was a weird mix of blonde and what appeared to be ashen-colored streaks. Her skin was smooth and flawless. She seemed rather youthful and at the same time ageless, every part of her incongruous with what Mila had expected.

But what had she expected? She should have known Marlène would be breathtakingly beautiful. She was after all the beauty editor of *Vogue*—someone to emulate and admire as Stacey had done for years. So this is where Stacey had gotten the crazy idea of coloring her hair platinum.

Damien was the first to notice her standing in the lounge, her face afire to the roots of her hair.

He dropped his hands to his side and raised his eyebrows. "Mila."

Marlène's gaze narrowed on her, unfazed by being semi-naked.

"Damien," Mila greeted him, her voice a soft croak. James was not going to like this at all.

"You've met Marlène?" he asked as he handed Marlène her shirt.

"No." She wanted to flee. Go back to the Louvre and disappear in the crowd, and not return until the apartment was back to what it had been when she'd left earlier that morning. The knot that had been slowly building in her gut gave a snarky little twist. *Get real.* Things were never going to be the same again.

Marlène strutted over. "You must be Stacey's friend?" she asked. "I've heard a lot about you."

She had? Mila swallowed. She'd heard a lot about Marlène too, but only the one-sided idolized view Stacey had of her. What she'd heard from James she hadn't liked.

When Marlène stuck out her hand, Mila could do nothing but reach out her sweaty palm and shake her hand. At least they weren't attempting the multi-sided French kiss-thingamajig that Damien had given her the other night.

"Well," Marlène said as she let go of her hand. "You're enjoying Paris?"

"It's just lovely," Mila blurted out. "I've never been overseas before." Dear Lord, did she have to sound so inexperienced? Untraveled? Young? Idiotic?

Marlène was pulling the red stretchy top over her head, her curves and toned stomach almost rippling, her cleavage pressing close with the movements of her arms, letting her studded nipples press tight against the mesh of her bra.

She couldn't really say, but Marlène's breasts were just a tad out of proportion with the rest of her. A bitchy little murmur in her head whispered that it was because they were fake.

Mila dropped her gaze, crossing her arms over her own breasts. Was that the only place Marlène was pierced? Did James like it?

"Once Stacey is here we should go out one night," Marlène said, a little smile playing on her lips. "Have you experienced some of the nightlife?"

"I did come around two nights ago—" Damien started.

"Stacey's only here next week," Mila interrupted. And by then she would have made other plans. "She has to write one more exam."

"Oh? All the more reason to celebrate once she's here." Marlène shot a glance at Damien. "We can go clubbing."

Mila swallowed the urge to spit out that she wasn't the clubbing type.

"There are some nice clubs around this area," Damien said, winking at Marlène.

"We can make a night of it with James if he's still around." Marlène smiled, but it didn't quite reach her eyes. When her gaze dropped to Mila's breasts, and lower to where the red heart watercolor stain had seeped into her pubic hair, it felt as though she was naked and Marlène could see every inch of skin that James had touched and had made love to. "We can have so much fun together."

Damien raised his hand and squeezed Marlène's shoulder. "Let's leave James out of this. We only take the girls."

The look he cast her way made her flinch inwardly. She wasn't a woman, just a girl.

"Stacey's been sending me messages," Damien continued.

"She can't wait to have a night out. James breathing down her neck might be awkward."

Oh no, Stacey. And with Marlène talking as if nothing had happened between her, James and Damien, she was sick to her stomach.

"I—" She broke off. She needed to buy time. There was no way she was going to commit to an evening out with Damien and Marlène. But she didn't have any proper defense on hand. "Let's wait until Stacey's here to make plans—"

"Sure," Marlène interrupted. "We can talk later. Let's go, Damien. I'm really hungry."

"Do you want to join us?" Damien asked. "Early dinner?"

"No, thank you." Her gaze traveled down Marlène's figure. She was still clad only in her panties and a top.

Marlène laughed. "We had to get out all the furniture so that I could get to my wardrobe. It's like Christmas unpacking all these things." She turned and sauntered off to the corridor and the rooms that were once locked up.

Damien rested his hands on his hips and studied her. He was not blocking her way, but the situation was too weird and she couldn't walk past, ignoring him, without seeming rude.

"James is taking good care of you?" he asked after the silence stretched uncomfortably long.

She blinked, having no clue what to make of his statement. "I'm nobody's to *take care* of," she said, a bit more bite in her tone than intended.

"You should be," he said softly and reached out to take the tip of her hair that curled on her breast between his fingers.

The movement was slow, not sudden enough to make her jerk away by instinct. It was done with measured and delicate intent as if she was a wild thing that would bolt at his first touch. His hand hovered there, so close to her breast it was intrusive, but she'd been hypnotized by the infinitesimal movement of his fingers as he rubbed her hair between them, so that she only felt his touch at the roots of her hair.

"But sometimes it's fun to do the rounds," he finished his sentence. "James would know."

She gathered her hair and he let go with a wry smile.

"Excuse me. I'm tired." Did she have to give some excuse? The way in which he touched her had been more than enough to walk away.

When she got to the corridor Marlène came out of her room. She was dressed in a beautiful summer skirt, which spread from her waist to below her knees, white with enormous bold pink and red flowers on it. Her outfit screamed catwalk and designer and was rounded off by red high-heeled sandals.

Mila would curse with every step she took on the cobble-stoned roads of the inner city if she wore those. Maybe Marlène knew something she didn't.

And Damien—what the deuce was he thinking after the other night? Coming into the apartment and making comments about James *doing the rounds*. That Damien was still having a thing with Marlène was clear.

She walked into the master bedroom, closed the door quietly, plunked down on the bed, and waited. She clasped her hands over her breasts, feeling overprotective.

It wasn't long before the apartment turned quiet.

Chapter 31

JAMES CHECKED HIS WATCH AGAIN. Usually, he made it home earlier and he pursed his lips as he got into the lift. He disliked being held up by work when he had much more enjoyable things to do. The whole freaking day all he could think of was Mila and her smooth, creamy skin. In the morning, he'd idled a considerable time away researching kolinsky paintbrushes on the Internet and had at last settled on a neat little beginner's kit that set him back a few hundred euros. A pity they'd only arrive later in the week, but they still had time. And he was planning to use them creatively.

He dropped his bag and keys and walked into the lounge only to come to an abrupt stop when he saw the scattered furniture.

Fuck. Fuck. Fuck.

"Mila?" he called out, his gaze jumping over Marlène's heirloom furniture, which had been carried out from her room and dumped in disarray.

There was movement coming from the kitchen, but his blood took flame as Marlène appeared in the lounge and came towards him.

"Where's Mila?" he asked. He didn't doubt for one second that Marlène had already met her. From the smile toying on her lips, he knew.

"She is a very pretty little rebound, James," Marlène laughed.

He pushed against the anger that burned through him. It wasn't worth it.

"Where is she?" he asked, trying to keep his cool. How much time had Marlène spent with Mila? What had she told her?

"I'm not sure, but the door to your bedroom has been closed since I came back." She yawned and rubbed her nose. "To be honest, I don't have the energy to make small talk with her right now."

Small talk. For fuck's sake. Most probably inviting Mila to one of her orgies would be more like it.

He glanced over the room. Did she have to pile her furniture all over the place without arranging it in some kind of usable order? "When are you packing up?"

"And getting out?" She sniffed.

"Yes. That's pretty much what I'm asking." He narrowed his gaze to her nose, focusing on her beautiful, delicately turned French nostrils that were one of her best features.

"I was hoping… we could talk. I don't know… patch things up?"

He blinked. Was this why she'd delayed moving her things out of the apartment? She'd been pushing his limits from day one. Now she'd gone too far. While he was traveling the situation hadn't bothered him much, but now he wanted her out. "There's nothing to talk about. How does tomorrow sound?"

Marlène shook her head. "I can't. For months now I've been thinking only of us, James. Please."

Hell would freeze over first. "Where are you staying?"

She frowned at him. "Here." Another sniff. "Since I own

218

twenty percent of this apartment, I assume I can stay here for a couple of nights."

"That wasn't the deal, Marlène. I offered to buy you out eight months ago."

She rolled her eyes. "Things have been busy, as you know."

He didn't want to dig into her life. He wanted to find Mila and see whether she was all right. He started walking past Marlène but she stopped him with her hand on his arm. He closed his eyes, wanting to shrug her off, but there was something desperate in the gesture. Marlène was never dependent; she was always sure of what she wanted, certain that things were going to turn out just as she'd planned.

"I miss you," she murmured. "I miss *us*."

Funny that. He took in her face. He might have missed her at some point, but for a long time now he'd gone bland towards her and the memory of them together.

She sniffed again, not the telltale sniff of hovering tears. Those delicate nostrils told their own story.

James couldn't care less, but he couldn't help himself either. "How did it work out for you, in the long run?"

"As you predicted." Their gazes clashed and in hers there was desperation.

"I told you you'd make a habit of it, and then you'd have a habit."

She leaned closer to him, dropping her forehead on his shoulder. "So what if you were right? Maybe I wanted a habit."

"Well, con-fucking-gratulations. I prefer if you keep all your habits to yourself." He shrugged her off and stepped away. "Stay the hell away from Mila. And don't even think of introducing any of your shit to Stacey." He had no control over whom Stacey decided to hang out with at home, but he sure as hell wasn't going to encourage her to spend time with Marlène while she was in Paris.

At least there was a whole ocean between Stacey and Marlène on a good day. He intended to keep it that way. Marlène better be long gone by the time Stacey arrived.

James left her standing in the lounge and with each step towards his bedroom took a deep breath and huffed it out. His bedroom door at the end of the corridor was closed, and as he passed Marlène's rooms, he glanced inside. The wardrobes gaped open and clothes were strewn on the floor. She was such a fucking teenager sometimes.

He knocked on his own door for some reason he didn't quite understand himself. There was no answer and he opened the door with his heart stuck in his throat.

Mila sat on the bed. Through the skylight and windows, the setting sun threw beams of light over her like a halo. She looked so calm and serene, studying the pad on her lap, her hand poised mid-air with a dainty paintbrush between her fingers. She always seemed so deeply content, as if her heaven was contained in a piece of blank paper. Seeing her there let his world shrink to her and that moment and everything became secondary to being with her. He let out a breath, relieved that she hadn't run off yet.

She looked up at him. "Hi." She tugged her headphones from her ears. "I didn't hear you." She smiled and he dropped his gaze, overtaken by the unwelcome feeling that he was deceiving her. He was going to lose her the minute he told her the truth and he wasn't ready to let go.

She was still here, and for now, she was still his.

"What are you painting?" he asked as he sat down next to her and picked up a small painting on hard paper. She had several already finished and they were scattered over the bedcovers, drying.

"Postcards. For my family. As a surprise."

He grinned. Only Mila would paint her own postcards. Each

one had a different landmark of Paris on it—the Eiffel Tower, the Louvre Pyramids; he recognized L'Orangerie's exterior and the outside of Shakespeare and Company. "They're gorgeous, fit for printing."

She said nothing, and her gaze rested on him as heavily as everything else that weighed him down.

He forced himself to look her in the eyes. "I didn't know Marlène would be here so soon."

She searched his face. "She was here when I came back from the Louvre."

"Did you talk?" He had to know how far Marlène had pushed the boundaries with his *pretty rebound.*

"Not much. Damien was here with her." She covered his hand with hers. "I'm sorry."

"What for? I'm over her, Mila." When was she actually going to get it? It was as if she couldn't accept that Marlène and everything in his past was just that. The past. It was time he stood up to it, acknowledged it to himself. Told her. "Damien did me a favor. Honestly. Made it easier for me to break up with her."

When the words were out he knew they sounded shittier than he'd intended. If it weren't for Damien, he would still be with Marlène, if only for the sake of being with someone who allowed him to live life in a damage-controlled environment.

"It's okay. I don't need to know." She let go of his hand and gathered her hair from her face. "She seems nice." She dipped the fine point of her paintbrush in the water and shook it clean. "She mentioned we should go out one night. Clubbing."

His stomach clutched tight. "Clubbing."

She shrugged. "When Stacey's here. She said we should all go out together."

For fuck's sake. "Did she say where?"

"No, but it doesn't matter. I'm not going." She arranged her painting things on the bedside table, making sure each brush was clean and dried. "Clubbing is more Stacey's thing. She can go and enjoy it."

He got up and strode to the window, gathering his thoughts. The cat was not out of the bag yet. But he needed to do this, tell her, before she heard it from someone else.

"That's if we're still here." She met his gaze. "I was thinking a side trip to Versailles or Giverny would be nice."

"It would." He leaned to the window, unlatched it and threw it open to let some fresh air in. His chest constricted, tightening with the pull of courage.

"Mila," he started.

From the lounge there came a shriek. Then two. He turned to the door with a frown. Mila shoved her things to the side, her eyes wide. "That sounded—"

"Just like Stacey."

He strode out of the room, Mila tailing him as the laughter and shrieks from the lounge intensified.

"I didn't know you'd be here!" Stacey's voice said, followed by Marlène's husky laughter.

When he walked into the lounge Stacey and Marlène were hugging like old friends and doing a little turning dance in the process.

Stacey opened her eyes over Marlène's shoulder and seemed to freeze in Marlène's arms. They stepped apart, Stacey's eyes widening and a blush rising to her cheeks.

"Jamie." She bit her lip. "I didn't realize you'd be here."

Her words curdled his stomach. Things were afloat that he hadn't been aware of. "I live here." His gaze jumped between Marlène and Stacey and settled again on his sister's flustered face.

"What are *you* doing here?"

Stacey looked away. Arriving like this meant only one thing: she'd ditched rewriting her last exam, giving up the last chance to actually pass. He steeled himself and boxed the disappointment doused in anger that wanted to ignite. Instead, he stepped up and gave Stacey a kiss and a hug, if a bit stiffer than usual. He'd discuss her nonchalant attitude towards her studies when they were alone.

When he let her go Stacey all but pounced on Mila, who'd stood quietly to the side. Mila avoided his gaze, whispering something in Stacey's ear.

He was outnumbered. Three to one. With the exception of his sister, the situation, which would have made him grin in the past, made him grimace. They were going to play musical chairs over beds. And no chance in hell that he would get involved.

A fucking coward. That's what he was.

"We'll talk later, Stacey." No way she was getting out of that conversation. He looked at Mila, trying to convey to her that he was, what—sorry?—for the mess. "I'll leave you ladies to catch up."

He shot a freezing glare at Marlène to warn her off. If she attempted to get Mila or Stacey even halfway involved in any of her shit she'd spend the night on the street with her heap of antiques.

He turned to walk off.

"Where're you going, James?" Stacey asked, her tone rather strained.

So they'd progressed to James. Good. Stacey knew she was knee-deep in trouble.

"To the gym." That edgy feeling was hovering over him like a close-range missile.

Chapter 32

MILA STARED AT STACEY, PROBABLY mirroring her wide-eyed consternation. An awkward silence followed as they listened to James packing his things in his room. Marlène had gone after James, but if there was any conversation between them they couldn't hear it.

A minute later, he stomped past them, inclining his head mid-stride as if bowing. "Princesses." His tone said everything. He was teasing them, maybe in an attempt not to sound as stern as he had minutes ago. Mila could not help but chuckle, but that only earned her a scathing look from Stacey.

The front door closed and Mila let out a strained breath. "You should have warned me. To arrive out of the blue like this—"

"What? *You* should have warned *me*." Stacey pulled a dining room chair up and sank onto it. "I had no clue. If I had known James was here I would have stayed put."

"And actually finished your rewrites?"

Stacey dropped her gaze. "When I told him about the rewrites three weeks ago he promised he'd be here next week instead. So we could get to see each other."

"When you were *actually* supposed to be here." Mila sighed. Stacey hadn't answered her question about finishing her exams. "What happened?"

Stacey bit the tip of her forefinger nail. "James is seriously pissed off."

"What did you expect?" Mila still couldn't believe Stacey had gone and pulled the plug on another opportunity. "What's your dad going to say? He can't keep footing your studies like this, Stacey."

"I need a drink." Stacey got up and went to the kitchen.

Mila shook her head but followed her. "You were going to tell them you failed, weren't you? Without ever mentioning that you didn't bother to take the rewrite?"

Stacey pulled open the fridge and stared at its contents. "Really? There's zero alcohol in the fridge."

"That's what you get for showing up without warning." The situation was grating against her. Stacey hadn't answered her. Had she gone too far this time? And with her discussion with James the night before... Stacey had pulled the plug on her and James too.

"I didn't come here to fight with you, Mila," Stacey whispered. "I just had to get away, okay?"

Stacey was running. Mila had no idea why, from what or where to. She never used to be like this. Something triggered her to make the worst possible decision every single time.

"Stacey, you can't go on like—"

Marlène walked into the kitchen, dressed in a pale pink satin pajama set. At the sight of her Mila's muscles tensed from her toes to her shoulders, which hitched up an inch.

"I'm so glad you're here," said Stacey, hugging Marlène close.

"We can make work of you and Jamie."

Mila bit her lip. Stacey still hankered after reconciliation between the two. As Stacey's words percolated, a low warmth rose up Mila's neck. The last thing Stacey would want to know was that she'd slept with James.

Marlène smiled at Mila as she let go of Stacey. "Stacey has become like a sister to me. We haven't seen each other since James broke up with me." She sniffed and wiped her cheek. "I missed you."

"I missed you too," Stacey said, looking as if the world's worries rested on her shoulders.

Marlène sighed. "Give James time to cool off. He'll come around."

"I don't know if he ever will," Stacey said and bit deep into her fisted knuckles. "I can't carry on like this. I'm my own worst enemy."

"Sweetheart," Marlène murmured. "We *must* get you out of this mood."

Mila met Marlène's gaze, a shudder of foreboding trickling down her spine.

"I'm knackered now, but let's go out tomorrow night," Marlène said. "Damien already said he will take us to his club."

"Really?" Stacey's face lit up as if she was a four-year-old who got her first snow globe. "That would be awesome. We can take Jamie with us and see what happens between you two."

Marlène laughed a naughty little chuckle that made her eyes sparkle. "Leave James out of it. I don't want to drag a growly bear around Paris."

Stacey chuckled; Marlène gave them both a top to toe inspection. "What are you going to wear?"

"I did bring some things," Stacey started.

Marlène gave Mila the downward inspection. Again. The

question was clearly aimed at her and not at Stacey.

"Let's raid my wardrobe," Marlène threw out. "I haven't worn anything in there for ages and it's loaded with treasures."

Mila groaned inwardly. She wasn't going. She cleared her throat. "You go ahead Stacey, clubbing's not my—"

Stacey grabbed her hand and tugged her along. "You're coming with. Time to get a life and no better place to do so than in Paris."

A useless protest wanted to spill from her mouth, but Stacey clamped her down. "You owe me one, okay?"

She couldn't fight that logic. If it weren't for Stacey she wouldn't have had access to James's apartment. She wouldn't have been able to afford to be here in the first place. She was tired, not in the mood for a tiff either, and reluctantly caved in. "Okay, but I'm not getting drunk tomorrow night." Mila hated drinking with the aim of getting smashed.

Marlène smiled drily. "Damien's club only serves champagne."

She tried not to groan in anticipation of the cost of one night out with the likes of Marlène. She could hardly afford fake bubbly, let alone the real thing.

An hour later Mila had tried on more than ten outfits. All of them had made her wince. The amount of skin the dresses exposed, never mind each dress's price tag, which was stationed on its hanger so that Marlène could keep track of which dress had cost her what, made her eyes bulge. It was too much.

"I can't wear this." Mila couldn't even breathe in it. The dress was too tight. "What if I spill wine on it?" It was a little white number, more fit for a slutty bride than a night in town.

"That's cute," Stacey said, giving her the once-over. "But I preferred the red on you. And champagne doesn't stain."

Mila rolled her eyes at Stacey, who rewarded her with a told-you-so stare.

"The aim isn't to look cute. The aim is to look sexy." Marlène brushed her platinum strands from her face. "Tell me you have contact lenses?"

Ugh. She should have known. "Yes."

"Wear them tomorrow." Marlène gave her another skin prickling inspection. "You should wear the red Prada, and Stacey should wear this." Marlène pulled a green slip dress from its hanger and handed it to Stacey.

Mila unzipped the dress and stepped out of it with a deep inhale. She plunked down on the massive bed, exhausted and exasperated. Red it was. She'd been transported back to some traumatic middle school event which involved age-inappropriate clothes and going out with boys. Only this time it was the inverse—she wanted to cover up as much as possible, whereas Marlène wanted to get her as naked as possible.

"Tell me that's not the only underwear you have," Marlène probed, eyeing her simple white underwear.

She'd lost most of her inhibitions over the past hour. It was a miracle she'd managed to keep her panties on this long. Her bra was long gone with the number of midriff-exposing, naked-back things she'd been forced to try on.

"Plain Jane," Stacey murmured as she slipped into the little green number. "I'll sort her out tomorrow."

"Oh no, seriously?" James hadn't minded her plain cottons. His words were that they were *fucking sexy*. The memory made her smile, but she paused at the thought. Something else had shifted in her in the past hour. James had been with Marlène for years and now, having spent time with her, Mila knew she was no Marlène.

Confident, sexy, in charge and knowing what she wanted. Sexed-up, without even trying.

Next to her, Mila felt wilted. She missed James. Heavens. If it started like this, how was she to carry on when she went back home?

Her feet were tired, her head spinning with the overdose of fashion. She picked up her own clothes and dressed.

She wanted to go to bed but that posed a problem. With the apartment full, she had no idea who'd be sleeping where. James wasn't back from the gym yet and hadn't dictated who'd go where in his apartment. With the Marlène–and–Stacey duo on hand, it wasn't her place to make decisions.

"Where are we sleeping, Stacey?" she asked, stifling a yawn.

Stacey shot her a brief glance, but Marlène's gaze rested on her a moment too long for comfort.

"In James's room," Stacey answered, as she zipped up the cocktail dress. "This just screams Valentino." She sighed and turned to inspect her neat backside in the mirror.

"Where's James going to sleep?" The words slipped out before she realized the implication.

"Where has he been sleeping?" Marlène asked and raised an eyebrow, waiting for her reaction. The glint in her eyes dared her to break the truth to Stacey. Damien must have told Marlène about the night he came over because Marlène knew she'd been sleeping with James.

Stacey couldn't ever know. It was a sickening feeling, to be in cahoots with Marlène.

"Has he been here? With you?" Stacey eyed her.

"We've been cohabiting in perfect harmonious… disinterest." Dear Lord. Since when had lying become her forte? "He hasn't slept here since I arrived." Now she was lying to her best friend too.

Stacey pouted and crunched her face to Marlène in what was her sympathetic look. "I'm so sorry, Marlène. I'd love…" She stalled. "We should do all we can to—"

"My sleeper couch is in the lounge." Marlène cut her off. "And there's this double bed here. I'm not going to push him, Stacey."

Stacey shrugged, but her gaze dropped, filled with regret. "I'll share his room with Mila and leave you two to sort things out."

Mila got up, glad that things were settled. She wanted to get out of Marlène's company. But poor James; ousted to the sleeper couch in his own apartment. "Shouldn't we take the sleeper couch?"

"Maybe he won't be here tonight." She waved James off with her hand. "There's two of us and only one of him."

Mila gave up. "Can we go fix up the furniture? I'd hate to kick him out of his bed and he is going to be home tonight, Stacey. You're here."

There was an uncomfortable silence as Stacey digested this. Did she honestly think her brother was going to let her off the hook? "Okay. You're right. Let's go fix up the lounge."

She walked out of Marlène's boudoir with Stacey right behind her.

"The sleeper couch is awful. I've slept on it before," Stacey said. "That would definitely prompt him to go snuggle up with Marlène."

The notion made Mila's stomach turn. He had said he was over Marlène and had been quite exasperated with her when she'd kept on pushing the Marlène button. Maybe Stacey was having blurts of wishful thinking.

Marlène came and helped them, directing them to put the furniture back in the original layout. Together they shoved everything into place, covering the pockmarks in the carpet where

230

the chairs and sofas used to stand.

They folded open the sleeper couch and Marlène fetched some linen and extra pillows. "I'll leave you to it," Marlène said, and with a sniff excused herself for the night.

"We've made his bed." Mila sighed as she dropped a puffed pillow in its place. She'd give anything to reverse the clock to the previous night. The way James's kisses had made her feel was etched under her skin. Just the thought of him made desire ripple through her.

Stacey chuckled and winked at her. "Now let's hope he doesn't sleep in it."

Chapter 33

W HEN JAMES GOT BACK TO the apartment it was dark, only the city lights beaming through the windows to mark the furniture with ghostly shadows. As he entered the lounge, he eyed the sleeper couch, and noticing that it was empty, sighed with resignation. At least he'd had the foresight to shower at the gym. Some windows were still open and he went over to close them. Stacey sat alone on the terrace, busy on her mobile, its light reflecting on her face.

Both Mila and Marlène were nowhere to be seen and must have gone to bed. He should get this talk over with now, while he had a moment alone with his sister. As much as Mila was Stacey's friend, he'd hate to take her to task in front of an audience.

He opened the French door leading outside and Stacey looked up.

"I couldn't sleep," she murmured, shifting in her chair.

"No surprises there." He should keep away from sarcasm, but he'd allow himself this one slip.

"Don't be mean, Jamie."

"Don't be petulant, Stacey." He checked his temper. "You're going to get expelled at this rate. Why are you doing this to yourself?"

"I… I don't know, okay?" She dropped her phone on the side table and brushed her hair from her cheeks.

Sometimes Stacey could be too much Millennial for him. Or maybe she was just completely lost. He stopped short of groaning. Somewhere along the line, Stacey had fallen through the cracks of his parents' issues and all the shit that had mutated in between. She'd once been a stellar student, earning distinctions. Her promising future had gone up in flames after their mom's passing.

"I can't support you if you go on like this." He hated doing this, but it was for the best. "I won't. I'm no longer funding your studies. Go find a job. Sort your head out." He was one to talk.

"Don't cut me off, Jamie. Please." Her voice constricted and she reached for his hand.

He hugged her hand with his and wanted to let go, but she clung to him.

"I don't know how you got through it all unscathed, Jamie. How did you?"

He couldn't look her in the eye, he couldn't admit to her how fucked up he really was. She'd always looked up to him, thinking of him as this infallible hero who could do nothing wrong. His lifestyle might have been his saving grace, but he couldn't let Stacey go there… what kind of example would that be for her? One visual of his secret life and he would shatter, and she with him. He shrugged, failing to answer her.

"I'm not like you," she murmured. "You always know where you're heading, career-wise, love-wise. You're always in control. You always achieve what you want."

He wanted to laugh. He'd never had so little control over his life as he did right now.

Mila. He was going to be lost without her and yet he had no control over what was going to happen between them. It scared him shitless and already he hurt like hell. "That's not true. When it comes to the most important things I can't get what I want."

"And what are the most important things?" She was probing and he'd let himself into the trap.

"Love. Happiness with the perfect woman."

She pulled her hand away to wipe at her eyes. His stomach twisted as he caught the shine of a tear running down her finger. He couldn't have Stacey crying. He'd cave into anything she wanted.

"Is it Marlène? Why?" she asked. From the strain in her voice, she tried to hide her tears. "Why did you let her go then?"

"No. It's not Marlène. I broke up with her for all the right reasons." He looked away over the view of Paris. "It's someone else."

"Someone you've been spending the past few nights with?" She glanced at him. "Mila told me you weren't here."

He hung his head, the implication of her words working his innards. Mila hadn't told Stacey about them, sticking to her resolve from last night. She was not interested beyond the few days they'd had.

"Yes." This was the easiest way out, but it was killing him.

"Will I get to meet her?" Stacey's tears had stopped.

He blocked the bitter laugh that threatened. "It's still early days."

Stacey leaned forward in her chair. "Bring her tomorrow night. We're going out. It would be awesome."

He scanned her face to see if there was anything he needed to be wary of, but Stacey was sincere and innocent in her invitation.

"I can't commit now." Not unless he pulled a new girlfriend out of his magic hat. "If I can go out it would only be later. Need to wait for the New York stock exchange to close."

"Ugh. Did you really have to get yourself that job?"

"*That job* is paying for your messing around, Stacey." He couldn't help the jab, but she had it coming. He didn't relish working strange hours either, but it came with the salary package.

She stood and her chair scraped angrily on the tiled terrace floor. "Wow. One low blow after the other. Marlène had it spot on when she said you're a growly bear."

He lifted his gaze, staring at the odd star that managed to shine through the polluted air that hugged the city. "Best you stay away from Marlène, Stacey."

"What?"

"I don't want you to hang out with her, okay? Marlène is not what she seems."

"Really? Jeez, you've totally lost it. To think she still cares for you!"

"Should make you think she's really stupid, doesn't it?" The conversation was turning ugly and he had to cut it short. "It's not up for discussion." He stood and walked back into the apartment, leaving Stacey to stew.

He'd barely gotten under the covers of the sleeper couch when she strode back inside and closed the French doors behind her. She stopped short of going down the corridor to the bedrooms. "Marlène is like a sister to me. I can't cut her off just like you did." She exhaled sharply. "Best you make peace with our friendship."

She padded down the corridor, leaving him to stare at the checkered shadow pattern the scant city lights threw on the ceiling.

Women. He could do with a fucking universal manual instructing him how to deal with them.

235

Chapter 34

James woke up to the clanging of cups and the rumbling of his coffee machine. He felt like shit, having hardly slept. He tossed the covers to the side and got up. They'd banished him to the lounge and sleeper couch, the least they could do was give him some silence at six in the morning.

He strode to the kitchen to find Marlène, in her signature satins, making some coffee.

He should have known. Only she would be so thoughtless as to wake him up by banging and crashing around in the kitchen. He stretched and yawned.

"Would you like some?"

She hadn't even turned to see who it was. But she knew him and had probably woken him up on purpose. His mind returned to the aborted conversation he'd had with Stacey the night before. He had to do everything possible to separate Stacey from Marlène.

"Sure." He sat down on a bar stool by the kitchen island and watched her every move, steeling himself. Her hands were shaking and he suspected she needed a shot of something stronger than coffee.

"Slept okay?" she asked as she pushed a cup of coffee towards him.

He twisted his neck, stretching his stiff muscles. "Perfectly."

She finally met his gaze. Her skin was still smooth and flawless, but the color had taken on an undertone of grey. He strengthened his resolve. "I'll arrange for a removal company today. Get your things into storage."

"James. Please."

He was no longer feeling up to any more niceties. "Don't you get it, Marlène? We were over before you even started with Damien." He dragged in a deep breath. "I'll ask Jean-Pierre to help with the legal side of buying you out." He might have to let go of the apartment completely to get rid of her.

"Give me the weekend."

He shook his head. "No." He couldn't risk Mila, Stacey, and Marlène together. "Are you working today?"

She took a sip of her coffee, studying his face. She turned away to put the milk back in the fridge. "Yes. Tonight I'm having dinner with my parents."

"Can't you go stay at their place?" She wouldn't, but it was worth a shot.

She didn't respond but took up her cup again, drinking her coffee at leisure as she leaned against the counter.

She was scrutinizing him, trying to see what was going on in his mind. "This Mila," she said eventually, "does she know everything she needs to know about you?"

Fuck. He should have known. Was she jealous of Mila? Of course she would be. She'd be thinking that despite her transgressions he still belonged to her, and her alone. That was the weirdest thing about this swinging business, they might have been out there fucking other people, but at the core, they'd still been one hundred percent committed to each other. It was the only way it worked.

She'd been the one to break the rules, not he.

He ground his teeth, clutching his coffee between his hands. Marlène had a malicious streak in her and wouldn't hesitate to expose him to Mila. And somehow Stacey would be dragged into it and get to know the real James Sinclair. His blood curdled, the coffee turning to acid in his stomach.

"Mila and I—" he faltered. In the few days he'd been with Mila, they'd become so much more than just sex. He got off the bar stool and took a few indecisive steps. His mind was racing, but he needed to do something to stop this game so he could get Marlène to back off.

She'd strolled out of the kitchen towards the terrace and he needed to hold her back, make her understand. Mila was sacred.

He paused as the only solution that could possibly work charged through his mind. Marlène would let go of Mila if he could make her believe he didn't care. That's how it had worked when they were together.

"Mila and I... we're nothing and I'd prefer to keep her uninformed of my past life."

Marlène turned to face him, but her gaze jumped to look over his shoulder. "Is that so?"

A ripple of dread ambled at leisure down his spine. He could feel her gaze on him, her beautiful brown eyes as she studied him. He turned and his stomach crunched up as if he'd been hit by an iron fist.

Mila stood outside the kitchen, in the corridor that led to the rooms. Her hair was rumpled but she looked gorgeous in her floppy *Hello Kitty* bed shirt and socks. She dropped her gaze, but he'd already seen every pain his harshly spoken words had inflicted reflected in her eyes. *Fuck.*

"I just wanted to know if you want to use the shower?" Mila gathered a few stray hairs from her cheeks, staring at the floor.

"Use my shower, James," Marlène said, dismissing Mila. "Don't you need to be at work early on Friday mornings? You know, last day of trading and all that?" She sauntered to the French doors, threw them open wide and took a deep breath of the cool morning air. "Who knows what could be crashing today if you're not there to take care of it."

She walked out to the terrace with a swagger, as if nothing could faze her, as if she'd staged their whole conversation and had enjoyed a perfect first run without a dress rehearsal. Marlène had been conscious of Mila coming out of the bedroom and had known she'd hear their conversation. Marlène had been playing him.

He looked up to find Mila turning away. He had no idea how much she'd heard.

He groaned. "Mila."

It was too late; she'd heard his last words. He needed to stop her and explain. But what was he going to explain? He'd known this was going to come, but he hadn't known it would be so soon. And not like this, with Marlène the puppet master and he all but limp and hemorrhaging from the inside. "Baby—"

Mila raised her hand in warning. "I'm no baby, James. Please don't call me that." She shook her head. "I'm going back to bed."

He was left standing in the lounge, raking his hands through his hair. Bloody hell. He used to like women aplenty, but now he couldn't seem to deal with even one of them.

The rotten apple needed to go first before it spread its poison to the others. He squared his shoulders and walked out to the terrace. "I don't care where you stay, Marlène, you can go stay with fucking Damien for all I care. He has rooms aplenty. But you are not staying one more night under this roof. Understood?"

She didn't look at him, didn't say a thing.

He stomped away, straight to her room and picked his way through discarded shoes, accessories and clothing items that didn't have a place on a hanger in her open wardrobe. He showered at speed in the en suite, hating every moment of inhaling Marlène's signature musky scent from her toiletries that crowded the shower. Marlène was forever plotting and might corner him in her room. He found a clean towel and dried himself, rapidly dressed in his jocks and made a quick escape.

He hovered outside his own bedroom door, which was closed.

He had to protect Mila and Stacey. They had no idea who Marlène really was. They had no idea who *he* was. But he no longer felt good in that old skin that had protected him for years, and shedding it would be the first step in pulling himself out of the swamp of his past. He took a deep breath and knocked.

"Come in." Mila was back in bed, sitting up straight, pen in hand and seeming to write her postcards. She dropped her gaze immediately as he walked in and he had to clamp down the urge to stride over to her, take her in his arms and kiss her.

Stacey reclined against the headboard, busy on her phone. He'd interrupted a cozy tête-à-tête, because Stacey looked up at him and gave him a glare.

"I thought you were bringing us coffee in bed," Stacey murmured, but her eyes sparkled with naughtiness.

Heaven helped the man who fell for her.

"Just getting my clothes," he mumbled, wishing Mila would acknowledge him.

The pen paused and she looked up, making his heart bleed.

Her gaze was cold, so unlike the ones she'd given him the past few days. "I'm sorry, we didn't think all the logistics through last night," she said, perusing his naked chest. A blush rose to her cheeks and he forced his body not to react to the thought of them together.

"No worries." He went to his wardrobe and picked out what he needed. "What are your plans for today?"

"I'm taking Mila shopping." Stacey stretched languidly, smiling up at him. "I suppose you don't have time for us today?"

"I can do a quick lunch if you want to meet somewhere?" He could check in on them, make sure they weren't dangling after Marlène as Stacey would love to do. Stacey had spent a couple of days at the office with Marlène when she still worked in Paris and had even connived to get to a show during Paris's fashion week. No wonder Stacey idolized his ex. He should have curbed the whole business.

Stacey glanced at Mila. "We can do lunch?"

Mila hid behind those thick-framed glasses, her hair covering most of her face as she looked down to her postcards. "I don't mind coming back here for lunch after your shopping spree?"

"Do perk up, Mila," Stacey implored. "It's just lunch."

He groaned inwardly. He knew what bothered Mila. She was not swimming in cash and hated to be beholden to anyone. "I get to treat you ladies at least once while you're in town. Meet me for lunch at *Galeries Lafayette* at twelve."

He closed his eyes and turned, unable to stomach the rapture on Stacey's face. It was going to be so much more than lunch. He strode out of the room, but couldn't go deaf.

"Eeeeek!" Stacey called out. "Shopping with Jamie! It's the best!"

He cursed under his breath. He might be sending out mixed messages here. And he should really stop spoiling his little sister.

241

Chapter 35

MILA SAT ACROSS FROM JAMES, trying her hardest not to zone out of Stacey's conversation about shopping and the light lunch they'd just finished. Ever since she'd heard James tell Marlène that they were *nothing*, she'd been holding herself together by a thread. If it hadn't been for the three hours she'd been forced to shop with Stacey, she'd have had a broken heart bobbing in a puddle of tears by now.

Those words… it was one thing to think them quietly to herself, but to have heard them from him had been a stab and twist to the heart with a blunt knife.

And yet, whenever his gaze rested on her, which was often and longer than she could bear, regret shone in his eyes. It was killing her because that morning James's words—inconsiderate and spoken in a mean tone he'd never used on her—were completely unlike the James she'd known and gotten to know again over the last few days.

At least the famous department store was worth a visit in itself, but she prayed that this wasn't how Stacey planned to spend the next few days. Stacey had insisted that they try on a pile of expensive, breathtakingly beautiful dresses, each item in the range of the average student's monthly rent. It was fun, entering an impossible dream world of affluence for a few hours, but it was so far out of her comfort zone she felt as wretched as Cinderella as the clock struck twelve.

Stacey nursed her wine, oblivious to the tension between Mila and James.

Mila felt like a fifth wheel. James and Stacey's conversation flowed naturally and they'd chatted about people and things she didn't have a connection with. Her efforts to remain cool and unfazed by everything that had passed that morning were paying off, but for how long could she keep going with this charade? She wished for nothing but to be alone and lick her wounds. She should have known it was all too good to be true. Men like James Sinclair didn't happen to the Mila Johnsons of the world.

"What are your plans for tonight?" James asked.

"I'm taking Mila to The Sommelier," Stacey said, as she picked up her wine glass. "Should be fun."

Mila looked up. The Sommelier was one of the places James had recommended to her a few days ago, frequented by the English-speaking crowd. Where the lingo wouldn't be an issue. It didn't sound like Damien's club.

"I'll join you there after work," James said. "But it will only be later."

"But—" Mila started. A heeled foot dug into her toes and she closed her mouth, biting her lip.

"Sure," Stacey answered. "We might be home if it's too late, so maybe check in on us before you head over. We don't plan to go big."

Right.

"Excuse me," James said as he got up. "I'll be back in a minute."

He walked past her, his fingers ghosting over her hair where it hung over her shoulders, the whisper of his touch echoing onto her back, to her skin and rippling to deeper, darker parts of her. She closed her eyes for a second, treasuring the sensation, and listened to his footsteps that hadn't broken their rhythm despite the lingering of his touch.

When she was sure he was gone Mila tuned her eyes in to Stacey. "Why did you tell him some tall tale of The Sommelier?"

Stacey hitched her shoulders. "James can be super dull sometimes. And he doesn't approve of Damien."

"Probably with very good reason," Mila retorted.

"Don't worry, we'll be in bed and neatly tucked in by the time James gets home. When he does this month-end Friday night thing for work he's always awfully late."

Mila shrugged and told herself to ignore the unease that had settled in her stomach.

"Bottoms up, dearest," Stacey said as she took up her wineglass and emptied it in one go. "When James comes back he's going to be in a hurry."

She sipped at her wine. One glass down and she already felt heady; between herself and Stacey they'd been supposed to finish the bottle. James had only drunk water during lunch.

She thought he'd gone to the gents', but when he strolled in a minute later pocketing his wallet she pursed her lips. He'd gone to pay on the sly.

"Do you always let him pay like this?" she grumbled to Stacey as they got up and gathered their handbags.

"Only in times of severe financial strain," Stacey whispered back.

Mila rolled her eyes. "Which is pretty much always."

Stacey laughed and flung her arms around James's neck and hugged him thoroughly. "Thanks for the lunch, Jamie."

God only knew how much she wanted to do that. How much she wanted to feel his body against hers one last time, how much she wanted to have his hands travel down her back and pull her close. She wanted to savor his strength, harvest it and use it to get through this day. She couldn't do this for longer. Not after what they'd had and his words that morning.

"Thank you… James. For lunch," she managed and gave James a cursory nod.

"Jeez, Mila. Lighten up. It was just lunch." Stacey had pulled away from James, and they were both staring at her.

She inhaled sharply as she realized she'd hardly breathed.

James reached out for her, taking her hand in his. "Too much wine in the middle of the day?"

The gesture was so caring, so gentle, her hand wanted to snuggle with his, get cozy and never let go.

"Yes," she said as she pulled away to brush her hair from her face, hating the emptiness that hollowed her out. "You spoil us."

His gaze didn't leave her face and for a moment he studied her so intently she didn't know where to look. Heat settled on her cheeks, making her feel five years old again.

With a sigh, he turned to Stacey. "Come on, this needs to be quick, I've got to get back to the office."

She trailed after them into the department store and they took the lift to the floor with women's attire.

There was no way she was going to stick around for Stacey's spending spree with James. She had to get away, let them do their thing on their own.

When the lift's doors opened, she didn't exit with them. "I'm going to the gift section upstairs." It was several floors up and as far away as she could get. "Meet me there once you're done?"

Stacey gaped to protest, but Mila pressed the button to close the doors again. "Thanks again for lunch, James!" she called as the doors swept closed.

With a heavy heart, she idled the time away, aimlessly walking between the displays of stuff she didn't need and couldn't afford to buy. Trying not to keep track of time, she almost caved in and left to find the Sinclairs when she spotted Stacey coming up the escalator.

Stacey's smile was contagious as she stepped up to her. "James is a darling."

"I bet he is," Mila said, taking a glimpse at all the bags Stacey clasped in her hands.

"I couldn't help it. I couldn't stop him." Stacey's eyes sparkled and she bit her lip, the corners of her mouth tugging up in a suppressed smile. "Jamie insisted."

Her eyes widened as her blood seeped to her feet. "Oh no, Stacey. What?"

"We got you that simply gorgeous black dress. The strapless one that makes your shoulders look so sexy."

She shook her head. "Why? I can't possibly—"

Stacey handed her one of the bags and Mila took it hesitantly. Stacey hooked an arm through hers. "Don't be difficult," she begged. "James said you'd need something for the opening night of your exhibition, and this is just perfect."

She skipped a breath. "Stacey, really, I can't. It's too expensive. I can't possibly wear that dress to the opening night. My mom would have heart failure."

But he'd thought of her. The dress was short and so sexy, she'd been a goddess in it, ruling the world. What she would give

246

to let James see her in it. For a few simple minutes, wearing that dress, she'd felt she could compare with Marlène.

"Good thing your folks won't be at your opening night. Rugby first, remember. Johnson and Johnson will be playing in Durban that weekend." Her voice reduced to a conspiratorial whisper. "They'll never know."

Mila laughed. "You're plotting against me." She was already too deep in debt with James for someone he'd *had nothing with*, except her whole heart and soul on a platter. It wasn't like him at all, but she couldn't shake the feeling that this was a 'thank you' gift from James as if she'd been his kept woman for a few blissful days.

Stacey shot her a grin. "Never plotting against you, Mila, but with you. Best of all is, you can wear it tonight too."

That dress was way too precious to spoil in a wine bar.

"Can't we wear jeans? And a nice top?" Mila probed. She'd brought exactly what she'd needed from home for a night out. Plus, there was the red dress from Marlène's vast selection, but she'd hate to wear something of hers. "It's just a club, after all?"

"Apparently this one has a dress code. It's very exclusive." Stacey didn't meet her eyes. "Marlène said women wear dresses. Men go in suits."

"Wow. Okay," Mila chuckled. "Only in Paris."

As they left the department store behind, Mila suppressed a sigh of resignation. At least she had something else to wear, and wouldn't be in Marlène's debt.

Chapter 36

Mila ran her hands down the thick silk fabric of the dress for the third time. The dress was the sexiest thing she'd ever worn. It hugged her curves, accentuating every feminine bit of her. Looking at the mirror, her heart pounded wildly. James had picked it for her, knowing every inch of her body, and with his expert eye had known it would fit her like a glove.

The style left her shoulders bare, making her smile with a tinge of heartache. The bits that had driven James crazy the other night, when she'd worn her cheap strapless summer dress, were fully exposed for his enjoyment. But he wouldn't be there tonight and with all Stacey's scheming, they'd miss him completely.

If nothing else a girl should take home a little black dress from Paris, and a broken heart.

Why did she suspect this club wasn't like the clubs either she or Stacey were accustomed to? She had no idea what Stacey was expecting, but reading between the few lines Marlène and James had spoken, thinking about what had happened between James and Damien—she couldn't put her finger on it. There was also the conversation she'd had with James a few days ago about clubbing, of which she hadn't made much until now. Something was off, but she wasn't sure what.

She suppressed a sigh as Stacey walked into the bathroom and appeared in the mirror.

"You look stunning," Stacey said, her gaze running down her body.

"I really wish you didn't talk me into this."

"You only live once," Stacy murmured and slicked a layer of cherry red lipstick over her parted lips.

Stacey looked striking. Her dress was equally simple, with a halter neck and elaborate collar that spread seventies-style to her shoulders. The whole back was covered with mesh. Both dresses allowed only strapless bras, and since neither of them had brought any, they were naked except for panties underneath.

"So, whose funeral are we going to?" Stacey joked as she checked her make-up and hair one last time. "All dressed in black as we are."

Mila chuckled but wanted to weep. They'd be putting to rest the liaison she'd had with James.

"Your brother sure knows his way around haute couture." Any other response would open the Pandora's box of secrets she'd been sitting on, trying to keep the lid on.

"Marlène's influence," Stacey stated. "But he always had exquisite taste. I'll give him that."

"How are your heels?" Mila asked, in dire need to steer the conversation away from Marlène.

"High."

Mila laughed. They didn't splurge on shoes and already Mila's were biting into her heels and toes. Her feet were going to have a hard time tonight. "I don't know if I can do a whole night in these."

"Maybe we can take them off at some point," Stacey said. She rolled on a final layer of lip gloss. "I don't mind dancing barefoot."

"Let's see how it goes." She was ready; there was nothing more to do.

They went out of the bedroom and found Marlène sitting in the lounge, wearing the slutty bride dress. She was on a call, her voice husky and low as she spoke in French. She became aware of them and looked up, her hooded eyes widening.

"*Mais, voilà, les filles,*" she laughed into the phone. "We'll see you soon." She hung up and stood, taking them in from top to bottom, stripping them naked. Mila shuddered inwardly. Marlène studied her just a little too closely, a little too intimately with her eyes as they roamed over her body.

Why did she wish James were here, giving her an excuse to stay at home? She licked her lips, nervous, the oily sweetness of her lipstick invading her tongue. If she carried on like this her lipstick would be obliterated by the time they arrived at the club.

"*Mon Dieu*, you are perfection." Marlène sauntered over, her every curve swaying in time with her hair. She took hold of Stacey's hand and pulled her closer in a hug. "Thank you, for always being there for me."

Stacey blushed, a sweet smile on her lips. "Anything for you, Marls."

Ugh. It wasn't her place to say anything, but she wished— how much she wished—that Stacey would see Marlène's true colors and no longer idolize her.

Marlène glanced at her, and a slow blush stole over Mila's cheeks. Did she really have to be so pathetic?

"Let's go have fun," Marlène said, her lips smiling, but her eyes cold. "You don't need anything. Damien is meeting us at the club."

Mila checked her cash before slipping her wallet back into her bag. "Are we taking a taxi?"

"It's not far to walk. You're in for a pleasant surprise." Marlène gave her a sly smile. "Just leave everything. Also your phones."

Stacey's eyebrows shot up at this comment. "I don't go anywhere without my phone."

"I've noticed, but we're together and you won't need it," Marlène said. "Damien's treat."

Mila rolled her eyes. First James, now Damien. "I prefer to look after myself." Damien's words, asking her whether James had been looking after her as he should, made her shudder.

"Trust me, it's not necessary. You can leave your things with the concierge, but no phones are allowed inside the club. And when Damien looks after his guests… he looks after them."

Mila pulled her phone from her bag with trembling fingers and placed it next to Stacey's on the coffee table. They exchanged wary glances. There was a multitude of reasons why phones wouldn't be allowed and an unexpected tingle spread over her skin as she acknowledged the most blatant of them: photos.

None would be taken tonight, that was for sure.

Marlène led the way to the apartment door and held it open for them. They took the lift to the ground floor in silence, the claustrophobic space soon filling with the suffocating exotic blend of Stacey's and Marlène's perfumes.

"This way." Marlène opened the lobby door and started walking down the sidewalk in the direction of the restaurants, the same way Mila had gone with James a few nights ago.

Mila glanced at Stacey, who was nibbling her lower lip, looking concerned for the first time since they'd signed up for this.

They turned left into a narrow pedestrian walkway. The street was empty with the exception of a few doors. An odd twenty meters further Marlène stopped at a black door, which seemed to have a single watching eye. It was only a little plaque, but in the twilight, even darker in the narrow street, she couldn't read what it said.

Marlène raised an eyebrow at them. "Ready, girls?"

Stacey bubbled up a nervous laugh. Mila wished she'd let James know where they'd gone. At least the apartment was only minutes away. But still. Why did this seem like a bad idea?

Marlène held the door open and Mila shook her head, but after a second followed Stacey into a marble lobby. There was a cloakroom and a mirror that looked double sided. Security cameras eyed them from at least two corners of the room and Mila's innards tightened.

An antique escritoire stood to the side, a laptop looking out of place on it. Damien looked up with a smile, shuffling some papers together. "Ah, voilà!" He got up and crossed the marble floor in easy strides.

He was dressed in a slick grey suit, molded to his body in the perfect fit. Every bit of him looked as if he'd stepped off an undeniably French fashion shoot. Too suave. Mila blinked. Underneath all that money was a frog that no amount of kissing would ever turn into a prince.

He perused Stacey, soaking up every detail of her delicate frame, her thick blonde hair and those big, innocent blue eyes. Mila shifted on her feet, reading every feeling Damien's intimate inspection made Stacey feel: sexy, wanted, desired. Groaning, she tried to tear her gaze away from Damien's expert tactics but was compelled to watch as he stepped closer.

"Stacey?" he purred. "*Enchanté.*" He leaned in, took hold of both of her hands and gave her two of those invasive pecks on the cheeks. But Stacey seemed to love him this close, in her personal space, and didn't pull back. He smoothed his hands up her naked arms, slowly, with such intent that Mila just knew Stacey relished every inch of his caress. The touch was too slow, too intimate, to be anything but the first note to a sexual tune.

Mila looked away and swallowed compulsively.

"Damien?" Stacey chuckled. "We finally get to meet."

"Indeed."

A bout of silence followed, then Damien turned her way, his hand still cupping Stacey's elbow as he tucked her close to him.

Mila stalled. Stacey didn't know how often she'd already met Damien. That there had been a tiff between James and Damien... about her. She had to keep that information to herself.

"Hi Damien," she said, extending her hand as far as possible. She'd shake his hand and block any attempt at getting closer to her with a palm to his chest.

His gaze lingered on her for a fraction of a second before he reached out with a cool hand. "Welcome to our club. I look forward to showing you around."

Marlène had moved to the escritoire and was flipping through the papers Damien had left on the desk.

"You've made two copies?" Marlène asked.

"*Oui.*" Damien hadn't let go of Stacey's elbow but led her closer to the escritoire. "Please. Take a seat. I need you both to sign these documents before we go inside."

Stacey glanced at Mila and sat down. "What is it?" She fingered the stack of papers. "Does it have to be so long?"

"It's a non-disclosure agreement," Damien answered as if every club in the world required this bit of paperwork before one could enter.

Stacey looked up at him, her face pale in consternation.

"Nothing to worry about, Stacey. You need to initial each page and sign the last page. We'll witness." Marlène smiled as she called Mila closer. "Jean-Pierre is a pedantic perfectionist... in everything he does."

"Jean-Pierre?" Stacey queried.

"You might meet him tonight. One of the co-owners. With James and Damien. And a few other people."

Mila's face burst with thousands of pinpricks. James?

Damien smiled, but his eyes were hooded. "No entry without paperwork being done."

She tried to suppress the slow twist in her stomach. How did James fit into all of this? Surely this was another James? His words from that morning, which previously had no frame of reference slotted perfectly in place. *We're nothing and I'd prefer to keep her uninformed of my past life.*

There was no escaping the logic. Flushed, she took up the papers and tried to read the magnitude of fine print. Her eyes darted over the pages, but nothing quite made sense. Her breathing stalled, her hand quivered as she initialed the pages and signed the last one.

Damien took the documents from her, scanned them briefly, then handed them to the man who stood silently behind the concierge's counter. He had an uber-strong build, looking more like a bouncer than a docile coat handler.

The man scrutinized the documents, checking that every t was crossed and i dotted. Eventually, he nodded to Damien and shot them a disinterested glance. "We'll open for you," he said in English, nodding to the mirror. "If the ladies have anything to leave behind? No phones are allowed."

Mila handed over her frumpy handbag, which she'd clung to like a shield until that moment. She offered her empty hands for his inspection, feeling almost naked now that the moment had come. Stacey had left everything behind, showing her unwavering trust in Marlène.

"Thank you, Pascal. Come, ladies," Damien murmured, his hand settling into the low hollow of her back. "The champagne awaits."

Reality had sunk in. She might be inexperienced, but she wasn't naïve. Imagine her, Mila Johnson, in one of those places her father loved to condemn as devils' hives. Not that he'd ever mention those by name, but the Lord help her, she knew exactly what he'd spoken about and it made her body flush hot and cold at the same time.

She turned to Marlène, trying to read her expression. "Is this one of those clubs where people get tied up and whipped?"

"Why? Does someone need a whipping?" Marlène smirked and a chuckle escaped from deep in her stomach. "*Non, ma chérie,* but if you ask Damien nicely he could arrange it for you."

Chapter 31

HALF AN HOUR LATER JAMES entered the apartment's lobby and impatiently called the lift, checking his watch for the hundredth time. He'd phoned Mila and Stacey several times, but each time both their phones had just rung without going over to voice mail.

He'd finished earlier than expected. One of his juniors had done most of the groundwork, and after they'd pulled in the numbers, checked that everything made sense given that there was no volatility in the market, they'd knocked off.

A swift tour of The Sommelier had produced no Mila and no Stacey. He doubted his sister would have called it a night so early. Not when she was in Paris.

He got out of the lift and unlocked his apartment, hoping to find their laughter filling the emptiness. But there was not a sound and his body contracted.

He crossed the empty lounge, calling their names. No response. Not even from Mila, who he knew would rather spend a night cozy at home than with Stacey out on the town.

He cursed under his breath. He had to get Mila alone.

It had been impossible to have a private word with her since that morning. Twice he'd been on the verge of calling her, but he had to speak to her in person. He'd wanted to corner her during lunch, but it had been impossible. He needed to make her understand, to drill down into her mind that what had happened earlier that morning was not his truth. It wasn't their truth.

She'd come upon him in the midst of a negotiation with Marlène. Why had he even been negotiating with his ex? Shouldn't he know, from experience growing up, that nothing stayed hidden, that truth and honesty was always the only road to take? Because every other way led to pure destruction.

He should have told her. From day one. And now, as he strode through the empty apartment, he couldn't shrug the notion that his past was catching up with him three times as fast as he could deal with it.

The master bedroom was empty but disheveled with evidence of females preparing for a night out. The doors to Marlène's rooms leered open, showing off neatened-up interiors. None of her clothes were scattered on the floor anymore. What the fuck did that mean?

Inwardly he quivered with unease as he came to a stop in the kitchen. On the counter, three cellphones blinked. Mila's, Stacey's and Marlène's.

Hell would freeze over before Stacey went anywhere without her phone.

And Marlène only went one place without hers.

He dragged his hand across his face. Dinner with her parents had either be cancelled or had never been on the cards. *Fuck fuck fuck.*

Mila.

She was stuck in the middle of all of this. Marlène's little introduction to the 'real him'. Her petty revenge. Did she really think he'd ever get back with her?

His jaw ticked as the thought of Mila burned every notion of Marlène to the ground. He'd never deserved to have her, but if something would put her unadulterated soul off him, it would be an evening at the club.

His mind raced as he rushed out of the apartment, slamming the door with undue force. Taking the stairs two at a time, he exited to the street and swerved through pedestrians to reach the narrow alley as quickly as he could.

He buzzed the bell, staring straight at the security camera. Pascal wouldn't let him wait. The door clicked open and he stepped inside.

"Monsieur Sinclair," the concierge greeted him from behind the cloakroom's desk. "How nice to see you again."

Eight fucking months. He would never have put a foot here again if he weren't forced.

"*Bonsoir*, Pascal. Are Damien and Marlène here?" Why did his voice sound so anxious, so out of breath?

Pascal didn't blink, trained to keep a straight face. His bouncer bulk shifted behind the desk, giving him the once-over.

"They came earlier. Two new ladies were with them."

He nodded and rushed his hands through his hair. He'd fucking known as soon as he'd seen the empty apartment, where Marlène's scent had still hung thick amongst the shadows. "Open for me, please. Those two ladies shouldn't be here."

Least of all with the likes of Damien and his ex. His stomach was twisted as tight as the wet towel he was about to be whipped with.

Chapter 38

MILA COULDN'T SHRUG DAMIEN'S HAND off her back, the tips of his fingers burning in their subtle guidance. He'd led them to the antique double door and someone buzzed them in.

She drew in a tight breath as Damien held the door. Marlène smiled at her, very kindly, but it made her skin creep. A short-lived giggle escaped from Stacey's throat, her eyes twinkling as if she was about to have the treat of her life.

They walked into what looked like a high-end cocktail party at a classic five-star hotel. The floor was carpeted; antique mirrors graced the walls and comfortable sofas and settees were scattered strategically. Women wearing elegant dresses and men in expensive suits graced the tasteful space, jewels catching the light from the chandeliers.

Mila exhaled. So far nothing hairy.

"Everybody looks so stylish," Stacey murmured. "And the room is exquisite."

Mila nodded, not sure where her voice had gone. Waiters circulated amongst the people who'd grouped together and were chatting, serving champagne and *amuse bouche* on silver platters. Nothing else was served and there didn't seem to be a bar anywhere. Music played in the background, subtle and classic, underlining the atmosphere of gilded sophistication.

Her ears pricked. Heavy bass pumped from somewhere, but she couldn't place it. The sound was an underlying heartbeat from deeper in the building.

"Here." Damien handed them each a glass of champagne which he'd lifted with a perfected swing off the waiter's tray, who himself looked like he was a model who hadn't quite made the cut yet.

Glass in hand, Mila glanced around. The room was not as big as she'd initially thought, and the illusion was amplified by the lights softening to the deeper recesses of the room.

She took a tentative sip, her first champagne in Paris. Her first champagne ever. It was dry and light, the bubbles bursting on her tongue in a thousand teases.

"Like it?" Damien asked, his eyes warm as he studied her.

She took a deeper sip to avoid giving him a shy smile. "Of course." It was decadent, warming her. As if on cue she relaxed a bit, the drink filtering into her veins.

Damien turned his attention to Stacey and Mila lifted her gaze to the walls, which were covered in several antique paintings. She stepped away from their little group, wanting to study the works of art.

"These were all bought at auction," Marlène said next to her. "Decorating this place was immense fun."

"You were involved?" Mila shot her a glance.

"Intimately." Marlène edged closer to the wall and Mila followed. "This one here is eighteenth-century. Not quite a Fragonard. But you can see the theme."

The painting had a naked woman lounging in rumpled bed-covers and could have been a Fragonard to the untrained eye.

"I met James working on this project."

Mila dragged her gaze from the painting, her stomach clutching. "Really?"

"God, he was a mess when I met him. A disaster on every level but his job." Marlène shrugged. "He owns a share in the club. I was still with a decorating magazine at that point."

"I see." She didn't see at all. Blinking, she retreated two steps, wanting to give Marlène the slip. She glanced over the room, searching for Stacey, wanting to leave before she got to know anything more. Anything that would burst James's bubble, which had been floating precariously close to a field of thorns.

Stacey was nowhere to be seen. Damien had disappeared as well. Mila bit her lip hard, containing the pressure on her chest and in her throat. She peered deeper into the ill-lit room. Was it her imagination or had the lights dimmed more?

As she scanned the room she noticed a corner where a woman had sat down on a settee. Two men stood with her, gazing down at her body that draped over the flow of the chaise longue. The three seemed to share a joke, because they laughed softly, intimately. One of the men sat down next to the woman and pulled the thin strap of her dress down her shoulder to completely reveal her breast. Mila inhaled slowly, raggedly, her gaze transfixed by the threesome, spellbound. "Heavens."

The woman's puckered nipple hardened more on exposure, and she laughed, raising her shoulder as the seated man kissed and stroked the top of her arm. The man that still stood leaned in slightly and poured a drop of champagne in the hollow formed by her collarbone. The droplet lingered a second before it gravitated, finding its path down her breast. The seated man closed in, licked the champagne off her breast and caught her nipple in his mouth, sucking deeply.

"Goodness…" Mila turned her back on the threesome, clutching her champagne glass as blotches of heat invaded her face.

"Hmm," Marlène hummed. "Turned you on, didn't it?"

The weight of Marlène's gaze dragged her down, but she met her eyes steadfastly. "Did you see that?" Mila whispered.

"Foreplay. Just foreplay."

She had to look away but had to swallow, her eyelids aflutter. She looked to the floor, swaying on her feet, but it was too late. The heat on her cheeks intensified, only finding reprieve by dissipating to her neck and her whole body, to her core, where she was invaded with tingles.

Mere meters from them a woman had released a man's rigid cock from the constraints of his trousers, stroking him gingerly in front of other onlookers who were only mildly interested.

"Do they even know each other?" Mila's throat sounded constricted.

"They're regulars here; some people come at funny intervals, depending on their personal lives." Marlène sighed. "Some become life-long friends. It is easy to mingle here. We've made sure to keep the tourists and the sleaze out of it."

"The sleaze?" Mila frowned, incredulous. "Whatever is the sleaze?"

"The sleaze factor?" Marlène shrugged. "We French, we have standards. It's not unusual for the upper crust to engage in this type of *affaire*. It is seen as a… right… to indulge due to your status. It's hardly frowned upon, you know."

But James wasn't French. Mila didn't understand at all how

he fitted into this place, irrespective of what 'a mess' he was a few years ago. She couldn't even imagine that.

Marlène swept her arm to indicate the whole room. "Look at this place. Beautiful, is it not? We kept the tourists out. If you want to go to a club that takes tourists, there is one in the *7ième arrondissement*. But you won't like it."

Mila eyebrows shot up at her last comment. "I'm lucky then? To get in here?" She shook her head in disbelief. "And what else happens here—" She broke off to raise her champagne in the direction of the man, who would soon be the lucky recipient of a blow-job. "On the other floors?"

"Ha, let me take you and show you. There's a dance floor upstairs." Marlène's hand was on Mila's naked arm, caressing her softly, possessively. "I know you'd like it. Maybe we'll end up together, in Damien's hotel next door. There are plenty of rooms, and the linen is always clean. We can share a man—"

Mila had to block out her voice, her words. She twisted away, the image that those words had conjured up as Marlène spoke in her husky tone chilling every part of her. "Let me go!" Mila croaked and tore loose, wildly searching for the door.

Her heart was in her throat, her pulse ringing in her ears as she spotted the double doors leading to the exit. She strode away, her dress too tight, the slit too narrow as Marlène's laugh haunted her.

Halfway to the doors, she disposed of her champagne class on a waiter's tray, blinded by tears of confusion. People's eyes were on her, scrutinizing, lingering on her body and sweeping over her revealing dress, stripping her naked, whispering comments as they did so.

The double doors swung open, and she froze as James stepped inside and met her gaze, his face pale and his jaw tight.

Chapter 39

JAMES RELIVED FOR A SPLIT second the first time he'd stepped into a swingers' club. Every inch of that seedy room, which he recalled vividly, was in exact contrast to the opulent space Mila stood in the center of, but at the core, it was the same. He'd known exactly what he was getting into, and why.

As James walked in he hardened his stance. The usual Friday night crowd was there, turning their eyes to him, then back to Mila, who'd solidified on the spot like Lot's wife.

Marlène sauntered up to Mila and he shuddered involuntarily. Subdued whispers rose in the unnatural quiet as he crossed over to the two women. He knew every single thought that zapped through the brains of the swingers observing them in that crowd. He read it in the looks people shot at him: James Sinclair was back after so many months and the new flesh might just be his.

Now the men scrutinized Mila shamelessly in that fucking dress he'd bought for her, their gazes sliding up and down her body. Several women eyed her with interest, but turned away sooner than any of the men, possibly sensing it was Mila's first time, and that she'd be allowed to set the pace. The men would fuck her irrespective, given half a chance.

The sickening churn in his stomach intensified, spreading over his skin.

Mila was his.

He reached her before Marlène and cupped her face in his palms. Moisture teetered in the corners of her eyes as she gazed up at him, her body quivering in his hands. "Mila," he whispered. "You don't belong here."

She blinked, parting her lips. "No."

He leaned in, kissing her gently, reverently, mooring her body against his in the only signal that would talk to this crowd. She let him kiss her, but as her hands crept up his chest he knew it was over. She applied pressure, wobbling on her feet, and he took hold of her hands to steady her.

Over Mila's head, he met Marlène's cold stare and shook his head at her, huffing out a slow breath. She'd brought Mila here to be ogled, introduced to and seduced by random people to get him back—or get back at him? The notion was making him physically sick, his body quaking with the need to contain the aggression that pumped through every tightened muscle. He'd never felt like this before, never needed to protect anybody from the ramifications of the club, least of all Marlène, who made sure they came to the club at least once a fortnight.

"Where is Stacey?" His tone said everything. Marlène didn't dare fuck with him now.

"I don't know. Upstairs? With Damien?"

Fuck.

There was no way he could take Mila with him on a search

265

and rescue mission through the club, drawing her deeper into depravity as they went higher with each floor. He'd have to come back for his sister, but right now he was aiming to get Mila the hell out of there and still be on speaking terms with her afterward.

"Look for her and get her the fuck out of here, or I'll make them shut this whole fucking joint down." He turned his back to Marlène, letting go of Mila's one hand and pulling her towards the door with the other. "I'm taking you home."

She followed but strained against his hold. "James." Mila's soft voice broke on his name. "You are squeezing my hand into the afterlife."

He loosened his grip with a muttered apology. He'd clung on to her as if she was his lifeline in that moment. Maybe she was.

The double doors swung open as if by magic and James led the way into the lobby, heading for the black street door.

"My bag," she said, drawing her hand from his.

She went to the desk, red to the roots of her hair as she faced the bouncer whose eyes oscillated between her and James. The man turned and went to fetch her bag, not even asking her for the number.

"Thank you, Pascal," James said, closing the space between them in a few swift strides. He clasped her elbow in his hand. "I'm walking you home."

She tried to shrug him off. "It's hardly a block, James, I can manage alone."

He gave her elbow a small squeeze and let go, stuffing his hands in his pockets. "You're not okay. So I'll see you home all the same." He nodded towards Pascal and the street door clicked open. "I'm coming back for Stacey. I can't leave her here."

She exited to the street and waited for him to close the door. "What type of club is this, James?" Mila asked although her blush told him everything.

Mila hadn't figured it out yet? "It's—" He broke off as the ghost of Marlène's cold gaze brushed over him. She'd been waiting for him to fall, to shatter to pieces what had developed between him and Mila.

James closed his eyes briefly. What a fuck-up. Inside him, a battle was raging—half of him wanted her to never know his past that held him captive, the other half knew she was entitled to know this about him before developing anything deeper.

He sensed Mila's flitting eyes travel over him, swallowed and manned up. There was no turning back.

"It's a swingers' club." He opened his eyes and looked straight into Mila's dark chocolate pools. "Great long-term investment."

She grazed her lower lip with her teeth. "Yet you are on a first-name basis with the concierge?"

He nodded. There would be no chance for a relationship with her after this.

Chapter 40

Mila BARELY MANAGED TO SWALLOW the sob that wanted
to explode and strode away from James without a backward glance.

Her whole body was flushed, not only because of the embarrassment of being in a sex club but because she was undeniably
turned on.

What she felt for James and for what had happened between
them before Stacey and Marlène had arrived, had somehow been
sacred. And now… she didn't know what it had been. She'd known
from the start that this was a sexual interlude of some sort for
him. He'd fucked her almost randomly that second night. But then
things between them had changed… and now this?

She hadn't seen that coming. She hadn't expected to be
aroused so quickly by the two scenes that still flooded her mind.
The woman on the settee looked so relaxed, so happy and even
more liberated as she enjoyed the attention of the two men, who
got pleasure from the situation too. The woman who was on her
knees to suck the man's cock was so confident, so sure and at ease

with what she was doing as if it was second nature.

She didn't want to look too deep; she didn't want to acknowledge it. But deep down in her dark soul, she wanted to be that skilled woman who knew how to please James with such confidence and ease.

His hand slipped into hers, interlacing their fingers before she could pull away. She shot him a woeful glance. "How could you have a share in a place like that?" The whole idea frightened her. The freedom with which the people in the club approached sex head-butted with her ingrained sense of shame. She was suffocating under the weight of her upbringing, which dictated that sex happened only between married people and that it was something sacred, done only to procreate and not to be enjoyed.

She couldn't quiet the whisper that surged through her body, insisting that the past sinful week had been exactly the opposite.

"It's a solid investment." He sighed. "It's been more than a solid investment."

"Is that all?" she blurted out. "Do you mean to say you were into this type of thing before you invested? Or did you invest first and then get involved with... all these debauched people?"

Her innards tightened as her words resounded in her mind. The way her treacherous body had reacted to what she'd witnessed—was she debauched too?

"This is hardly a chicken or egg situation, Mila." He'd slowed down and let go of her hand. "It's a matter of self-defense."

She walked faster and he picked up his pace. "Self-defense against what?" She'd never been so defenseless against her own feelings. Her body was a mess, wanting things her brain tried hopelessly to squeeze back into that little box they belonged in. Like a map that would never fold back neatly, she sensed her body was never going to fit back into that little box her brain was trained to make it stay in.

"Against this type of situation." He raked his hands through his hair and chuckled mirthlessly, sounding almost helpless.

She didn't understand what he was talking about and right now she didn't want to dig deeper. She wanted to go where she felt safe, where she felt like her old self and where the rules were clear-cut.

From the start, there had been no question about James having years of sexual experience. If she were honest, there was a lure in his knowledge, which was in contradiction to what she'd been taught to look for in a partner. She shot a glance at him. His face was pulled into a grimace and his jaw ticked. He raked his hands through his hair again, seeming to be on the verge of trying to explain something to her.

She didn't want to hear it, not now. There was only one thing she wanted to know. "What I don't get is… if you and Marlène were into this partner mix-up business… swing—" She swallowed, the word stuck on her tongue. She took a deep breath. "Swinging and going around having sex with random people…" She chewed her lip. "I'm sure it's all more complicated than that." She hoped it was more complicated than that.

"It is and it isn't." He raised his hand to reach for her cheek. "Mila."

She stepped to the side, effectively keeping a distance between them. "What I don't understand is how Marlène could have cheated on you with Damien?"

Damien had been there tonight. Apparently, he owned the hotel with the rooms where the people in the club would continue what had only started on the ground floor. Now, she didn't doubt for one second that James, Damien, and Marlène had had a liaison that had gone sour beyond what James had explained to her.

He closed his eyes with a grunt and came to a complete stop, blocking her way. The apartment's entrance was only a few meters from them. She wanted to go up, lock herself in the room and re-calibrate.

"You really want to know?" he asked softly as he opened his eyes and stared at her. There was no pain in his countenance, only an absolute despondency, which tugged at her heart.

"Yes. Unless there's something else you need to hide."

He stepped closer, but she mirrored him backward, feeling the wall of the apartment against her back. "I'm not hiding any-thing from you, Mila. I don't want to hide anything from you. I would have told you, eventually. When the time was right."

She blinked and bit her bottom lip hard to get a grip on the quick rise of tears and the merciless tightening of her throat. "There's no time like the present."

"I have my own limits. I don't take stupid risks. Some things are just not worth the return."

"And you know all about risk, don't you," she murmured. She was not going to like this.

He looked up and down the sidewalk, which had become quieter since she'd left earlier with Stacey and Marlène. "You might not believe it right now, but there are things I won't get into and won't do."

When he met her gaze again he didn't blink. "Marlène want-ed to try every illegal drug she could possibly get her hands on and see which would give her the best sex." With a groan he turned towards the door of the apartment. "I wasn't getting into that for anybody, but Damien offered to take her on every possible ride. Same thrill, different rollercoaster. The amusement park for the sexually sated."

The wall behind her was warm, the rough texture of the old stone somehow comforting as she leaned her shoulder against it, needing something to give her some strength at that moment. She'd gone numb. Not that she knew what to say in any case.

"I want to stay with you." He cursed under his breath. "But you understand why I need to fetch Stacey and get her out of Damien and Marlène's company?"

She nodded and pushed off from the wall to take the last steps to the apartment's entrance.

"Please, Mila… don't hate me for this." His eyes begged, his brow furrowed. "I haven't been to the club for eight months. For what it's worth."

She couldn't think further; the knot in her stomach tightened and she turned away from him.

He opened the door for her and she tugged her apartment keys from her bag.

"I'll be back as quick as I can. Please wait up, okay?"

She could only respond with a nod, the need to be alone overpowering every other faculty.

"Mila." He paused in the doorway, waiting for some response from her.

"Just go, James," she mumbled as she pressed the call button for the lift. It was already on the ground floor, and as the doors slid open, she stepped inside, pressed the button to his floor and got the hell away from him.

Chapter 41

JAMES REENTERED THE CLUB WITH a chilled heart and an uncomfortable feeling of foreboding. He couldn't allow Stacey to be lured deeper into Marlène and Damien's dark world. Sex was one thing—it was normal—but drugs were a hellish quicksand his sister wouldn't be able to crawl out of.

He scanned the ground floor reception area, already busier than what it had been half an hour ago, but didn't find any sign of Stacey, Marlène or Damien.

He rushed up the stairs to the second floor and the dance area that pumped with music and whatever else. The room was hardly dark, the flashing lights and lasers giving ample opportunity to scout who was on the dance floor.

After a fruitless round, he cursed. If Stacey was wearing the LBD he'd bought her that afternoon, like Mila had, he would have a hard time spotting her. And he didn't want to look too closely at any writhing white flesh that was getting sweaty on the floor, hoping that Stacey was still fully clothed.

He was heading for the third floor when he came face to face with Marlène, who was still dressed, her mouth pulled into a grim line.

"Where have you been?" she hissed. "Stacey's up here." She wanted to tug him along but he shrugged her off.

"What's wrong?"

"Fuck knows." She rushed up the stairs, opening the door to an open space with subtle lighting, filled with several king-sized beds and mirrors.

The erotic moans of the only threesome at it hit him first, but then he heard it—uncontrollable whimpering interrupted by the odd staccato sob. *Stacey.*

"She won't move," Marlène whispered, but he'd already zoned in to where the crying was coming from.

He navigated the beds, going straight to the dark corner where Stacey huddled. Damien sat on the edge of a bed across from her, still fully dressed, leaning with his elbows on his knees, unaware of his approach. Damien was speaking to her in soft tones.

James grabbed him by the scruff, jerked him up and rammed his fist into his shitface. Damien yowled as his lithe frame slumped back onto the bed, clawing his cheek. "*Mon Dieu*, James!" he spluttered. "I didn't touch her!"

"That was for bringing Stacey and Mila here, allowing them in, you motherfucker," James growled. "I'll slit your throat if you even think of touching my sister."

He cast a glare at Marlène and she edged away as Damien sat straight. James's chest heaved at the rush of adrenalin and sudden exertion. The fucking coward wouldn't even lift a hand to defend himself.

He went on his knees next to Stacey. "Sweetheart," he whispered. "What happened?"

Stacey hugged herself tighter, her sobs intensifying. He'd never seen her like this, and he tried to smooth her hair. But instead of calming her as his tender strokes always had, she yanked away from him, finally looking up, eyes swollen and wide.

"Jamie?"

She hadn't realized he was there.

"Shh, angel face. I'm here." He swallowed at the fear reflected in her stance; her whole body was shaking. "I'm taking you home."

"James," Damien said, his tone pressing.

The man's hand was on his shoulder, and he wanted to lurch up and strike him again. But something in the pressure in Damien's gesture made him pause. He looked up, reading only urgency in the pull of Damien's mouth.

He rose. "What?"

"She must have had some past trauma that got triggered when we stepped in here. She just broke down like this. Nothing I did helped."

The devil had cursed them. Stacey wasn't unscathed. And the previous evening she'd hinted at it. But how? What? When? James stared at Stacey's hunched-over frame, her whole body coiled up to protect itself. He shrugged off his jacket and settled it over her shoulders, then hugged Stacey close, and this time she didn't pull away. He couldn't look up, couldn't face Damien's or Marlène's concerned hovering. "Leave us," he murmured and listened until their footsteps faded.

"Can you walk home, sweetheart?"

She glanced at him and he gathered her hair from her delicate features. She nodded with a wobbly lip and he helped her up. She still shook and for a moment he held her tight, waiting for her to get a grip on her crying.

They made their way out of the club, not making eye contact with anybody else, their bodies intertwined as he supported her.

She let go as they entered the apartment's lobby and waited for him to call the lift.

"Jamie—" Her voice broke.

"It's okay, but we are going to talk about what happened." What had she been hiding from him—and for how long? He took her hand and held it until they reached his apartment's door. Her fingers quivered in his, a butterfly caught in his gentle grip.

"Where's Mila?" she asked as he unlocked the door.

"She's here. I brought her back before I came looking for you." They entered the apartment where all the lights were lit but no human presence gave life to the place.

The emptiness was almost eerie.

"I lost track of her when Damien took me to dance. God," she whispered. "I'm so sorry I went tonight. I should have told you. I… Marlène—"

"It's okay, sweetheart." Gone were the days of pretense. He didn't want to think about what Marlène and Damien had connived behind his back. "Do you want to check up on her quickly?"

"Yes, please. I feel wretched for leaving her behind." Stacey walked off, and he dragged in a deep breath, watching as her shoulders heaved with an ill-contained sob.

He followed two steps behind her, having no idea how to deal with the situation. With Stacey in a state like this. That Stacey had been thrown by what she'd experienced at the club, little as it was, made his innards crunch together in fear. He wanted to talk to her—now—but he wasn't sure whether Mila should be privy to what they were going to talk about. Whatever Stacey had gone through wasn't going to be pretty. Or did Mila already know?

Fuck. He needed a drink. Instead of going for the cupboard where he had some whiskey he paused at the kitchen counter. Mila's watercolor of the view from the apartment, still unfinished, was next to the only two phones left on the counter—Stacey's and Marlène's.

He picked up the drawing and the paper quivered in his hand. He turned it over, his stomach dropping.

I'm leaving you and Stacey to spend some quality time together. Hate to be the fifth wheel and Stacey deserves to have you all to herself. Thank you for a lovely week in Paris. Will treasure the fond memories.

In self-defense.
Mila xoxo

His chest clutched tighter with each word. Self-defense? A lovely week? Fond memories?

She was the love of his life.

The sudden insight chilled him to the bone. He'd never expected to fall in love. Had never wanted to fall in love. He felt his pockets for his phone, intending to call her, but Stacey's breathing next to him pulled him out of his shock.

"Mila's left. All her things are gone." Stacey stared at him, chewing her thumbnail. "God, Jamie. What have I done?"

James took a deep breath. "None of this is your fault, Stacey."

The tremors that ran through his body intensified and he went out to the terrace to get a grip. The fault was all his.

He scrolled to find Mila's number on his phone and dialed. It didn't even ring; the phone just killed the call by itself.

Mila had blocked his number.

"Can you call her?" James asked. Stacey had followed him to

the terrace. "I can't reach her." He'd lost every bit of control over the situation. Mila was gone, and he had no idea where she went.

Stacey nodded and got busy with her phone, her hands trembling. After a minute she withdrew it from her ear. "It's ringing but she's not answering. I can't leave a message. Possibly because we're in France."

He hung his head. At least there was that. Mila would still speak to Stacey, but not right now. She must have gone somewhere close to sleep. Even if he spent the rest of the night tracking her down at one of the youth hostels in the area, he had to find her.

He scanned Stacey's face. She looked haggard; all the spark that usually twinkled in her eyes when she was with him had disappeared, the sweet gusto completely sucked from her. He'd never seen her like this. Or had he never looked closely at his sister?

"What happened tonight, Stacey?" He had to know. If he didn't wrench it from her now she might never tell him.

She fiddled with her dress, stroking over the curve of her hip with a nervous hand. She'd shed his jacket, but despite the warm evening, goose bumps spread over her skin. She bit her bottom lip hard, and he flinched at the blood-drawing pressure she applied.

"Stacey, I can't watch you like this. It's tearing me to shreds."

She dropped her head. "There was this song playing tonight. I wanted to get away from the dance floor before it got any worse... before it got to me. But then Damien took me one floor up and there were all these white beds and mirrors and everything just came crashing back to me."

With every word her voice narrowed, until he had to lean in to hear her.

"What crashed back to you?" He didn't want to know, didn't want to hear what she was going to tell him, but already every truth shone from her pale face and her eyes that avoided him.

He cupped her cheek in his palm and it was wet with tears she'd silently let go. He lifted her chin to make her look at him.

"I was raped, Jamie, a week before Mommy killed herself."

His hand circled her neck, pulling her to him in an all-consuming embrace. He wanted to take every drop of pain away, by some magical osmosis let it travel from her body to his. "Why haven't you ever told me?"

"I just couldn't. Jamie—" She was all choked up, hardly able to breathe.

"Who was it? Do you know?" He wanted to kill the motherfucker who'd touched his sister. Who'd stolen her innocence and still suffocated her spirit. This was where she'd been, in the dark abyss of abuse where he'd been unable to follow and find her.

She'd pushed her face into his neck, hardly breathing. "Nick."

An angry sob tore from him, releasing the stifling pressure on his chest. She clung to him, her fingers digging into his back.

Nick. The lover who'd died with his mom in a gruesome accident that had been no accident at all. Had Stacey just admitted it too? His quiet suspicions, which he'd kept buried deep inside, crash-landed in this warped reality in which he didn't want to breathe the poisoned air.

"How?" he croaked. He had to know everything, irrespective of the pain it brought her.

"Dad had gone on a business trip. Mom had invited some of her friends over. I was supposed to stay in my bedroom and study. But he came to find me. Mom was too high to notice he was gone. Too high to care." She hushed and he wanted to block the memories for her.

"He was so strong, Jamie, I tried to fight him off but I couldn't breathe." She gulped, pushing away from his neck where her tears had spread in a warm film. "It happened so quietly, but he took his time. He held my mouth so tight, forced me to watch in the mirror."

She shuddered and he closed his eyes, but the image still burned.

"Did you tell anybody?" At least she was talking. How was it possible that she hadn't told him before?

"Does dad know?"

"No," she sobbed. "Please…don't tell him. Not until I'm ready."

She hadn't told their dad? At that time, James had long left home for good; he'd run as far away as possible. Literally. Leaving his sister exposed. Of all the horrors, he'd never imagined this would ever have happened to her. In their home.

Stacey had known he was always there for her. Had he really been?

"But she knew." Stacey's voice broke. "Mommy knew. I told her the next day, when she'd sobered up. And then she made sure that they were both dead one week later."

And in the aftermath of their mom's traumatic suicide, everything else had tumbled through the cracks.

Chapter 42

MILA TOSSED *JANE EYRE* TO the side with a discontented grunt. Why didn't she see it coming? James was just another man with a secret. Were all men like that? Rochesters, all of them?

The subtle sway of the train was lulling. The other passengers in her carriage were asleep, leaning their heads against windows or against each other. Couples held hands, tucked in close, which tore at her because she'd never felt so alone in her entire life.

Not that she needed to be. Her phone had been vibrating in her pocket as if was about to rocket-launch. She stared out of the window into the night, which wasn't dark at all. The train was passing through the outskirts of Paris, and the scenery was incongruous with everything she'd experienced from James's luxury apartment in the heart of the city. High-rise apartment buildings blinked at her with a thousand eyes as the poorer side of town encroached on her very soul. It wasn't pretty.

Nothing that night had been pretty, but it had been real.

She was in love with James Sinclair. With a man who had

lived so far outside her comfort zone that she was as lost and frightened as Gretel without Hansel. She was in the void between two worlds, clueless as to which direction to take. She couldn't navigate her way back to where she came from, but she wasn't ready to plunge into James's world either. She'd never be able to go there again.

What had the past few days been like for him? She still couldn't figure it out, despite all the comments he'd dropped. About eight months. Marlène and whatever had been happening between them had nothing to do with his ex. That night he'd said *It drives me crazy that you're all I need.*

He would have told her about the club himself sooner rather than later. That much she knew about James. He didn't like secrets. This thing they had was too fresh, too pure, too new to bring to a sex club.

What if she'd never known? Would it have mattered?

She swallowed and rubbed at her brow. She'd never been so confused.

Maybe to bolt like she'd done wasn't fair on James. One thing was sure—she'd never be the same person again and keeping her heartache from her family was going to be torturous if not futile. She simply didn't want to go back home and face any of them. Never mind the doses of shame she'd be forced to swallow for her actions, her family would expect her to conform to the same mold of perfect saintliness she'd been squashed into from birth, despite a broken heart.

She'd be living a lie.

Those days were over. She couldn't live in pretense, as if nothing had changed. Even if she never told them about James, even if they never guessed, it was more than that. The past week in Paris had liberated her on more than one level.

When her phone vibrated again she pulled it from her pocket with resignation. Paris was long gone and that deep into the night nobody would pack up and follow her.

Stacey's happy face smiled at her from the screen. A warm rush of relief swept through her. James had managed to pull her from Marlène and Damien's clutches. The least she could do was to let Stacey know that she was all right. She'd pass the message on to James.

"Hi, Stace."

"I'm so sorry, Mila." Her voice sounded exhausted, broken by too many tears. "I should never have taken you there. If I'd known—"

"It's okay, Stace. Good Lord," she chuckled mirthlessly, trying to de-stress the situation. "To think we got in there for free. You saw the club fees on that document we had to sign? They're crazy."

"I feel bought. Cheap."

Mila closed her eyes. Of all the things Stacey should feel, those were the last she'd wanted for her friend.

Stacey breathed into the phone. "Where are you? I feel horrible for having left you alone with Marlène."

"I… I'm going out of Paris for a few days." Mila swallowed, now knowing she'd left both Stacey and James in the lurch. "I'm sorry. It was all just too much."

"You're telling me. James is a caged beast. He wants to talk to you too."

"I—" She broke off, biting her tongue to stop every emotion pouring into the phone. "Stace, I can't. Not now. Please."

"Okay…" A beat of silence followed. "Is there something I need to know here?"

Mila lowered her head, groaning. "Can we talk tomorrow?" she whispered. "It's late, and I really, really need to digest a few things."

"I have to tell you something too," Stacey admitted softly. "But tomorrow is better, honestly. I'm drained."

They rung off and Mila stared out of the window. The landscape had changed; gone were the bright city lights. As the countryside sped past, she seemed to have entered a tunnel, in which the little lights of a hundred exits beckoned. She had no clue which one to take, as if she had a choice in changing the direction of the train.

James brushed his hand down Stacey's arm and gathered her in a sideways hug. "She's okay?"

"Yes, but she didn't tell me where she's going. But she's safe."

He sighed but gave way. He had to also respect Mila's feelings and actions in this imbroglio.

"What's going on, James?" Stacey slipped from his grip. Her eyes scanned his face, searching. "Mila said she had something to tell me… and surely she wouldn't have run off like that if nothing had happened?"

There was no getting away with it—how could he not tell her the truth when she'd bared everything to him? He was going to look like a monster, and in his sister's eyes, one of his princesses, that was the last thing he'd ever wanted to be.

"I slept with Mila." He ran his fingers through his hair. "Well, it was more like we slept with each other."

Stacey's eyes widened as she scanned his face, emotions flashing back at him like mirrors to his own soul. Did she think exactly the same of him as he'd thought that first morning? He was a debauched, defiling son of a bitch who had no right to Mila's sweet innocence.

But then there was more. Her gaze softened and she bit her lip. "Were you easy on her? She was a virgin."

After her revelations about Nick, these were the last words he wanted to hear from Stacey. She'd been a virgin too.

"She didn't tell me until after the fact."

Stacey's eyes widened. "Really? Well… I hope you made it memorable."

"Jesus. Of course I did."

She looked away for a moment, gathering her hair in a twist that she let fall over her shoulder. When she met his gaze again, she shook her head. "You shouldn't have… James—" She huffed a sigh and swallowed. "James. You can't mess with Mila."

"You think the worst of me after tonight?" He'd never wanted Stacey to know. He would have hidden this dark corner of his soul from her for his entire life. And yet, between them there were no more secrets, their baggage zipped open and the fraught contents exposed.

They were both equally fucked up.

She reached for his hand and he took it gingerly in his. "You live your life like this because of Mommy. Because of how she hurt Dad. Don't you?" She groaned. "You're scared to get hurt—staying with Marlène was just to be safe."

He shrugged, his throat tightening. She read him like a book. What did he expect? If anyone would get it, it was Stacey.

"You're nothing like her, Jamie."

He wasn't like their mother, and never intended to be. Their mother wasn't a swinger, she was a sexed-up, cheating egoist who'd walked over their dad as if he was a set of train tracks that crisscrossed her life again and again. Random, permanent, immovable, but to be picked over with her daintily shod feet until she could fall into her next lover's arms. Swinging might have been his dad's saving grace, but he hadn't bothered getting involved.

"I… fuck it, Stacey. I don't understand why he never did anything to stop her. Why did Dad allow her to do that to herself? To him? To us?" He gripped her hand tighter. She was the only one who would understand the warped upbringing they'd had.

"Because she was abused herself, Jamie. When I told her about Nick it all came out. She was brutalized early in life and for such a long time, it was the only thing she knew." Stacey let go of his hand and wiped at her cheeks. "Until she met Dad. And he loved her despite everything. Just as she was."

Stacey broke down, and he had to pull her to him to clamp down on his own emotions. "And here I am, following in her footsteps, sleeping with any random guy in his messy, dinky dorm room, to get the memories of Nick out of my head."

"Fuck it, Stacey," he breathed. "I wish you'd have told me sooner."

"I was raw... too broken to tell you. The guilt of Mommy's death—"

"That wasn't your fault, Stace. It was her choice. Please." This was killing him.

For a long time, they stood in each other's embrace, then Stacey whispered, "She's perfect for you, Jamie. Mila is pure gold. She'd never do a thing to hurt you."

He let go and held her at arm's length. "It's a mess. I'm a mess? I can't even dream of someone like her ever wanting to be with me. To want me." *To love me.* "Not once they know who I am."

Stacey rolled her eyes. "Is that attitude supposed to get you anywhere?"

He chuckled. At least Stacey was battle fit for him, even if she had no energy left for her own uprising.

"Let's get a bloody drink." Getting his head around dealing with this situation was going to take some liquid support. Only one thing was certain: he wanted Mila Johnson by his side, and he'd do anything to get—and keep—her there.

Chapter 43

Mila woke up, reluctantly. It was bliss to be in a fog of sleep, where everything was only a bad dream. She rubbed her eyes, sat up and pulled the stained curtain to the side. Bright sun flooded the room, making dust sparkle and dance. At least something was in good spirits.

She groaned as James's image popped up in her mind's eye, and she fell back against the pillow to get a grip on her emotions. *Close that tap.*

Her phone vibrated and she felt for it under her pillow. Glancing at the time, she blinked. Good Lord. It was almost eleven in the morning. She had to be out of there in no time, or pay for an extra day.

There were several messages from Stacey; it was a miracle that she hadn't woken up earlier.

She rolled out of the bed, careful not to bump her head against the bunk above her. Luckily she hadn't shared the dorm room with anybody else. Rouen didn't appear to be the hot spot for backpackers that weekend. Propping her glasses on, she unlocked her phone and read Stacey's messages.

Can we meet for breakfast?   *Sent 08h13.*

Where are you?   *Sent 08h32.*

Brunch would work too. Or lunch.
Whatever. Just let me know!!!!!!!!!!!   *Sent 09h54.*

Are you ignoring me?   *Sent 10h43.*

PS: I know about you and James,
so no need to hide.   *Sent 10h45.*

A smiled tugged at Mila's lips as heat rushed to her face. How much had James told Stacey? Possibly everything. She pressed a hand to her sternum, willing her heart to calm down.

She was too far out of Paris to meet with Stacey. Slumping back into bed, she dialed her number. There was no way out of this one.

"Jeez, Mila, you made me wait," Stacey answered. "Where are you? I'm freaked out with worry."

"I'm sorry. I overslept and need to be out of this youth hostel by eleven."

"Well, come back to the apartment. We can talk—"

"I'm no longer in Paris, Stace. I can't come back today." She wasn't ready to face either James or Stacey. "How is... how is James doing?"

"He's going to be bald at the rate he keeps dragging his hands through his hair. I told him to go to the gym to burn off some energy."

"Oh. So you're alone?" She didn't want James to hover in the periphery of their conversation. How did Stacey feel about what had happened between her and James?

"Yes."

"I'm sorry about James. Truly, I am. I know you had hopes of him getting back with Marlène—"

"Fuck Marlène."

Mila flinched. To hear Stacey swear, the words popping out of her sweet doll's face mouth, was always weird.

"She never cared for James. She never cared for me... she tried to bait me with Damien! I've been so bloody blind. Fuck it, Mila, that woman is poison."

"Did James tell you why he broke up with her in the first place?"

"About the drugs?" Stacey sighed into the phone. "Yes. It's too close to home for comfort."

"What do you mean?" Too close to home?

"Let Jamie tell you everything, please. Jamie and I spoke for a long time last night. Mila—" She broke off. "I've changed my ticket; I'm leaving tonight. I need to go home, back to university to go see a psych... try to fix this mess I've dug myself into."

"What?" She'd known Stacey had issues and had realized long ago that they were deep and dark. But Stacey had never confided in her, keeping everything bottled up. But now, if she was ready to see a psychologist, maybe Stacey would talk to her too. "What's wrong, Stacey?"

"Please, you need to look out for James," Stacey whispered, side-stepping her question.

"I—I'm not ready to see James again." Would she cave in, doing anything he wanted? She couldn't live that life with him.

"Please, Mila. Give him a chance to explain. If... if you can find it in yourself to listen and be there for him... If you feel anything for him, you will give him one last chance. That's all I ask."

"Okay." Tears were flowing freely down Mila's cheeks, but she forced her voice to sound unaffected.

"Where are you?"

Mila bit her lip. "You can tell Jamie that I'm going to visit his flowers."

He knew her and he'd know exactly where she'd be.

Chapter 44

Jᴀᴍᴇꜱ ꜱʜᴏᴠᴇᴅ ᴛʜᴇ ɢᴇᴀʀꜱ ᴛᴏ his car into reverse and the tires screeched as he sped out of his underground parking bay. He tapped on the steering wheel with both thumbs, checking the clock on the dashboard whilst waiting for the garage gate to rattle open. Energy sizzled through his veins.

Stacey had told him about her phone call with Mila and it was no brain tease where Mila had headed. She'd wanted to go to Giverny ever since he'd taken her to L'Orangerie. The road trip there would allow him a good hour and a half to rehearse what he wanted to say. He needed to go into this with a clear head, despite having had very little sleep and after having pumped iron weights in the gym for the last two hours. How on earth was he going to deal with his past?

With Mila by his side he could deal with anything, an inner voice whispered.

He closed his eyes for a second, trying to shove the ghosts and demons that still encroached on him away, despite Stacey's pep talk. Everything she had disclosed still ate at him. But at least they'd worked out a plan for her to go forward. With some help, support and love, she would find her path again. He would make sure of that if it was the last thing he did.

James steered his car into the empty street and, after navigating through the city center, got on to the highway.

Arriving at Giverny in the early afternoon had its drawbacks. There was no parking available; the whole place was packed with tourists. The gardens at Monet's house would be chaos and he had no idea how he was going to find Mila among the dense crowds.

When he arrived at Claude Monet's country house a thick throng of people still queued outside the entrance. He should have known—weekends were worse than weekdays. He walked past the line slowly, searching each face for the one he wanted and needed to see most.

Mila wasn't in the queue.

His chest tightened with panic. What if he'd misread her intention? What if she wasn't here and hadn't planned to come here in the first place?

He bought his ticket like the rest of the tourists standing in the line and entered the garden, quickly spotting a bench where he could sit and wait with his eyes glued on the exit and entrance.

Half an hour later, his pulse rushed, his heartbeat reverberating throughout his entire body. Mila was walking in, her signature bag with all her painting things slung comfortably over her shoulder. Her long hair was loose and brushed over her breasts. She wore sexy little shorts that allowed him to drink in the beauty of her long legs.

James rose from his seat but she didn't notice him as she scanned the map in her hands. He strode over to her and stopped short of taking her in his arms. Instead, he covered her hand with his. "I believe the bridge is this way."

The map started to quiver, but she didn't pull away.

"James." She looked up hesitantly, and when their gazes met her eyes filled with tears.

"Don't ever run from me again, Mila. Please." His fingers edged up her forearm, cupping her elbow and luring her closer into his embrace. "I know last night was... a lot to digest." He hesitated. She wasn't fighting him, she wasn't pushing him away and he hugged her tighter. "Can we talk about it?"

He let go to search her face. Her eyes were downcast, her cheeks pale. Her eyelashes glittered with moisture, but she didn't blink a single tear down. Trying to be so bloody brave. He could resist a lot of things, but not that sweet trembling lip that she was about to trap with her teeth.

He leaned in and kissed her. A soft, melting kiss that drove every feeling home. He wanted her. He needed her. He was in love with her. He poured every emotion into their kiss and she pressed into him.

People moved past and crowded them. Mila pulled away and glanced to the side. "There're so many people here," she said softly as she stepped away and straightened her shirt.

Her eyes flittered over the crowd that ambled through the garden and a ready blush stole to her cheeks. Their intimate kiss had caught a few curious glances. He should have known Mila would be shy in a setting like this. His heart chanted *mine, mine, mine.*

He took her hand and led her to a path in the opposite direction of where most people were going.

"It smells so heavily of roses," she murmured, shooting an

uncertain glance at him.

"It's the best time of year to visit the garden." And the last place on earth he'd ever thought to do this. "Mila—"

"Can we sit down?" she interrupted. "My legs are shaky and they might give way soon."

He glanced at her, concerned. "You've eaten?"

She chuckled. "Yes. It's just… you. And seeing you here so soon. I just checked my things in at the youth hostel, never thinking you'd come today."

"You thought I'd be able to stay away?"

She licked her lips and hunched up her shoulders. Did she really not understand how he felt about her? The love in his heart swelled and he wanted to scoop her up in his arms and fly away with her. Instead, he nudged her towards an empty bench in the shade, out of the throng of tourists.

"I never thought this would happen," he said as he sat down next to her.

"What?"

"Us. Falling in love."

She gazed into his eyes and shot him a sad smile. "No, it wasn't the plan."

"I've guarded against it all my life, Mila," he sighed. "With the home I was brought up in… with my mom, my dad… Love was pain. I suppose you must know some of it, having been in Stacey's life."

"Only some."

"Can I fill you in?"

Mila nodded. She fiddled with her bag as the story poured from him, every detail that she'd never been privy to. When he told her about Stacey, she broke down completely and the tears she'd been relentlessly checking washed down her cheeks.

The shade shifted as they sat quietly for a long time. He was spent but felt lighter for it.

"That's what you meant by self-defense?" she whispered. "That you got into… swinging because you wanted to protect yourself from falling in love? And getting hurt?"

"Probably. The thinking was that an open relationship would protect me from a cheating partner. I'd figured that she'd have no reason to go behind my back."

She nodded, her hand finding his; he clutched it tightly between his own.

"Mila. That's not what I want. I can't see myself wanting that ever again. Not now… that I've met you. Not ever again."

She searched his gaze, faltering.

"I can't change my past, Mila," he sighed; he had to look away from her gaze that spoke so openly to him, telling him she was scared.

She didn't respond and everything he'd hoped for slipped from his grasp, which had been weak from the start.

"No, you can't," she murmured eventually. "I'm actually a bit jealous of the freedom and… uninhibited way you go about this whole sex thing."

He chuckled. "Let's get one thing straight. I don't intend to go back to the club or any other similar club. Ever. I'm going to sell out."

"Really? You said it was a good investment."

"I'd rather invest in this thing we have for each other." He faced her and cupped her cheek in his palm. "I don't want just once, Mila. I'm in love with you. I want this…" He let go of her cheek to indicate the garden, the sunlight, and the beauty that surrounded them. He wanted her forever. "I've never had this feeling with anyone else." He closed his eyes for a second, breathing out the relief of telling her how he felt. When he looked at her again she'd licked her lips and they were begging for his kiss. "And this..." He glanced shamelessly further down her neck and her chest, pausing at her breasts before sweeping lower to where her legs were crossed, concealing her hidden treasure.

She said nothing, the heat of embarrassment staining her cheeks a delicious pink. He cursed under his breath and pulled her close to crush her mouth with a kiss that he deepened slowly. He had no other means to make her understand how serious he was. She opened for him in an agonizing tease that made him want to pull her onto his lap in a straddle if for nothing else than to hide his arousal. When he eventually pulled away he whispered hoarsely to her, "What can I do to convince you? What do you want?"

She swept her hair from her rosy cheeks, flustered after the intensity of their kiss. "I want to live in... sin. With you."

His pulse raced, the heat of the moment tightening every muscle in his abdomen. "Then come to New York with me. Next week. And then Singapore. Back to Paris. Come see the world with me. Until we get dizzy from going around and around."

She dropped her head back and laughed. To hear her so happy was food for his soul. She turned to him with sparkles in her eyes. "You're crazy."

"You travel light. You'll have everything you need. Kick-start your career in New York." He searched her eyes, begging with his own for her to say yes. "I'll look after you. There's nothing I want more... the idea of not having you by my side—"

"You're so crazy." She shook her head, still chuckling. "But I kinda love your type of crazy."

He chuckled and she leaned in to kiss him, deeply. After a wistful moment, she broke away and brushed his cheek with her fingers. "Now, Mr. Sinclair. The last time I checked, this garden wasn't going anywhere in the near future," she murmured. "But do you think we could go somewhere...?"

Sassy Mila Johnson had read his thoughts, read his body, just as he'd read hers. "You're crazy, but I kinda love your type of crazy too."

He stood and helped her up, and hand in hand they strode out of the garden.

Epilogue

Three Months Later

MILA SMILED WISTFULLY AS SHE ran her finger down the frame of a watercolor she'd done of Stacey. Taking a few steps back, she made sure the painting still hung straight. Not that it mattered anymore. She glanced around the gallery. In the perfect lighting, her art literally shone and she exhaled in elated relief. Every single painting had a red dot next to it, indicating that it had been sold. She was making a living out of her art and the reality of it was liberating.

An arm wrapped around her waist and she leaned against James's chest. He pressed a kiss to her temple. "Congratulations, my love. You've been a roaring success, as I knew you would be."

He was her biggest fan, her cheerleader, her anchor. She turned her face towards his, relishing the sweet scrape of his cheek against hers, his lips trailing kisses in search of her mouth.

"Has everybody left?" she whispered against his lips, a certain heat building in her body from being in James's arms. He held her with a bit of reverence, his fingertips stroking down her sides and hips in a gentle tease. She caught his hands in her own, pausing the slow burn in its tracks.

"The catering company is cleaning up. They'll be done soon."

She turned into his embrace and hooked her arms behind his head. "Thank you. For everything. I couldn't have done this without you."

In the end, she'd never gone home until a few weeks before her exhibition. Instead, she'd hopped the globe with James, staying with him in New York, Paris, and Singapore. When he'd had some leave, he'd taken her to the Maldives as if they were on honeymoon. Heat rose to her cheeks and a delicious tingle whispered between her legs. The time with James had been just that—a long extended honeymoon. He had set her free on so many levels. Her experiences of the past three months were exhibited on the walls for anyone to see between some of her earlier paintings and drawings, and she was proud of every piece that hung in the gallery.

"Anything for you," he murmured, then kissed her, deeply. Around them, feet were scuffling, glasses clinking as they were gathered onto trays, but they didn't stop the slow exploration of each other's mouths.

When it grew quiet around them he pulled away. "All these watercolors you did of Stacey sold too."

"I'm surprised." The watercolors were raw, somehow deprived of Stacey's natural beauty. Instead, they scraped under the surface, at Stacey's soul, exposing her heartache and loss. Doing these paintings in New York during Stacey's recent visit had been therapeutic for both of them.

"The same man bought all four of them."

"What? Really?"

"I checked the list earlier, I didn't think they would go so quickly... I still wanted to keep them." James's voice was strained.

"Why didn't you tell me? I would never have exhibited them if you wanted them."

He shrugged and she knew why—he was dealing with what had happened to Stacey, too, but in his own way. If seeping their pain into art and sending it into the world helped James, then she'd do a million more.

"Who bought them?" Mila asked, her curiosity piqued.

"Ivo Linder," he answered. "A certain *Doctor* Ivo Linder."

Mila paused. "Dr. Linder?" The man Stacey had referred to on more than one occasion, mostly in scathing terms. He was the university counsellor Stacey had to see twice a week until the semester was done. Or until Linder signed her off, whichever happened first. She glanced at James, but his eyes studied the watercolors, his jaw tight and not revealing that he knew any more.

"Did you by chance meet him?" Stacey had arrived at the exhibition on her own, but earlier Mila had watched her sneak off with a man Mila had never met.

"No. But there was this guy Stacey walked circles around for about two hours. Then they left together."

So many things were off with that situation that Mila closed her eyes for a second. Three months until the semester was finished. One set of final exams. One last chance for Stacey to get things right. *God, Stacey, please stay out of trouble.*

A shudder ran down her back at the thought of Stacey tossing everything to the wind on a whim. Dr. Linder was there to stop her from burning her future at the stake, not to lead her by the hand to the stake to tie her to it. You didn't visit art exhibitions solo and leave with your university shrink when something wasn't afoot. Something that could only leave a pile of ash behind.

"Are you cold?" James asked, interrupting her ill-directed train of thought.

Summers were slow to come in the Cape—it was as good an excuse as any. "This dress is a bit skimpy for this time of year." She wore the little black dress James had bought for her in Paris.

"I love that dress on you." He shrugged off his jacket and draped it over her shoulders. "But I love it better off, to be honest."

She chuckled. "Thank you." Was it possible for her to love James deeper? More?

"Let's walk the gallery one last time."

"Yes." She slipped her hand in his and he led the way. She'd never see these art pieces again and many of them told the story of her journey. There were her small cityscapes of New York, Singapore, and Paris, framed in layers of white on white, clustered between drawings of people she'd met en route.

"I'm sorry your parents weren't here." James gave her fingers a soft squeeze.

She shrugged. It didn't matter, despite it being her first solo exhibition. Her parents and brothers, with the exception of Ruben, had been glaringly absent.

"It's for the better, really."

James chuckled. "Yep. Way too much of my naked flesh exhibited here for Pastor Johnson's eyes."

"You didn't mind, did you? Having them all here..." Mila hadn't exactly been shy in introducing her model to anyone asking. James's nudes were pieces that poured out of her, like nothing could hold them back any longer.

"Of course I don't mind. You're just satisfying my exhibitionist streak."

She laughed and swatted playfully at his arm. "You may exhibit all you want, James Sinclair." She loved the ease he felt within his own skin.

He rubbed his thumb over her hand, quietly assuring her that any exhibition was for her eyes only. Around them, the gallery grew quiet and empty. They were all alone.

They stopped in front of her most expensive painting, an oil she'd ended up doing in New York, painting in a studio belonging to one of James's art world connections in the city. It was a project that had taken up a lot of time, but she could leave it to dry between their trips to the city and pour all her energy into it when they were there for a few weeks.

"I rather like this one. And the fact that you had the time and place to do it."

"It was fun." And something different.

"Mila…" James turned and took her hands in his. "The sale of the Paris apartment has gone through."

"So quick?" Her heart tugged. She loved being in the center of Paris, surrounded by history and art, but understood that James had to sell the apartment to let go of his past.

"The sale of my share in the club will go through in a matter of weeks."

Mila nodded. He'd let go of everything for her. She slipped her arms around his neck and pulled him close.

He smiled down at her when they broke apart for a breath. "We can get another apartment wherever you choose. So, your pick. Do you want to set up house in New York, Singapore or Paris?"

Her breath stalled in surprise. "Set up house?" This living in sin thing was rather delicious, but she'd love to have somewhere to settle that would be theirs.

"Set up house, with you. That's all I can think of."

She hitched her eyebrows at him. "I knew you only had one thing on your mind, Mr. Sinclair. But I hadn't imagined for one second that it would be setting up house."

He laughed. "When you're around, yes." He gave her a peck on the tip of her nose. "When you're not around, all I can think of is how to make you the happiest woman in the world." He let go of her hand and slipped his into his jacket's inner pocket, caressing her breast on the way.

Every time he'd hugged her since she'd put on his jacket, there had been something hard pressing against her breast. She blinked when he pulled a little square box from the inner pocket, her mouth suddenly dry.

"So where's it going to be? New York, Singapore, or back to Paris?"

"New York," she managed to whisper. Of course, it had to be New York. She'd give anything to live with him in a city that was drenched in creativity and art.

"Mila Johnson, make me the happiest man in the world, and say yes."

"To what?" she teased him. She wanted to laugh and cry at the same time, her throat tight with emotion.

"To marrying me."

She bit her lip and closed her eyes. She didn't have to see the ring; she didn't care what it looked like. All she wanted was to say yes.

So she did.

The End

Acknowledgements

No matter the path you take in life, many people influence your journey. I have so many wonderful people who have walked the road with me, helping me get where I am today—thank you!

My husband Richard: Thank you for all the craziness. You are my heart. I never knew it was possible to love someone like I love you.

Supreet Kaith: what a privilege to have met you and to have worked with you. Every book just gets better. Here's to many more to come! No pun intended.

Tilla: for all the proofreading. And Stephen, of course, for tirelessly providing opportunities for copper buckets in the past few years. And now I got you to read a part of my book. Thank you both for being our anchors and sharing some of our best crazy adventures. Where are we going next?

Isolde Dittrich: we've come such a long way from our early days in tourism. Thank you for proof reading and always being there for me.

Allison Dobson: My personal cheerleader! Thank you for being such a wonderful and supportive friend.

Laurie Sanders: for being the lookout rock in this maze of writing.

Stephanie Létourneau: friend and life coach—thank you for giving me the kick in the butt exactly when I needed it. I miss you and wish that we could still be neighbors.

Caitlin Bronaugh: critique partner extraordinaire and book angel! The person who literally helped me save this book. I would not have been able to do this without you. Not only are you a wonderful critique partner, you are a fabulous writer too. I'm looking forward to the day when you wow the world with your first book.

About the Author

I've always been drawn to the magical escape of books and the journeys they take us on without leaving the comfort of home. I've been fortunate to have traveled a bit, and this book was inspired by a visit to Paris some years ago. We were walking in some narrow alley in the 1st *arrondissement* of Paris, when I noticed a door with a single plaque with *Club Privé* written on it. My imagination got going, and at some point, things got pretty wild.

I've wanted to write for a long time, but life had plans of its own. I'm grateful to finally have time to write, and love writing contemporary and erotic romance in far-flung settings. Taking readers on a journey of their own with my books is part of the plot. *Bon voyage!*

A Note to the Readers

I hope you loved this trip to Paris! If you enjoyed this read, I'll really appreciate an honest review on Amazon, Goodreads or Bookbub, whichever is your home in the internet book world:

Amazon | Goodreads | Bookbub

Follow me on Social Media:

f @sophiakarlsonwriter

⊙ 🐦 @SophiaKarlson

sophiakarlson.com

Subscribe to my newsletter to receive a free short story and keep up to date with new releases!

sophiakarlson.com

Also by Sophia Karlson

THE SHRINK

Stacey Sinclair lives a charmed life of affluence and ease. Her mother might have died in a brutal car accident six years ago, but really—she's good. So why does everybody think she needs to have some shrink rummage through her head?

Her psychologist, Dr. Ivo Linder, is a strait-laced stickler, but too decent, too handsome and too caring to allow into her head. Her unexpected feelings towards him make her retaliate—she taunts him, never dreaming of falling with him into forbidden lust.

As their affair intensifies, the old adage stands: what does it matter, as long as nobody finds out? But the real world catches up on their liaison—they will not go unpunished and the cost of their love demands a paramount sacrifice.

PERFECT MISTAKE (PERFECT #1)

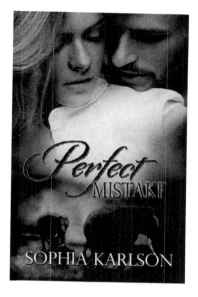

Simone Levin had a dream job as a safari pilot until an unexpected pregnancy clipped her wings. Tired of juggling motherhood with her demanding flight schedule, Simone applies for an office job, unaware that her new boss is Carlo Carlevaro, the man who'd ditched her before finding out he'd knocked her up.

Carlo returns to East Africa only to kill another fire—Ivory trafficking from his lodges threatens to destroy his company. Finding Simone back on the payroll comes as a pleasant surprise. As his employee, Simone is off-limits, but she is the only one he trusts to help with his undercover investigation.

With time running out, Simone and Carlo strive to expose the trafficking ring, but working together rekindles their mutual desire. When Simone is implicated as a trafficker, revealing her daughter's existence to Carlo seems inevitable. Acting on her instincts might come too late as the syndicate retaliate and hone in their threat. Will they survive to give their love a chance?

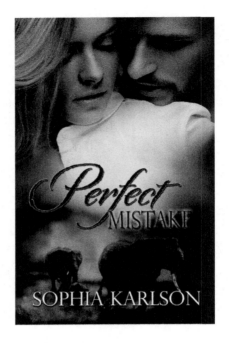

PERFECT MISTAKE (PERFECT #1)
COPYRIGHT © 2018 by Sophia Karlson

First Crimson Rose Edition, 2018
Print ISBN 978-1-5092-2023-6
Digital ISBN: 978-1-5092-2024-3
Published in the United States of America

AN EXCERPT FROM
Perfect Mistake

SIMONE WENT TO STAND NEXT to him. "Why am I here?"

Carlo turned to her. The dark shadows under his eyes were somehow more accentuated in the play of lamplight than in the bright sunshine. "Let's talk somewhere else."

"Where do you suggest? The guests are bound to arrive soon and you know we can't walk around by ourselves after dark."

"Come to my room."

She inhaled sharply, her hands clenching into fists. "Is that why I'm here? Do you really think–"

With a soft groan, Carlo curled his fingers around her arm and pulled her onto the deck, away from the other people sitting in the lounge. "To your room then," he whispered, "although I much prefer mine. And no scenes, if you please." His hand was a ring of fire around her arm, propelling her to the wooden walkway.

He walked next to her but let go of her arm.

A few steps from her tent she stopped. "I don't care who hears this. If you think we're going to carry on where we left off four years ago you are very much mistaken."

He didn't blink an eye. "You seem to be singularly one-track-minded, Simone."

Heat rose to her cheeks; it spread down her chest to her treacherous heart, which pounded at the thought of him. Why was he still able to do this to her? Being alone with him was the worst possible idea.

"Well, if not for that, why march me to my tent as if you would have your way—"

"You may still be devilishly tempting, Simone, but now that I'm your boss you're completely off limits."

BUY NOW FROM
Amazon | Barnes & Noble | Kobo | Google Play
The Wild Rose Press

Printed in Great Britain
by Amazon